I0761861

Back to Normal Series Book Four:

CROSSOVER

RANDY

MCWILSON

Moving Images
Publications
Cape Girardeau, Missouri

Crossover

Published by Moving Images Publications
Cape Girardeau, Missouri
www.MovingImagesPublications.com

Lightning Photograph by Erica Murphy-Burrell

ISBN-13: 978-0-9977917-1-6

Dedicated to

C.S. Lewis

For inspiring a curious reader with enduring tales of timeless characters thrust into impossible situations with remarkable outcomes.

The Four Accords

First Accord: *Walk Without Footprints*

Second Accord: *Filter the Future*

Third Accord: *Prevent Personal Profit*

Fourth Accord: *Avoid Meeting Yourself*

CHAPTER 1

Sunday, January 21, 1979 3:07 a.m.
Victory Memorial Hospital
Brooklyn, New York

Four words would change his life forever.

Terry gazed out across the sleepless skyline, his breath fogging up the cold and wind-rattled windows of the fifth floor waiting area. The intensifying tempest delivered more than irregular hot streaks of lightning and waves of unsettling thunder along a chilly 7th Avenue. Having grown up along the East Coast, it wasn't the first time that he had seen an electrical storm during the coldest month of the winter, but this squall line seemed different.

As the thermometer flirted with the freezing point throughout the night, large patches of wet snowflakes danced among and through the pouring rain in a fickle mess. During the stressful race to the hospital (in what felt like an eternity ago), the heavy clumps had splattered across their windshield from time to time, overpowering his past-due wiper blades.

If it unnerved him, he never let it show to his past-due wife.

The only thing louder than the annoying scrape and squeal from the other side of the windshield was the horrible moaning from the other side of the front seat. Valerie had experienced three rounds of false labor in the past two weeks, but tonight's crisis was anything but false.

They reached the hospital in time, but it was a disheartening case of hurry up and wait. And then wait some more. Five hours of waiting.

A brilliant flash and crash from the storm distracted Terry; he didn't notice at first as a nurse slipped up behind him. The worker's silent arrival was heralded by her reflection in the window just before she tenderly tapped his shoulder.

"Congratulations…it's a boy."

January 22, 1979

SECURITY LEVEL: TOP SECRET

FOR: Chief Neal Schaeffer, Project SATURN
FROM: Richard Forsythe, Northeast Section
SUBJECT: Operation Caretaker Phase I

At 12:02 a.m. Eastern Time on Sunday, January 21, Denver Wayne Collins was born at Victory Memorial Hospital in Brooklyn, New York. Parents have been identified as Terry Lee Collins and Valerie Rose Collins.

END

DCI/PS

CHAPTER 2

Friday, November 30, 1956, 11:27 p.m.
Just outside of Normal, Illinois

Denver's options were rather limited.

The only significant movement open to him involved turning his head. But considering the lethal reality that Hank's razor blade hovered inches above his jugular, he avoided even attempting that typically harmless maneuver. Waves of searing pain compelled him to twitch against his bindings at times. The emotional misery of being betrayed and used by a callous friend was intense, but the gaping wound in his throbbing right side was a close second.

McCloud hadn't budged.

As far as Denver could tell, he hadn't even blinked.

"I'm gonna give you one last chance to drop the knife!" the Chief delivered low and slow. "Trust me, this bullet'll travel about a few thousand times faster'n your hand. It's a no contest, Bodenschatz. Only way this ends well's for you to lose that blade."

To an immobilized Denver, the entire scene smacked of an Old West standoff. The primary difference consisting of the uncomfortable fact that he himself was the hapless damsel in distress. He lacked a clear view of Hank's face, but the tense silence between the two standing men (armed with deadly weapons) provided ample pigment to paint that mental picture.

But that wasn't the only image pulsing in his mind's eye.

Thoughts—thirty-year-old thoughts—mingled violently with his current crisis in a swirling chorus of fear and pain. Hank's gray concrete room dissolved to a lush green park and then back again. He caught a murky glimpse of himself. Young Denver darted in and around the massive oak trees that lined the area like towering sentries. He could still remember running his tender palms across their fractured bark.

That yellow and white outfit! I looked like a sissy.

Two Polaroids had survived the decades as embarrassing evidence supporting the notion that Valerie Collins must've wanted a girl. Even the length of his blond hair was gender-deceptive.

The only thing I'm missing is a purse and heels.

He studied his mother's contented face.

Thanks, mom. Thanks, a lot.

But she didn't hear his playful rebuke.

She didn't hear the car pull up.

She didn't hear the dark-suited man advance upon young Denver.

By the time his immature vocal chords began screaming through the man's strong hands, there was nothing Valerie Collins could do but begin screaming herself. People came running, a few dogs barked in confusion, but it was all for naught. The kidnapper whisked Denver away like a package kicking and thrashing, and tossed him into the backseat of a late model, silver four-door Chevrolet.

Reality and memory were converging and tormenting Denver's still-drugged consciousness. He could make out McCloud's poker face, but the only sounds were his own mournful sobs emanating from the backseat thirty years before.

But then a voice barked at him. A familiar voice. "Shut up, kid! Stop your crying or I'll kill your mommy and your daddy!"

"I will kill you," another voice said, miles away, yet so near. "So you better start movin' that knife away from his throat on the count of three."

Denver felt Hank's left hand loosen somewhat in its grip on his shoulder. The knife hand, though, hadn't altered its deadly position.

McCloud wasn't playing games. "*One…two…*"

"Wait," Hank snapped. "*Wait.*" He released Denver's shoulder and eased the blade away in a slow but deliberate motion. Denver arched his head back. Hank had hoisted his arms in a semi-surrender fashion.

"There," Hank offered. "There. See? I did what you asked. No need to kill a man in cold blood."

The Chief inched forward. "Little late for that, Bodenschatz. My feet are already steppin' in cold blood. And if I hadn't shown up, there would've been more." McCloud straightened up and squinted. "I oughta save the state all the trouble and skip our flawed judicial system. I could pull this trigger'n send yer ass straight to a much higher court. One without appeal."

Denver detected a nervous vibrato rippling through Hank's response. "You're a sworn officer of the law, *Officer* McCloud. *Police Chief* Mc—"

"This ain't about law…it's about justice. And you're still holding a weapon. A weapon that was used in a recent case of murder'n the first degree. Ain't a jury in the world that'd convict me of anything more than self-defense."

"Shoot him," Denver said. "I'll take the stand and swear on seven stacks of Bibles that he came at you first."

Hank laughed. "A killer cop and a witness lying under oath. You two make quite the team."

"Shut yer mouth, Bodenschatz!" the Chief bellowed. "I don't think a psychopathic murderer's gonna lecture me about morality! Now drop the knife and kick it over to me."

Hank hesitated for a few seconds. "What assurance do I have that you won't still shoot me afterwards?"

"You're still breathing," McCloud replied in disgust. "I coulda dropped your guilty carcass three minutes ago."

Hank held the knife out at arm's length and began bending down towards the floor. "Fair enough. Fair…enough."

He dropped below Denver's peripheral vision.

WHOOSH!

Denver couldn't see the sudden motion, but he was horrified at the result. Hank's blade sizzled through the air and lodged into the Chief's chest. McCloud jerked back and a deafening explosion erupted as his pistol fired wildly into the ceiling.

Hank lunged above Denver and ripped the solitary incandescent bulb from its cord. In the ensuing blackness, Denver felt Hank's bony elbows crash down into his abdomen as the bulb exploded upon the concrete. Hank's heavy frame rolled across him and down into a scuffle along the floor.

Yelling.

Another shot.

Metal clunked to the floor.

More metal.

The violent noises subsided.

A hand grabbed Denver's arm. "You okay, son?"

"I'm alive, Chief. You?"

"Don't know. Think I'll live. Hurts like Hades."

"Tell me about it."

"Hold on, lemme find my dang flashlight."

A few muffled pops rang out from the distance.

Denver detected a faint rumble. "What's that?"

Pause.

It sounded like the Chief was picking a blind path over to the doorway. "Yep, it's what I thought. A truck. Hank just high-tailed it outta here. Tell me, what does he know?"

"Probably *everything*."

"That's...not...great."

A pool of light popped on and panned about before settling on Denver. "There you are, now that's better," the Chief muttered. He flipped the flashlight around and trained it on the expanding bloody mess just below his own right shoulder. "And that's...*not* better."

"Did it puncture your lung?"

McCloud snapped the tight beam up into his own face. "Now how the heck am I supposed to know that?!"

"You would know, trust me. I've seen it several times. You'd probably be hacking up blood by now, or drowning in it."

"Thanks for that—*encouraging*—tip, Trailer Collins."

"Just being honest, Chief. Listen, I need to get some pressure on your wound. Now cut me loose."

McCloud worked his way back, but the sight of Papineau's corpse sprawled out along the floor gave him pause. "You, uh, you saw it? His death'n all?"

Denver relaxed his head back and stared into the dark ceiling. "It was pretty sickening. I've seen a lot of guys die in a lot of ways, in war...but...yeah. It was bad."

McCloud retrieved Hank's knife and worked on Denver's restraints. "It's gonna kill Ellen." Denver's right hand broke free. The Chief looked up. "Did he suffer?"

"Uh, it was fast. Over in a few seconds."

"A small mercy." The Chief delivered the flashlight to Denver. "Aim this for me, it'll go a lot quicker."

"How in the world did you find me?"

The Chief scurried to the opposite side of the table. "Quit squirming, or I might cut ya!"

"It wouldn't be the first time tonight. So, answer me. How did you know to come here? Wherever here is."

McCloud leaned closer and sawed with careful strokes. "Well, Mr. Complicated…I guess you'd call it detective's intuition." Denver's left hand came loose and the Chief stepped over to his ankles.

"A few weeks ago I walked into The Basement. I coulda swore I heard ole Pappy on the phone." The Chief glanced up and Denver spotlighted his stern face. "Speaking *English*. Perfect American English."

He bent down with the blade. "Pappy hung up, real quick like. I acted like I didn't see or hear anything. After that, I assigned Billy to keep an eye on 'em. Evenings…and weekends, you know. After hours. You say that he was in cahoots with Hank?"

"He was the mastermind. At least according to Handyman Hank."

Both feet were liberated in under a minute. Denver focused the flashlight on the leather strap running across his chest. "So where's Billy?" he asked.

McCloud knelt close by. "He followed Pappy out here."

"Where's *here?*"

"We're on a farm, west o' town about two miles. Anywho, Billy followed Pappy out here. When he saw Hank's truck pull up and haul out a body, he drove back to town and called me." The Chief rose after the strap gave way. "So, I guess you owe Billy O'Connell big time."

Denver struggled to sit up. It was an uncomfortable process. "He, uh, he's high on my Christmas list."

"Better hurry on that one. Doc says we might be home before then."

"Well, Doc was counting on Papineau to help with that. I'm sure all bets are off now." Denver hunched forward.

"Take her easy now," McCloud cautioned while retrieving his flashlight. "Go slow." The Chief panned the beam down to Denver's side. He arched forward. "Have mercy! What'd he do to you? Deliver a baby through your right side?!"

"Felt like it," Denver moaned. "*Still* feels like it."

"I bet."

The Chief picked up Denver's weakened legs and helped slide them over to the edge. Denver sat and steadied himself for a handful of woozy seconds.

"So, what's this all about?" the Chief asked. "Why were they cuttin' on you like a fresh rump roast?"

Denver forced a smile.

"Well, because of something that Hank will do…about thirty years from now."

January 24, 1979

SECURITY LEVEL: TOP SECRET

FOR: Senior Staff, Project SATURN
FROM: Chief Neal Schaeffer, Project SATURN
SUBJECT: Operation Caretaker

With the recent confirmation of the birth of Denver Wayne Collins, I am directing all departments to transition to Operation Caretaker Phase II.

Affected personnel must complete relocation on or before 18 February.

END

DCI/PS

CHAPTER 3

Saturday, December 1, 1956, 2:57 a.m.

Ellen Finegan, like her mother, bore the curse of being a light sleeper. But tonight, she even snapped awake the moment footfalls scraped across her porch, long before the incessant rapping on the door began. She threw on the first housecoat her hands could feel and rushed towards her dark foyer.

It's either Shep or the Chief.

A muffled call sounded out. "Open up, Ellen."

Okay, it's the Chief.

Thank goodness.

With a quick flick, she popped the amber porch light on and twisted the reluctant deadbolt. She started to reach for the knob when McCloud barreled through, hauling another dark form past her before depositing it onto the living room couch.

"Chief!" she yelled out, scrambling over to turn on a few lamps. "What's going on?" The bloody form of the stranger now splayed across her furniture came into view. "Denver!"

"Or…at least about ninety percent of him," he moaned through a half-hearted smile.

She collapsed to her knees beside the couch and performed a rapid evaluation, with a healthy burst of adrenaline pushing her. She located the massive wound in his side and Denver lurched at her moment of discovery.

"Easy there, nurse," he cautioned through a clenched jaw.

"What happened to you?"

"It's…complicated," he replied, taking a deep breath. "It, uh, it started when I was probably about five years old."

Ellen ignored his answer and raced into the bathroom. She returned with a dark green medical kit and shoved it into the Chief's arms. "Open this and gimme a hand," she demanded.

Denver flailed his right arm a bit towards McCloud. "Hey, I'm not the one who needs your immediate attention."

"Like hell you don't," she responded. "Now hold still."

"I will hold still, right after you take care of the Chief."

"No, no, no. I'm alright," McCloud protested.

Ellen pivoted around and studied him. The dried blood below his right shoulder was difficult to spot against his dark blue uniform, but she caught sight of it and rushed over.

"Have you been shot?"

The Chief shrugged. "No. At least, not…by…a bullet."

"Take off your coat!" she yelled. "And your shirt. Now!"

"I appreciate yer interest," he teased. "But honey, not right here. Not in front of our kids'n all."

She sped off into the kitchen to grab a dishtowel and soaked it in warm water. "You're gonna wish you were shot if you don't take off your dang clothes."

He was halfway finished as she returned. "This looks hours old," she complained. "When did this happen?"

"Hours ago."

Denver struggled to sit up at a more convenient angle. "We would've been here a lot earlier, but someone shot two of our tires out."

Ellen tried to process everything as she attended the Chief's near-fatal wound. "What? Who shot your tires out?" She wiped more blood away as the Chief retreated under the onslaught. "Hold still, you baby. And would someone please tell me what happened before I break out the sodium pentothal?"

Denver slid over and up to a fully-seated position. "Long version or short vers—"

"*Any* version."

"Okay. *Any* version," Denver mumbled. He coughed and clutched his side. "Alright. Well, um, Hank Bodenschatz—"

"The handyman?"

"Yes, ma'am, the handyman. Hank Bodenschatz. He, uh, drugged me, kidnapped me, and cut me open."

Ellen glanced up at the Chief. McCloud winced and then nodded. "It's true."

"And *why* did he cut into your side?"

"It's complicated."

"You've already said that. *Twice*."

"And I meant it…both times."

"I'm a big girl."

McCloud exhaled loudly. "We need to call a meeting at the factory…first thing in the mornin'. Everyone."

"Except for Tori," Denver corrected.

"Good call," the Chief agreed.

Ellen snatched a few items from the kit and handed a fresh rag to McCloud. "Shove this in your mouth."

"Why?" he asked. "Cause it needs to be wet?"

"No," she replied. "Cause it's gonna *hurt*."

McCloud squinted and grumbled through the misery of stitches without the aid of anesthesia. "You think this hurts?" he asked.

"Ellen, I'm afraid this ain't hurting nearly as much as what we gotta tell you about Pappy."

May 28, 1983

SECURITY LEVEL: TOP SECRET

FOR: Chief Neal Schaeffer, Project SATURN
FROM: Richard Forsythe, Northeast Section
SUBJECT: Kidnapping

At approx. 4:30 p.m. ET today, young Denver Wayne Collins was abducted at Lincoln Terrace Park in Brooklyn by an unknown male with a silver, four-door Chevrolet. The child was with his mother. His father was not at the scene.

Witnesses describe the kidnapper as a Caucasian male of average height, late middle-age, in a dark suit. He was last seen headed north on Buffalo Avenue.

With your permission, I will coordinate our manhunt with the FBI.

Please advise

END

PS

CHAPTER 4

Saturday, December 1, 1956, 8:10 a.m.

"It…doesn't seem possible," Leah sobbed, gazing around at a roomful of somber faces. Her bloodshot eyes turned to the only person standing. "Chief, we've been through too much. Too much. Now this?"

Ellen folded and refolded her damp handkerchief over and over again. "I, uh, I just had dinner with Pappy last night." She blinked hard as Alexus tenderly rubbed her arm. Ellen adopted a conflicted grin. "I made him Veal Parmesan…his favorite meal."

Garrett smarted off under his breath, "You mean his *last supper*."

In an explosion of fury, Ellen launched out of her chair and clawed her way across the conference room tabletop. *"You heartless sonofabitch!"*

Denver and Shep bolted simultaneously to intercept her justified rage. Denver snagged an ankle as Sheppard caught a fist. "Let me go!" she screamed. "I'm not listening to one more word out of his hateful little mouth!"

Garrett refused to budge. "What's your problem, Finegan?!" He inched closer to her face as she struggled admirably against her human restraints. "That little French freak *sold…us…out*. Hear me? He sold us out!" Garrett folded his thick arms. "That traitor got what he deserved. If Hank hadn't done it, I would have. Gladly. Any frickin' day of the week."

The Chief marched over to the war zone, massaging his injured chest with every step. "Another outburst like that,

Mr. Frazier, and I'll lock you up downtown faster'n you can say '*goodbye freedom*'. Ya hear me, Garrett?!"

"I ain't afraid of a little jail in a Podunk town. Seen worse."

The Chief bent down. "And you'll stay there 'til Doc and Ellen find a way to get us home. Am I making myself clear, or do I gotta draw you a picture?!"

Shep released Ellen's arm and stepped back. "I think you're the one who ain't getting the picture, Chief," he ventured. "Once again we're in a crisis. And who's right at the center of it? Oh yeah…Colorado Collins. Am I the only one who sees the pattern, here? Every damn time something goes south, he's right in the thick of it."

Ellen composed herself. "You're way outta line, Sheppard. We can't hold Denver responsible for the sick and twisted plans of a confirmed psychopath."

"Oh, yes we can," Shep rebutted. "He shouldn't have started such a close friendship with a Local in the first place. He's treated the Accords like toilet paper. It was a helluva gamble, and now we all might've lost everything because of it. It cost us Pappy at the very least."

"You're forgettin' all about the super-metal or whatever you call it that Denver brought back from Area 51," the Chief observed.

"No, I didn't forget that, Chief. I didn't forget that *two* men left here for Nevada. *Two*. But…hmmm…only *one* came back. And that one was who? Oh, yeah. Colorado. Again. And since he got back, we've lost someone else. Pappy has been murdered. And who was there…again? Who told us about it…again? Colorado *again*. The writing's on the wall, and it's in blood."

"Hey! That's a bridge too far, Robert Sheppard," McCloud growled low and slow. "A lot of circumstantial nonsense. So back off. I was there. At Hank's farm. Hank killed 'em in cold blood. Period."

"Sorry, McCloud. You're a damn cop, you know better. You didn't see it."

"The knife was still in his hand. The knife that almost hit my ticker!"

Shep shrugged. "You. Did. Not. See. It." A wicked smile materialized along his smug face. "It burns you that the truth is on my side."

"The only thing on your side is *you,*" the Chief snarled back.

"I don't wanna get into all the rest of it, but Denver stole the goods for us, Shep," Garrett said. "No denying that. He's got my respect."

Shep paused. "He *stole* the goods, Frazier? Maybe. Or isn't it much more likely that he was *given* the goods? The odds were one-in-a-million, remember? The only story about the supposed break-in comes from Colorado. We don't have Terrance to confirm anything. How convenient. Almost too damn convenient." He hesitated long enough to survey the sullen faces around the room. "If each of you were honest with yourself, you would have to admit you've suspected this man of lying before. Or worse. Probably on more than one occasion."

Leah looked up suddenly.

Denver noticed.

Shep shook his finger. "He's more than a liar. He's dangerous."

Denver exercised great restraint as he ambled within inches of his hot-headed accuser. "You think I'm dangerous, Sheppard? Well, for once we finally agree on something. I am dangerous. Uncle Sam and Al Qaeda and Afghanistan have made sure of that." He slowed, collecting his thoughts. "But there is a difference between being dangerous and being a *danger*. The only people who have a reason to fear me are those who get in the way of my return to my daughter."

Denver glanced back at the group. A few met his gaze, a few didn't. "That's all I want. And if I've caused trouble or wronged anyone in the process…I am sorry. I just wanna get home."

Shep brought his hands up and clapped slowly; his face devoid of emotion. "Great speech there, Colorado. Quite moving. But it's just words. But me…I'm just reminding everybody of the *facts*. Not words. Facts. Is that okay? You gotta problem with the facts?"

"Nope," Denver muttered. "But I'm continuing to have a problem with you."

"Oh, nice little comeback there. But cute one-liners don't solve our much bigger problem. A problem that *you* caused." Shep brushed Denver out of the way and glanced to his right. "So, Doc…what are the ramifications of losing Pappy? What does that mean to us?"

Silence.

Shep sauntered up behind Stonecroft and leaned into his ear. "Tell us, Doc. Tell the Chief. Tell everybody. Tell every single person what this loss *really* means."

Denver returned to his chair as all eyes descended upon the elderly researcher. Doc's attention appeared to be occupied with yet another round of cleaning for his glasses. Betty Larson slid her chair closer and tapped him on the arm. Doc glanced around the conference table.

"What does this mean, Professor Stonecroft?" Alexus begged. "You told us that we should be home by Christmas. It's what you said. Home by Christmas."

Stonecroft froze.

"Go on. Tell her," Shep urged.

Doc frowned for a moment before donning his spectacles. "My dear, Miss Daniels, it would give me great satisfaction, if as Browning penned, I could '*foresee and could foretell…thy future portion, sure and well.*' But, my child, I have far too much affection for this group and far too much love for the truth to claim such patent foolishness."

"If we ever get home," Shep moaned, "I've made up my mind to punch anybody right in the face if they ever start quoting poetry." He relocated his stance and stared directly into Stonecroft's eyes. "I am so sick of the damn double-talk, Dr. Dictionary. Admit it. Without Papineau we are dead in the water. Going nowhere. Stuck."

"That's not true!" Alexus countered. "We all saw the future, just a few weeks ago. Right? Right?! Tell me I'm right, Professor."

"My dear child…you are correct. We all did *see* the future." He squinted and nodded towards her with a depth of compassion that was impossible to hide. "Against that glorious fact there can be no doubt raised. But—"

Bill O'Connell joined in. "But *what*, Doc?"

Another round of frustrating silence.

"But," Stonecroft continued, "without the benefit of Emile's apprehension of the complex nuances of temporal theoretical physics…I would say the probability of successfully overcoming our current obstacles is…not…high."

"Not high?" Betty echoed. "What does '*not high*' mean? I'm a reporter. I need something a little more specific. Black and white."

"It's his gentleman's way of saying '*no chance*,'" Shep smirked.

"Is that what you're saying?" Billy implored. "There's no chance? No chance now of getting home?"

Doc raised a hand as if to calm the confusion. "Officer O'Connell, that rash assertion is not entirely accurate."

"So there is a chance? A possibility?" Alexus asked.

"Yes, child. There is a chance. I could not, though, in good conscience, place a value on that probability. But hope remains. Indeed, hope remains."

Denver pushed up and out of his seat again and paced alongside the table. "Maybe it's not hope that we need, Doc. Maybe it's *help*. What about finding new help? Another physicist or whatever?"

"A valid question, for sure," Doc responded. "But by the mid-twentieth century there are or have been only a meager allotment of theoretical physicists with the credentials for this type of enterprise."

Denver grabbed for the low-hanging fruit. "Einstein?"

"Too connected to the government," Shep countered.

"I concur with Mr. Sheppard," Doc replied. "He could not be trusted with our…unique secret."

Betty leaned back in her chair. "If you could have anyone, Dr. Stonecroft—*anyone*—who would it be?"

"Without hesitation and without reservation, that choice needs no deliberation. If my selection was unrestrained, I would choose Tesla. Nikola Tesla. As an inventor and scientist, he is unequalled, and his accomplishments, unparalleled. Tesla accumulated eight honorary doctorates during his inspirational, and greatly misunderstood career. An accomplished polyglot as well."

"Poly-what?" the Chief asked.

"Poly*glot*," Doc repeated. "Tesla was fluent in several languages. Eight languages, if memory serves."

Denver smiled. "It's settled. Let's recruit him. Where do we go, Doc?"

"I believe he resides in Ardsley, New York."

"Ardsley. Great," Denver said. "Only about thirty miles from where I was born. Just north on Interstate 87."

"That is correct, Trailer Collins. But before you embark on your journey to the east, you will need to enlist the services of a strong back…and a stout shovel or two."

"What?"

"A shovel, my friend." The bulk of Doc's smile began to melt away. "You see, Dr. Tesla…is currently below ground."

"Underground?"

"At least his body," Doc clarified. "Nikola Tesla passed away at the outset of 1943. I believe that he was cremated."

Shep was livid. *"He's dead?* You just wasted all our time bragging about a dead guy? You see…it's this kinda crap that gets us nowhere. A lot of talk, with nothing to show for it. And people wonder why this man drives me nuts. We've got Colorado over there who just talks lies, and then Stonecroft who just talks. And talks."

Stonecroft clasped his hands together. "In my defense, our newspaper editor provided me with precious few restrictions. I took a more liberal interpretation."

Garrett straightened up in his chair. "Well, while you guys are arguing about a damn dead guy in New York, I'm more worried about one that is alive and kicking. And we have no idea where that idiot is."

The Chief finished his thought. "Hank Bodenschatz."

Frazier crossed his arms. "Bingo, daddy-o."

Doc squinted and rested his chin on his clasped hands. "Mr. Bodenschatz constitutes a very grave and present threat. One unlike any we have yet encountered."

"The way I see it," Shep offered, "we have two options when it comes to Hank. One…find him and stop him from either screwing up our damn futures or calling the Feds on us. Or—"

"Or two," Denver interrupted, "finish our portal and get out of here before he can turn us in."

"The first option ain't gonna fly," McCloud added. "We don't have the manpower or the resources to track 'em down. Bet your bottom-dollar he's long gone. He'll stay as far away from us as possible."

"But he's a murderer!" Ellen blurted out. "A cold-blooded killer. We have an eye-witness. Can't you do something with all that, Chief? He stabbed you for heaven's sakes!"

McCloud wagged his head and strolled in her general direction. "Notta chance, Ellen. Way too risky. If he gets busted, he could use information 'bout us as leverage. Feds would give 'em whatever he wants."

"I hate to say it," Shep began, "but it's all riding on you, Stonecroft. You and your little underground nuclear playground. You've been playing on an open tab for years. It's time to deliver on the investment."

"Speaking of *time*, Dr. Stonecroft," Betty inquired, "would you care to put any kind of estimate on how much time it could take? To finish the, uh, portal and all? Are we talking days, weeks? A few months?"

Doc shifted in his seat. "In all honesty, Ms. Larson, all of those may be insufficient for the daunting task before us."

"We are talking *years?*"

"Not necessarily," he answered. "But potentially. Emile and I had just finished the metallurgy on our superconducting elements not less than twenty-four hours ago. We have yet to install the cooling system for our magnets. We will need to purchase hundreds of liters of liquid nitrogen. The temperatures involved in our energy transfer will result in an inordinate quantity of nitrogen vapor. Once it enters the gaseous state, it will have to be replaced. Not to mention vented...safely."

Ellen scrunched her face. "Why can't we just collect the gas and then reconvert it back to liquid nitrogen again? Isn't that possible?"

His smile betrayed the futility of her request. "Oh, it is indeed *possible*, Miss Finegan. But it is neither practical nor financially responsible to attempt to do so. The specialized components for a nitrogen liquefier are prohibitive on so very many levels. It is more cost effective to simply increase our inventory of the coolant."

"Can we get the nitrogen?" McCloud asked.

"That will be among the very least of our concerns, I assure you, Chief McCloud," Doc replied. "It is quite plentiful."

"What about all of the cooling gear and stuff?" Denver requested.

"The vast majority of the cooling apparatus has been assembled. Thanks to the help of Mr. Sheppard and Mr. Frazier. Oh, yes…and Mr. Gaines. Before he departed."

Alexus glanced over at him.

Doc backtracked. "I am deeply sorry, a poor verb choice. I intended to say before he *left* for Nevada."

"So, where do we go from here?" Betty asked, minus her typical confidence.

"We get to work," McCloud boomed. "Everyone has a role to play. We help, and we hope, and we work. Like always. It's what we do. What we've always done."

An uncomfortable silence overtook the small assembly. A few started moving about, but with little discernible purpose or direction.

Ellen's eyes flared red as she blinked several times. "Not to, uh, sound morbid, or anything," she began, "but, what is, uh, going to be done with Dr. Papineau's remains?"

McCloud nodded. "Already taken care of, Ellen." He gestured. "Billy and I, we buried him. Early this mornin'. Out on the edges of Hank's property."

Doc pinched the bridge of his nose before folding his trembling hands on the table. "His recent indiscretions notwithstanding, we need to conduct a right and proper service for the poor soul," he urged.

Garrett jumped up out of his seat and shook his head with contempt. "Gimme a break, Doc! He was guilty as sin." He circled around towards the open doorway.

"If he got a load of fresh dirt over him, that's more than he damn-well deserves…my apologies to the dirt."

June 12, 1983

SECURITY LEVEL: TOP SECRET

FOR: Chief Neal Schaeffer, Project SATURN
FROM: Richard Forsythe, Northeast Section
SUBJECT: Kidnapping Update

Several leads being followed in the massive effort to locate Denver Wayne Collins have proved fruitless.

I recommend taking the investigation to the next level. In my estimation, we need to enlist the specialized services of the NSA.

END

PS

CHAPTER 5

Incurring Shep's managerial wrath seemed like an acceptable cost for a little intellectual diversion from time to time. Every moment below ground not only kept hope alive, it often allowed Denver to vent about the situation above ground. Life after Area 51 had become a delicate balance of keeping his hands busy and his tongue idle. Few could appreciate how difficult those simple tasks were to juggle on a daily basis.

Denver bounded down the last few steps into The Basement and crept up behind the researchers. He knew his echoing footsteps ruined all possibility of surprise.

Ellen swung her head around and slid a delicate hand onto her hip. "Well, behold! The gods have come down to us from above in the form of gorgeous men."

"I'm not a god," Denver admitted, giving it his best to avoid blushing. "Not even close."

"No," she replied, running her fingers through her lengthy red hair. "But you are still gorgeous."

"I'm not so sure about all that. But, uh, I am pretty sure that some people—*upstairs* people—think I'm the devil."

"The devil? Well, I can work with that, too," she said.

Doc adjusted his spectacles and laid his notes aside. "Good afternoon, Mr. Collins. Is this merely a social visit, my friend, or perhaps something more?"

Denver rested against the table and folded his arms.

Can't get much past Professor Stonecroft. He should've been a psychologist, rather than a mathematician.

"Well, Doc…perhaps something more."

"I cannot help but detect a question looming in your statement," Doc observed. "You have chosen a fine and opportune moment for such an inquiry. Nurse Finegan and I have been toiling over frustrating questions since sunrise. We would surely appreciate a respite from our own endless supply of quandaries."

"Oh, I don't know. It almost feels weird asking it. Even thinking it."

"*Weird*, as you call it, is the least of our concerns, Mr. Collins. Our very existence here calls into question any definition of weird, or fantastic, or strange."

Ellen grinned and winked. "He's right, Mr. Gorgeous. Spill it."

Denver pushed off the table and sauntered over to the refrigeration unit to his left. "When I first came down here, back in August, you guys ripped a patch of my hair out. Without warning." He tapped the side of the cabinet. "And stuck it in a little vial in here."

"Ah, yes," Stonecroft began, "your TRS sample."

Ellen squinted. "That was so that we could get a radiation signa—"

"*Signature*. So that I could be sent back to the exact same point in time or something. Yes, I understand. Sort of. I know…it's complicated."

Doc migrated towards him. "It may indeed be complicated, but I can assure you that both the mathematical framework and the temporal physics supporting our reasoning is quite sound."

"I'm sure it is, Doc. Quite confident, actually. Hardly a doubt in my mind."

It was Ellen's turn to take a few steps closer. "Then how can we help you?" she asked. "And don't get me wrong. I'm not playing *devil's* advocate."

"Cute," Denver responded. "I guess my concern is about the…*other* people."

Doc used a stubby finger to push his glasses up. "The *other* people?"

Denver chose his words with care. "The…*non*-TRS signature, sample-type people."

A noticeable change fell across Stonecroft's jovial face. He pivoted around and slid a chair away from the table. "I see," he said, dropping down into the seat. "Your question centers around those of us who arrived before we had the scientific sense to begin acquiring samples."

Denver took up a position directly opposite him and sat down. "Exactly." He lowered his voice. "I mean…think about Betty Larson, for example. There's no way you'd have a sample for her."

"Our dear newspaper editor is not alone in that dire club," Doc replied. "There are several of us who face some…difficult realities. Bleak choices."

"So I'm not crazy, right? I have a legitimate concern?"

Doc slid a chair out for Ellen and invited her to sit with a simple gesture. "Your concern, Mr. Collins, is more than legitimate. It is fundamentally spot-on. And one that has led to sleepless nights without number for this old professor."

"So you guys have thought of it? Talked about it?"

Ellen shook her head and folded her arms onto the table. "Oh yeah. We've talked. And then talked some more. Then, took a break. Drank a few pots of coffee. And then talked further."

"Dozens, perhaps hundreds, of hours of thoughtful discourse, Mr. Collins," Doc added. "As if the complexities of temporal displacement were insufficient to fill our every waking moment, this very issue that troubles you has rarely drifted far from our conscious efforts. It haunts us, plagues us. At times…mocks us."

Ellen exhaled and bit her lip. "I try *not* to think about it. But it doesn't usually work."

Denver's eyes raced between the two researchers. "Wait a minute…are you telling me that you don't have, or haven't discovered, a solution?"

"Oh, heavens no," Doc chided. "No, no. We have discussed many…potential solutions."

"None of them perfect," Ellen interjected.

"What do you mean *perfect?*"

"My female colleague has selected an appropriate description, Mr. Collins. Not one of our proposed solutions is perfect. Adequate, perhaps. Pragmatic. But none that could qualify as perfect."

Denver arched back in his chair. "For the sake of argument, since I don't understand, let's pretend I don't understand. Let's start there."

"The truth is, it's not good. No matter where you start," Ellen cautioned.

"What's she talking about, Doc?"

Stonecroft gazed at the table for several seconds. The fact that he typically responded without delay and with great eloquence disturbed Denver even further. "Mr. Collins, if we cannot discover a repeatable method of establishing a temporal rift to a specific point in time, then we will be forced into *another* solution."

"So you have another solution?"

Doc reached out and grabbed a piece of paper and a pen. He sketched out a line and scribbled three large dots on it. "Let us say, Trailer Collins, that these three dots represent three different Jumpers." He pointed. "The first, right here, represents me. I jumped from 2005. This last dot, here, represents you, Mr. Collins. Arriving from 2014." Doc hesitated and tapped his pen. "Now, let us submit that this middle dot represents a fictitious Jumper…I will name this new Jumper, *William*. William jumped from the year 2010. Are you following me?"

Denver leaned forward and nodded.

"Excellent. Now, let us also say that, for whatever reason, we could not obtain a proper TRS sample from William. We have one from myself, and from you, but not poor William. If we cannot discover a sustainable method of creating a rift to specific points in time, then William has, at best, three choices."

"Three?"

Ellen pushed a few strands of hair out of her face. "*Three.* First, William can choose to do nothing. He can just stay here, and continue to live out his life. That's one."

"That's not a great choice."

"But it is a choice," she affirmed. "Or, for option number two…he can choose to jump back with Doc. To 2005."

Denver searched their faces. "What? He would jump back to a time *before* he jumped? But that would mean there would be—"

"You got it. There would be *two* Williams," Ellen submitted. "Both living at the same time. At least, until the other William jumped in 2010. Then there would be just one again."

"So, wait…would the 2005 William have to hide out or something? Just wait around until 2010 William jumps, and then he would just slide into that life like nothing ever happened?"

"For all of its inherent difficulties and duplications," Doc stated, "you are essentially correct. It is fraught with dangerous pitfalls, but logically it remains as a tenable, though not optimal, solution."

"Our biggest concern," Ellen said, "is that there are no guarantees that William number two will jump in 2010. We may end up with two Williams, forever. No matter what."

"You lost me there. I don't understand."

Ellen and Doc exchanged glances. The elderly researcher fidgeted with the pen. "My dear Mr. Collins, our concern stems from the fact that the arrival of William number one to the year 2005 creates changes, however miniscule, to the temporal stream. The sum total of these deviations initiated by the unnecessary duplication of the two Williams' may alter future events. Therefore, due to these changes in time, William number two may not be in the exact same place and time to experience the initial jump. As long as the interactions between the two Williams' is minimized, the threat should be negligible, but there exists no way to guarantee the outcome."

Denver struggled to grasp it all. "Wow. Now that will give a guy a headache. I almost wish I hadn't asked."

"But you did," Ellen replied with a quirky smile. "Welcome to our world…on a daily basis."

"I guess working upstairs with Mr. Cheerful doesn't seem so bad all of a sudden."

"Come now," Doc interrupted. "All hope is not lost. There is at least one additional option."

Denver ran his fingers across his stubbly chin. "Okay. I suppose that choice number three involves William jumping back with me. Jumping back, or forward, to 2014?"

"Right again," Ellen confirmed. "Gorgeous and smart. I like that in my men."

"So, William mysteriously disappears for about five years, then magically reappears with me in 2014?"

"Yep," Ellen said. "But now how does William 2014 explain where he's been for the past four or five years? And we haven't even brought up the problem of people who jumped in the presence of witnesses."

"More problems?"

"Well, if Doc had jumped right in front of a group of people, even one person, during the lightning strike. But then, magically, right after the lightning bolt, there are now two people…Doc *and* William. Big problem."

"Yeah."

Ellen adopted a wicked grin and squinted. "And then there's the problem from the William who jumped in 2010. If there are witnesses during the lightning strike, then it would seem that he somehow disappeared."

"I was alone," Denver said. "In my apartment. So, no witnesses."

Doc hunched over the table. "As you can readily see, Mr. Collins, the situation is not entirely unlike a Russian Matryoshka doll." He took Ellen's right hand and encouraged her to make a small fist. Doc wrapped his left hand around it, and then covered both with his right. "Inside of each problem, lurks a series of additional problems." He peeled his hands away slowly. "And the deeper you investigate, the more you discover."

Denver fell back against his seat. "Wow. Wow. Now I see your point about things not being...*perfect*. Those would be some very difficult choices to make. I can almost understand someone choosing to stay."

"It is indeed highly probable, Mr. Collins," Doc began, "that many of us will have to select one of those three heart-wrenching and problematic choices."

Ellen sank back into her chair and gazed up without a trace of emotion in her face. "All three choices work, Denver. None of them work well."

Denver jogged back to the stairwell and craned his neck for a moment.

"Worried about Shep tracking you down?" Ellen said.

He crept back over. "No. Not Mr. Personality. Mister *Muscles*."

"Garrett?"

He nodded and kept his voice reserved. "I know that the prevailing rumor is that he jumped from the big house. From prison."

Ellen folded her arms. "*Rumor* is a bit weak if you ask me. I'd put the probability somewhere between certain and...guaranteed."

"Well," Denver began, "if that's true then there's no way he'd be willing to jump back. Would he?"

"Doc and I have talked about this at length. We feel that the only way he'll jump is if he only has a short amount of time left on his sentence."

He pulled up a chair beside her. "But if he's not going to return home, then why hasn't he left yet?"

Doc weighed in. "There could be any number of plausible justifications on his part, Mr. Collins. Perhaps it can be attributed to a more comfortable existence here in the

Jumper community. I would submit that forging an independent life would be difficult for any Jumper to undertake. Or perhaps he is seeking to keep his options open, so to speak." Doc adjusted his lab coat. "Please refrain from accusing me of resorting to clichés…but it may be that Mr. Frazier is wanting the best of both worlds."

"But if and when you guys discover how to send us all home, Garrett needs to go, too. Right? Like the military…no man left behind."

"My apologies to the future, but he needs to return," Ellen smirked.

"I harbor doubts that Mr. Frazier would concede willingly," Stonecroft added.

Denver mulled that over. *Interesting phrase, Doc.*

Concede willingly.

But what if he won't?

We probably need a plan.

June 15, 1983

SECURITY LEVEL: TOP SECRET

FOR: Lincoln D. Faurer, Director, NSA
FROM: William Joseph Casey, Director, Central Intelligence
SUBJECT: NSA Surveillance (NSSD 7-83)

I have been authorized by President Reagan (NSSD 7-83) to coordinate a cross-agency intelligence effort to locate a male child abducted on May 28th from Lincoln Terrace Park in Brooklyn. The child is Denver Wayne Collins, son of Terry and Valerie Collins of Midtown, Brooklyn, NY. Birthdate: 01/21/1979.

The location and safety of the aforementioned child is deemed vital and critical to the national security of the United States.

The President has authorized warrantless wiretapping across New York State in an effort to yield actionable intelligence on the location of this child. The President has also authorized the use of all available NSA resources, placing this effort at Strategic Objective Priority 1 status.

END

DCI/NSA/PS

CHAPTER 6

Marbles?

Why in the world does Doc want a bag of marbles?

An intrigued Denver Collins followed Leah and Shep down the stairwell into The Basement. They had almost reached the bottom when curiosity compelled him. "So, Leah, why did they ask you to go out and buy a bag of marbles?"

Shep slowed. "Maybe Stonecroft has finally lost his."

Leah kept moving and pushed past. "I don't know."

Denver pulled in a deep breath. *Well, at least she sorta spoke to me. That's better than the silent treatment I've been getting lately.*

"Thank you, my dear Ms. Swan," Doc offered affably as he took possession of the little pouch. "Miss Finegan, if you would select a single piece for us."

Chief McCloud, who was seated at the table, examined his hat. "So, Doc. What kinda magic show we gonna see today? Better'n the last one?"

"No illusions and no deception here, Chief McCloud," the researcher replied. "Just the application of sound scientific principles."

McCloud lowered the hat to the table and leaned his round head back. "And I thought I had ya pegged for a snake oil salesman. I was gonna ask to see your business license."

Doc migrated towards the open door to the portal chamber. "If everyone would join me for a moment, I will provide a brief explanation of our experiment."

"Brief?" Shep mumbled as they began moving. "Why start now?"

The four observers joined the pair of researchers and crossed the threshold. Denver noticed a tiny trough, about five feet long and a half-inch wide, which appeared to end exactly at the portal itself.

Looks like a section of a tiny roller coaster.

With cute little wooden supports.

Doc stepped out in front of the group, brandishing a single marble. "As you can see, Mr. Frazier has constructed a miniature rail system. This marble will be placed at this end of the track." He knelt beside it and lowered the glass ball. "There is a small gate here which prevents the marble from beginning to roll down the gentle slope and into the portal at the far end."

Doc picked up a roll of thin string. "As we exit the chamber, I will unwind this spindle and feed it beneath the door. At the proper moment, once the portal is energized, we will release the glass sphere. The acquisition of our superconductive materials by Mr. Collins has greatly enhanced our ability to maintain a relatively stable temporal rift." He slowly crept along the rail, moving away from them. "It will proceed along this trajectory toward the terminus, which is aligned precisely with the plane of the portal."

McCloud pushed forward. "So, what then?"

"That's the million-dollar question, Chief," Ellen called out from behind the small assembly. "The ball will continue into the portal. It will be our first test of actual mass, not just light, passing into the portal."

"Where will it go?" Denver asked. He caught himself. "Or *when* will it go?"

"Not a clue," Ellen admitted with an infectious smile. "We haven't a clue."

"But if the mass vanishes," Doc said, "it will be an event of immeasurable import. A truly spectacular milestone. One for the books, as they say. My research journal will never be the same once I record it."

Shep rolled his eyes. "Are you telling me that a little marble disappearing is some kinda big deal? To be honest, it sounds like you two are just lowering the bar. And expectations. Nice play."

"On the contrary, Mr. Sheppard, to make the transition from light, which is essentially comprised of pure energy, to transporting even the most meager morsel of mass, is an accomplishment worthy of the annals of physics."

"So says *you*," Shep retorted. "A man playing with marbles."

"It's time to begin," Ellen interrupted, shooting Shep a dirty look. "Would everyone mind stepping back into the control room so that we can seal the door? It may not be safe in here."

"You're serious?" Shep asked. "You're actually worried about a damn little ball? Really?"

Doc's platinum eyebrows rose above the frame of his spectacles as he inched closer to Shep. "Really."

Denver knew the routine well. He donned his eye protection and jockeyed for a better view through the undersized window penetrating the impressive door. As he studied Ellen engaging the power throttle, the reverberating roar of the apparatus was noticeably lessened.

"Thanks to the superconductive metals," Doc explained to the group, "our efficiencies in terms of power transfer are orders of magnitude ahead of previous experiments. This translates to obvious benefits. I have no doubt that you can both hear the difference, and *feel* the difference."

"Ain't no doubt about that," the Chief replied. "I can actually hear myself think this time."

Doc continued manipulating various dials and controls before finally reaching overhead and donning his own goggles. He glanced over at Ellen and she offered a quick thumbs up with a joyful smile. Through the window, the surreal lightshow intensified in all of its eerie splendor. A wash of blue light bathed the spectators as Stonecroft bent over to pick up the release string.

"Ladies and gentlemen," he began in an elevated voice, "we are on the threshold of an invisible entry into the history books. As they say, keep your eye on the ball."

All pressed forward while the researcher tugged on the wire. As predicted, the marble inaugurated its slow descent down the gradual ramp toward the maelstrom of colored fury before it.

Four seconds later the tiny, glass sphere intersected the surface of the portal.

Denver could have sworn he felt a shockwave slap his chest a fraction of a second before the deafening roar of the massive explosion. Regardless of his comprehension of the precise order of events, the radiance of the portal chamber had rivalled that of the sun for a few thousandths of a second prior to the blast.

Leah hurled herself away from the door, screaming.

Ellen immediately killed the power.

The Chief rushed over to console Leah.

A silent Doc Stonecroft strolled up to Shep and slowly raised his own goggles. He cleared his throat as he locked eyes with him. "Like I said, Mr. Sheppard. *Really*."

Denver sought to examine the aftermath through the window, but a smoky mist in the chamber clouded any real sense of detail. Doc pushed past him.

"Would you be so kind as to assist me in opening the door, Mr. Collins?"

"You got it."

Tiny rivulets of what appeared to be steam snaked towards them as the door initially cracked open. A distinct and unusual aroma of burnt-something followed closely behind. Denver's eyes began stinging at once and he struggled to blink away a rush of tears.

"It's perfectly safe," Doc assured, rubbing his own eyes. "The composition of the marble was primarily glass. Silicon dioxide. You have nothing to fear in terms of noxious gases or fumes. The haze will dissipate." Doc stepped through the doorway and navigated towards the portal.

"Most curious," he said, adjusting his glasses.

Denver coughed as he pulled up behind him.

"What's wrong, Doc? Besides the obvious explosion thing and all this smoke."

Doc gestured. "The rails."

"What about the rails?"

Doc faced him with eyes wide. "They are gone."

Denver glanced down, and then scanned the area.

The stunned scientist was correct. The marble ramp had indeed vanished.

"Where did it go?" Denver inquired.

Doc shook his head. "A mystery."

Shep's booming voice interrupted them. "There's no mystery here, Stonecroft. I found your damn ramp."

The two pivoted around and peered back through the lessening fog. Shep stared at several dark streaks on the backside of the door. Doc jogged down the transom and studied the anomaly.

"Heavens," he exclaimed. "The forces required to achieve this are…fearful."

"Achieve what?" a trailing Denver asked.

Then he saw it.

The metal rails which had previously comprised the majority of the ramp were embedded inside the thick metal of the door. Splattered puddles of blackened metal pocked the area surrounding the primary impact zone. The wooden support system which had cradled the rails was nowhere to be seen.

A glint in the wall just to the left of the door caught Denver's attention. He stepped forward and worked the shiny piece of debris loose with his fingernails.

"Well, Doc…was that scary explosion a success?" the Chief asked with Leah and Ellen in tow. "Did the marble meet the future, or did it meet its maker?" He grinned.

"I, I cannot even begin to venture a response, Chief McCloud."

"I can," Denver announced. "Look at this." He dropped the object into the palm of his right hand as the group flocked around him.

Doc retrieved the bit of evidence with trembling fingers and raised his spectacles. "Merciful heavens…this is conclusive," he observed, with disappointment punctuating each syllable.

"What is it?" Leah asked.

Denver bit his lip. "It's a chunk of the marble."

The Chief adjusted his hat. "It met its maker."

Shep snickered as he peeled away from the group and exited the chamber. "Wow. Now my expectations are even lower than before." He grabbed the edge of the door. "And that's really saying something."

"Shut up, Sheppard!" Ellen yelled. "Just shut the hell up!"

"It is alright, Miss Finegan," Doc consoled with a soft hand on her heaving shoulder. "Mr. Sheppard is entitled to his opinions. As we all are."

"Well, he can keep his damn opinions to himself," she retorted.

Denver scrambled to defuse the tense situation. "So, Doc, in layman's terms…what does this mean?"

Doc obviously forced a smile and dropped the tell-tale debris into his chest pocket. "It means, Mr. Collins…that I need to ask Mr. Frazier to construct a few more ramps." He sauntered towards the door, then looked back.

"As Edison admonished us…'*When you have exhausted all possibilities, remember this - you haven't.*'"

Research Log: Dr. Glen D. Stonecroft

DATE: December 10, 1956

The inestimable loss of Emile continues to manifest in our recent setbacks in The Basement. My optimism, though diminished, remains firm, but I suspect that Miss Finegan is succumbing to gradual despair. Her emotional pain appears to be hampering her ability to concentrate at times. I fear that my expertise in dealing with abstract concepts renders me a miserable comforter in the affairs of the heart.

Our demonstration and experimentation yesterday regarding the transference of mass remains an embarrassing failure, but recent calculations have shed new light on a possible solution. I have already implemented the changes to our magnetic tolerances. I am encouraged by the increasingly stable nature of the rift.

Mr. Frazier is committed to the construction of no less than 6 ramps in the next 72 hours, and has pledged to have one completed by 3:00 p.m. Thankfully, our supply of marbles is a non-issue.

G.D.S.

****

UPDATE:

Our second test of mass transference was attempted at 4:20 p.m. today. Only Ellen Finegan and I were present.

In spite of my calculations and the new settings, the lackluster results were nearly identical to our previous experiment. The sole difference being that the ramp, though mangled beyond repair, was not embedded into the door or walls of the chamber.

We also discovered and repaired a minor leak in the liquid nitrogen cooling system.

G.D.S.

CHAPTER 7

For three different hotels in Bloomington, Illinois, the Christmas travel rush seemed to have arrived a few weeks early.

To avoid arousing local suspicion, Howard Ross scheduled the massive influx of Project SATURN personnel to descend upon the area in several waves over a two-day period. All CIA staff had been instructed to speak in vague terms regarding an end-of-the-year business meeting for State Farm Insurance, a principal employer in the modest community of 35,000.

A defunct warehouse on the far-east side of town was rented for vehicle, equipment and weapons storage, and was soon retrofitted as a temporary incarceration center as well. A sizable and round-the-clock guard unit was established to discourage prying eyes.

A dozen or so senior staff members joined Howard Ross and Neal Schaeffer in a makeshift conference room deep inside the frigid facility. An outer ring of kerosene heaters added a warm glow to the convocation, but were ineffectual at moderating the air temperature to any real degree. To a casual observer, the unseasonably bitter cold temperatures combined with breathing created the illusion of a table surrounded by heavy smokers.

"I know I don't have to remind everyone about what exactly is at stake here," Ross began as he circled his captive audience. "We are acting upon the most conclusive intel SATURN has encountered in years." He paused. "I know we lost many good men, a lot of our friends, our SATURN *brothers*, in the recent assault at Dreamland. Trust me when I say we will not let that damn atrocity go unanswered. There will be justice."

Several heads bobbed in agreement.

"But also hear me when I say that our mission today, our mission now, is not about revenge. It is not about retribution. It is about *reconnaissance*. It is about *recovery*. Recovery of high-value targets and recovery of high-value technology." Ross stopped suddenly and leaned onto the table for effect. "We have the opportunity to do something truly transformative gentlemen. I know it sounds like a damn political slogan, but it's true…we can change the world. Payback will come later. You've got my word on that."

Neal rose from his seat and unfolded an impressive map of the area. One by one all of the agents pushed up out of their cold, metal folding chairs to obtain a better view.

Ross picked up a long wooden pointer and swirled it across the map. "At this moment, we are here. On the east side of Bloomington." He relocated the tip. "Our target area for initial reconnaissance is right here. On the north side of Normal. As you can see, there is a single, large building off the main road. Our intel suggests that there may be a significant portion of the site underground. Some type of temporal research facility below the surface, in a basement or similar."

Ross repositioned himself. "One building, one target. Keeps it clean and focused. On the down side, though, there are not too many opportunities for good cover. There are trees and a few side roads, but not much else. The damn topography isn't cooperating either, boys. Good luck finding any useful elevation to gain a decent line of sight with any real protection."

"Do we have any preliminary intelligence on the number of persons we may encounter at the facility?" one agent inquired from the opposite side.

"A legitimate question, for sure, Whittington," Ross replied. "But the short answer is…we don't know. I opted to forego an advance team…for several reasons. Not the least of which was my concern that early surveillance could alert our targets, leading to a high flight probability. What you see before you is just about all I know."

"Do we have any indication that Denver Collins is on site, or will be on site?"

Neal intercepted the question. "That is a distinct possibility, Agent Bollinger, and it does align with our best theories. But we have no specific *intelligence* on which to base that assertion. Just conjecture and probability."

"Any other burning questions out there before I continue?" Ross inquired.

"In the eventual assault on the facility, are we anticipating armed resistance?"

Ross rocked back on his heels and thought for a moment. "The old saying that the past is the best gauge for predicting the future comes into play here, Agent Hargraves. It would be reckless to disregard the fact that Denver Collins and an unknown female were able to kill over a dozen well-trained men within our SATURN security forces."

Ross folded his arms. "We are obviously dealing with a group of dangerous…of *lethal* individuals who understand and utilize firepower. And they did all that on *our* turf." He took the time to survey most of their faces. "Imagine what they could do on their own soil. They do have home field advantage."

Ross paused to let that thought soak in. The solemnity of the exhortation combined with the lull in the briefing led a majority of the staff to retake their seats.

Ross fired up his first cigarette of the meeting. "We can't blow this one, gentlemen. We gotta close up every loophole and seal up any possible leak. Nothing's gonna get through this net. I wanna know what transpires at this location, minute by minute. I wanna know the gender, age, height and weight of every person that walks in or out of that building. Hell, I wanna know their damn shoe size and whether or not they prefer chocolate or vanilla ice cream."

He stepped within inches of a kerosene heater and hovered both hands above it. "Mr. Schaeffer has already outlined shift and duty rosters for one day of twenty-four hour surveillance. *Whittington, Wilson, and Hovis*. Heads up. I wanna see a comprehensive plan, including vehicle recommendations, routes and alternate routes, staffing needs, and weapons recommendations for eventual human extraction by tonight."

He took a long pull on his cigarette and headed back towards the table. "*Hargraves…Bollinger*. I need background information on the property, the building, previous owners, and details concerning all adjacent neighbors. *Mitchell…Durbin*. Once surveillance begins in the morning, have a team in place to track down identities, vehicle registration information and residence information for all persons of interest."

A tolerable amount of quiet and focused conversation broke out sporadically as various agents relocated into functional groups. Ross overlooked the controlled chaos as he continued. "*Clark*. Where's Clark? I haven't seen him today."

Neal looked back as he distributed an armload of folders. "Oh, Clark. He's sick. Stomach flu. Pretty rough shape. Thought you knew."

"Make sure to notify him that he's been—"

"Assigned to aerial recon?" Neal asked. "Yes. He has been notified. And his team."

Ross sighed. "Does he have the list of general aviation airfields and the maps?"

"He will. By morning."

"Earlier," Ross demanded.

"By midnight."

"That's better. But don't mistake better for good."

"It's on my list, boss," Neal said.

"*Scarborough?*" Ross cried out.

"Yes, sir?"

"I need an update on Dr. Gottlieb and his staff."

The stocky agent jerked his sleeve back, studying his watch. "Their wheels touched down at Glenview about an hour ago. They will be checking into their hotel around eight o'clock tonight."

"Which hotel?"

"Bravo. Same as mine."

"Did you double-check their transportation detail?"

"*Triple*-checked, sir."

Ross blew out a lungful of smoke and pointed. "Make sure you and your staff assist him with absolutely everything he needs. Everything. I need to make sure our first round of interrogation is as...*fruitful* as possible. And don't forget the recording gear."

Scarborough nodded. "I understand. Most of the medical equipment that shipped with us has already been installed."

Ross kept moving and the noise continued to rise. "*James?*"

"Right here."

"It goes without saying that you need to coordinate the security personnel needs for each of the other details. Looks like your staff has things under control here at the warehouse."

"Yes, sir. Thank you, sir."

Ross yanked out his cigarette. "And I want hotel surveillance and security at all three locations. I wanna know if anyone is watching the watchers, Mr. James."

"Whatever you need, sir."

Ross dropped his cigarette and crushed it. "*Schaeffer*…who do we have on transportation and logistics?"

"Franklin," Neal hollered. "Oh, and Simpson is coordinating the grub. An army travels on its stomach, you know."

"Including the three tractor-trailer trucks?"

"Peterbilt 281s," Neal replied. "Almost brand new."

"Did we get the Illinois license plates, Mr. Franklin?"

"They are on a delivery truck from Chicago as we speak," the agent assured him.

Neal examined his watch. "Correction. They're probably already here. Along with a few extra cases of FBI badges and radios."

Ross shot the agent a well-understood look.

Franklin jumped out of his seat. "Right. I'll go check on it now."

"Who did you assign to be our liaison with local law enforcement, Mr. Schaeffer?"

Neal grinned. "I thought you would do nicely, boss."

"I don't do anything nicely."

"Good point," Neal quipped. "That's why I assigned Culbertson."

Ross stopped and cocked his head. "Culbertson?"

"*Bruce*. Bruce Culbertson. Black hair. Former Marine. Looks kinda like James Dean. Only taller. And he rarely wears jeans. If ever."

"But he's dead."

"*Dean* is, yes. But Culbertson…he is very much alive. At least, he was three hours ago. One never knows though, I hear Bloomington can get a little rough once the sun sets."

"I wanna meet with him. Right after breakfast."

Neal dropped into a chair to rummage through a briefcase. "He has a room three doors down from you. Hold on...Hotel Alpha...Room...2-1-7."

"Right after breakfast," Ross reiterated. "Make it happen."

Neal snagged a pen. "I'll add it to the list."

"Who's handling radios?"

"Uh, that would be Harris. And Brock. Like always."

Ross hesitated. "And I wanna meet with Gottlieb, and you, *during* breakfast."

"He's a vegetarian," Neal mumbled.

"What?"

"Dr. Gottlieb. He's a vegetarian. Didn't know if you knew."

Ross frowned. "Does that somehow affect his basic ability to simply share a morning meal with me, Mr. Schaeffer?"

"Just be sensitive, boss. And don't make any meat or animal jokes."

Ross glared at him. "I *won't* add it to my list, Mr. Schaeffer."

"Now that's the Chief Howard Ross we've all come to love and avoid," Neal teased before returning to his documentation.

"Did you put Lehman and Younce on TDS imaging?"

"10-4. Just like in Roswell."

"And what a wonderful memory that was."

Schaeffer glanced up and gestured over to the right. "The developing booth is about twenty yards that way. Or, it will be."

"What about the heroin and the cash?"

"Scheduled to be here by tomorrow afternoon."

"Better be. That candy will come in handy. Make sure."

"It's on my list."

After less than thirty seconds of silent assessment, a new cigarette, and a good deal of pacing, Ross clapped his hands. "Alright. Listen up, gentlemen. Listen up."

It took a few moments, but they did.

Ross approached the table, retrieved his pointer and rapped on the map. "This little building, this little business here, or whatever the hell it is on the north side of town…could be the temporal Holy Grail. I believe we are about to change the future, and if you can wrap your mind around it…maybe even change the past. Imagine a world map without any red. Instead, just red, white, and blue. Would you like to see Adolf Hitler swinging at the end of a long rope from a tall tree in the middle of the damn Sudetenland in 1938?"

Ross took a deep breath and stepped back. "How about sinking half a dozen Jap aircraft carriers headed towards Hawaii on December *sixth,* 1941? Anyone interested in embarking on a mission of discovery that'll make the one by Christopher Columbus look like beginner's luck in a trio of jon boats?"

He stared at a roomful of silent faces. The only discernible sound was the pulsating rumble emanating from the ring of heaters.

"Barring any unforeseen disasters, we will initiate one full day of surveillance and recon beginning tomorrow morning at six o'clock. Local time."

Howard Ross brought the stick up to his shoulder like a sniper's rifle. "And on day two…" He adjusted his head as if peering through a scope.

"…we take 'em all out."

Research Log: Dr. Glen D. Stonecroft

DATE: December 11, 1956

Overnight, my sleep was fitful at best. On several occasions I abandoned my bed and either re-evaluated our calculations or engaged in light reading. Poetry rarely fails in solacing a troubled breast.

I am quite perplexed concerning our inability to penetrate the portal. While we have maintained the ability to receive light, I fear that it may be impossible to transmit mass in the opposite direction.

As far as the mathematical models suggest, this should not present an insurmountable barrier. But I suspect that the symphony of nature cares little concerning the musical score that we have crafted through our equations.

Mr. Frazier delivered the remaining ramps a few moments ago. We are in the process of implementing phase changes to one of the magnets. Compounding wave alignment is one possible explanation for the mystery of an intangible yet impermeable portal.

G.D.S.

****

UPDATE:

Though not a success, our third attempt at mass transference yielded a most remarkable result. As the glass sphere intersected the plane of the portal, the marble began expanding outward as it halted forward motion. Before Miss Finegan could cut the power, the marble had grown to a diameter of 5.6 feet and had pushed the ramp back a considerable distance.

As would be expected due to the First Law (but still surprising nonetheless), its overall mass remained identical to that of a small marble. A clear, solid ball the height of an adult human, yet weighing only 45 grams is an oddity by any definition. The increased surface area, combined with negligible mass, led to considerable movement of the ball merely by the change in pressure as we opened the chamber door.

Unfortunately, the curiosity shattered after a short period of investigation and measurement. Miss Finegan was able to document the object through photography. The ramp was unharmed.

We still have far more questions than definitive answers, but any experiment which refrains from resulting in a destructive explosion is worthy of celebration.

G.D.S.

CHAPTER 8

The aroma of a busy grill announced that he had located the right place.

Neal Schaeffer exited the sidewalk along Main Street in Bloomington and jogged down the steps. A hand-painted sign caught his eye as he entered the subterranean establishment:

Cotton's Village Inn.

An underground restaurant?

Feels like I'm back at home in Nevada.

A late-middle aged hostess greeted him. "A table for one this evening, sir?"

Neal surveyed the cramped space with colorful murals gracing whitewashed walls. "No ma'am. I'm with the *Smith* party."

She nodded and whirled around. "Ah, yes. Right this way."

The hostess led him off to a series of smaller rooms around the bend which lined the back of the diner. Neal detected Ross' cigarette smoke long before he caught sight of his boss with a handful of other senior staff members. He slipped into a chair and continued to admire the décor.

"Well, gentlemen, this is...*quaint*," Neal observed as the hostess handed him a one-page menu and walked off.

"Welcome below ground in Bloomington, Illinois," Ross said. "And if everything goes according to plan, we will be underground again tomorrow. In Normal, Illinois. In about...oh...nineteen hours or so."

"Somehow, I doubt the accommodations will be this nice."

Ross gestured. "The manager tells me these little rooms back here used to be coal bins. Back in the day."

"It's fitting," Neal responded, enjoying the slight echo. "I mean, your lungs are probably black as coal, Chief."

"Not nearly as black as my heart."

"And I'm not touching that one." Neal assessed a quick inventory of the area. "Kinda quiet in this back-half of the place."

"Let's just say I've paid extra for the privacy," Ross commented.

"About your style. So, what's good here?"

Ross held up his menu and pointed. "I've had the Swiss Steak. It's tolerable. And we've already ordered. We didn't wait."

Agent Bollinger cradled his coffee in both hands. "The desserts are better than tolerable. Especially the pecan pie."

"Or the ham loaf," Agent Hargraves suggested.

Neal's eyebrows shot up. "Well, it appears that everyone but me has had plenty of time to evaluate the culinary delights of uptown Bloomington."

"Only my second time down here," Ross countered.

"But my *first*," Neal replied. "I've been busy."

"We've all been busy." Ross deposited his cigarette into an ashtray. "And I'm sure you have a fantastic excuse to explain why you're late tonight."

Neal continued to study the hand-typed menu. "Fantastic isn't the first word that comes to mind. I was thinking more like…*intriguing*." He lowered his volume. "Early this morning, an older man—a much older man—was seen going into the facility."

"The old man is old news, Mr. Schaeffer," Ross retorted. "I've been briefed on the day's recon."

"Several others have come and gone, Chief. But, as of fifteen minutes ago, the elderly gentleman has yet to come out of the facility." He paused. "Ten hours in one building? What's he doing in there? A bingo marathon? Feeding horses? What?"

"By tomorrow afternoon, we will have that intriguing answer, Mr. Schaeffer."

A waitress came around the corner and strolled up to their table. She stared at the latest arrival. "Welcome to Cotton's, sir. Are you ready to order, and can I get you a drink?"

"Oh, yes, let's see," Neal began. "I will have…the Swiss Steak. And a side salad. With Italian dressing. And a glass of wine. Red wine. Any red will do."

The waitress nodded and departed.

Ross retrieved his nearly-spent cigarette. "Has the…substance and money arrived yet?"

"Yes sir," Agent Whittington replied, almost whispering. "One hundred pounds of heroin, and thirty-five thousand in cash. It's at the warehouse now. Under heavy guard."

Ross wagged his cigarette. "Make sure it's loaded and ready to be hauled to the location no later than tomorrow morning. First thing. Let's see and hear the plan."

Whittington reached into his breast pocket and spread out a small map. "At two o'clock in the afternoon tomorrow, local time, our perimeter detail will take up positions," he pointed, "here, here, here, and right there. To keep prying eyes away, we will set up roadblocks five minutes prior to that…here and here. Phone lines, located here by the power lines along the backside of the property, will be cut right as the first assault team moves in."

Ross smiled and blew out a long trail of smoke as he looked across the table. "Phone lines. Dead giveaway." He paused. "Most of all that involves your people, Agent James. Are you ready?"

"One hundred percent, sir."

"Good," Ross replied. "I like it. Continue, Whittington."

"The first assault team moves in at 2:05 exactly. A six-man team, followed quickly by a second six-man team."

"I am still leading the first team, right?" Neal inquired.

Ross nodded silently.

Whittington kept his voice low. "Both teams will be equipped with semi-automatic weapons, chloroform, and restraints. Simultaneously, four delivery trucks will take up positions out front, ready to receive all suspects. There will be three armed guards inside the rear of each truck, and one up front with the driver. Two cars, each filled with security, will both lead and trail the convoy." He paused and covered the map with his arms as their waitress drew near with Neal's wine.

"Here you are, sir. Can I get anyone anything?"

"We're fine," Ross replied. "Make sure we're not disturbed again until the food arrives."

She clapped her hands together. "Whatever you like, gentlemen."

Whittington watched her disappear around the bend and then slid his arms back. "The four delivery trucks, loaded with human cargo, will exit the main drive and head west, then south. They will travel south along Route 66, and then the outer road, located here, and pull inside the warehouse at Dock 14. Once the delivery trucks are gone from the site, a pair of Peterbilt 281's, complete with trailers, will arrive and take up end-to-end positions along the front of the building to block line-of-sight of any passersby from the main road."

Ross interrupted as a new cigarette blazed to life. "What about our gear? The TDS cameras and all?"

"A third tractor-trailer, loaded with that equipment, will back up to the side of the facility near the large side door. The secure perimeter will be maintained during the remainder of the operation." He dropped his voice even further. "The heroin and the large sums of cash will be in the third truck."

Ross leaned back and took a quick hit on his smoke. "Does Dr. Gottlieb have everything he needs?"

Neal jumped in. "I just spoke with him, probably an hour ago. He reported that he and his staff are ready at the warehouse. Cameras and recording equipment as well." He smiled and took a drink. "I for one cannot wait to see what these time travelers have done with all that super-conductive metal Collins stole from us. Their technology and research could save us decades of research."

"Are there any indications that our presence or activities are being monitored by local law enforcement or other interested parties, Agent James?"

"Nothing of concern to report on that front, sir."

"I've heard that Mennonite activity has increased," Ross said. "Lots more of them damn black cars moving around."

"They're thick in these parts," James explained. "Amish are more toward the south. Mennonites up here to the north."

"Make sure all teams are equipped with powerful flashlights, Neal," Ross noted. "Once we go below ground, they might kill the power."

"It's on my list."

Ross leaned forward onto his elbows. "What is the latest intel on the number of suspects we should expect in the facility at 2:05 p.m. tomorrow?"

Neal took a small sip of his wine. "It remains at ten."

"How many females?"

"Just two."

"Well," Ross began, "we have two women, seven men, and one old man."

Agent James arched forward while Whittington stowed the map. "Is there a chance that one of the two women is the female who assisted Denver Collins in his escape from Dreamland?"

Neal swirled his glass and gazed into the small whirlpool of wine. "That…is a very distinct possibility. We could get both Collins and her. But just remember what those two did to us a few weeks ago. This won't be like taking candy from—"

"We have the advantage of surprise this damn time," Ross interjected. "Speed is the key here." He toyed with his cigarette for several seconds.

"Tomorrow, we hit them fast. We hit them hard."

Research Log: Dr. Glen D. Stonecroft

DATE: December 12, 1956

I may have stumbled upon a significant discovery related to the continued impenetrability of our sustained rift. I was meditating on our magnetic phases, when my mind drifted to thoughts concerning the Earth's own magnetic field. The magnetosphere, while simultaneously protecting the planet's inhabitants from fatal solar emissions, also allows for more beneficial particles and frequencies to permeate so that life may thrive.

As I held a marble, I pictured our own beautiful blue marble of a globe. My cogitations centered upon our two polar regions, and at that precise moment a potential solution presented: Polarity.

I have enlisted the aid of Mr. Collins and Mr. Frazier to assist Miss Finegan and me as we reverse the polarity in our system. I estimate that the process should not require more than three hours. Barring complications, we may be able to attempt a new experiment by sunset.

I am most encouraged by this new possibility.

G.D.S.

CHAPTER 9

2:04 p.m.

It's still 2:04 p.m.

He knew it wasn't physically possible, but it appeared that time itself had succumbed to the suffocating tension that was gripping his own trembling chest. As Neal Schaeffer checked and rechecked his watch, his thoughts raced with unparalleled nervous excitement. A decade-long manhunt was coming to a breathless head in less than sixty seconds.

He couldn't begin to imagine what Ross must've been feeling in the command vehicle just over a hundred yards to the north.

Neal took a moment to glance around at the five well-armed agents seated around him. These were the somber faces of the men who were about to alter the balance of world power in unconceivable ways. He felt the jolt as the vehicle's axles left the asphalt and pulled onto the gravel leading up to the structure.

This is it.

This is real.

He thought about the wallet. About Caretaker.

I have a thousand questions for you…Denver Wayne Collins.

Neal drew out his revolver and examined his watch.

2:05.

"Let's move out!" he ordered.

The door was thrown open and the assault team poured forth out of the vehicle in a precisely calculated and well-rehearsed, fluid motion. The lethal squad advanced to the entrance along the nearest side of the building. Neal offered a subtle nod and a stocky agent rushed up and kicked in the heavy door.

"Move in," Neal snapped.

Four agents slipped inside according to an established rotation, as Neal Schaeffer trailed behind for a few moments. The remaining team member scanned the exterior a final time, and then proceeded through the doorway directly behind his superior.

The drastic change in lighting was an unexpected hazard that temporarily caught Neal and his team off-guard. A calm voice called out to them through the murky and dusty darkness. "Greetings, friends. Can we help you with something?"

Neal's unprepared eyes began to adjust to the reduction in illumination. He saw at least three men approaching. They appeared to be clad in all black, with thick beards, and matching hats.

"I say, my friends," the comforting voice repeated, "are you in some sort of trouble or distress? We mean you no harm."

Neal waved his gun. "Secure and restrain these men." His team surrounded the trio and had them on their knees and handcuffed in seconds. He grabbed his radio. "Send in Team Two."

"Please, my friend," one of the men entreated, "for what purpose have you come? We offer you no resistance. As God's servants, we will not bring you harm."

Agent Schaeffer studied the expansive yet deceptively simple structure. *It not only looks like a barn from the outside…it is a barn.*

He sucked in a deep breath.

His nostrils were met by the unmistakable aroma of decomposing hay blended with the pungency of moist soil.

It even smells like a barn.

Three members from his team fanned out and conducted a rudimentary examination of the area. Neal trained his pistol on the hayloft to his left, relieved to find no trace of movement overhead. As he closed in on the detainees, he noticed a pair of rustic and well-used farm carts resting in the center of the damp, dirt floor.

A functioning barn?

Without warning, the area flooded with intense shafts of dust-filled light as the thick door crashed open for a second time and Ross advanced inside the farm building with his team.

"The area has been secured," Neal called out. "Three suspects neutralized. Over here."

Ross drew alongside his second-in-command and motioned to his own squad. "Check every square-inch, boys. Root out the remaining suspects. They're all here. Somewhere. Probably below ground. Look for trapdoors or stairs." He knelt down and locked eyes with one of the suspects. "Where are the others?"

No response.

"How do we access the sublevels?"

A new, soothing voice echoed from the farthest, darkest corner of the barn. "What is this talk of sublevels? Excuse me, sirs. May I help you?"

Several weapons raised up and were trained on the approaching figure. His own right hand waved from side to side in a non-confrontational manner. "Please, please, friends. Lower your weapons. We are a peaceful community of God's servants. Your violent ways are foreign to us, my friends."

Ross ventured forward. "I'm not your damn friend. Stop right where you are. And put your hands on your head. Or you will experience the very meaning of violence."

The bearded man halted and complied, but with an odd smile. "Forsake your weapons, my friends. I am Brother James. I am one of the elders of this community. We are Mennonites. Mennonites of the Weaverland Conference. From the Old Order."

"And I am Santa Claus," Ross retorted. "From the North Pole Conference of the FBI." He hesitated. "And you are under arrest. All four of you are. Cuff him and search him."

Three agents responded to the task with rough efficiency, but Brother James was unrelenting in his tranquil appeal. "I assure you that whatever grievance your…*agency* has with our farm, or our people, it is based upon a misunderstanding. And please, I beg of you, lower your weapons."

Ross squinted and sauntered up to the curious figure. "First, *brother*…you are in no position to ask me anything. And second, *brother*, we have conclusive evidence that activities, possibly dangerous to the welfare of the United States, have been occurring on this property."

The man almost chuckled. "Dangerous activities? Merciful heavens, since when is the simple practice of corn and wheat farming detrimental to the welfare of the good people of our great and blessed land which the Lord has given?"

"My evidence is beyond question." Ross turned away and raised his voice. "Have we found a damn door or a trapdoor yet?!"

"I will ask you, one final time," Brother James implored, "to lower your weapons. We do not wish to harm you."

Ross spun back around. "Harm *us?* What're you going to do, old MacDonald? Stab us all with pitchforks?"

The elder seemed unaffected by the verbal abuse. "We have been blessed to cultivate this fertile plot for over ten years, and we harbor no ill will toward any man. Please, consult with our neighbors, or ask the people of the community. We have sought to live simple lives of peace and godliness. We have nothing to hide."

Neal was impressed with the man's performance.

Wow. He's pretty convincing, I'll give him that.

Schaeffer trotted over to the pair of wagons and surveyed the barn once again.

All of this is pretty convincing. Clever disguise.

His hand slid along the rough, splintered wood of the cart's creaking frame.

It seems…perfect.

That single word began haunting him.

Wait.

It doesn't just seem perfect.

It is perfect.

A new, disturbing line of thinking refused to be ignored.

What if it's not an act?

Oh, no.

Neal rotated around and surveyed the aging barn once again.

I think we've just made a huge mistake.

July 8, 1983

SECURITY LEVEL: TOP SECRET

FOR: Chief Neal Schaeffer, Project SATURN
FROM: Richard Forsythe, Northeast Section
SUBJECT: Kidnapping Update

NYPD received an anonymous tip today concerning the whereabouts of Denver Wayne Collins at 7:25 a.m. ET. Officers responded and discovered the child, in stable condition, in a wooden crate in the New York Shipyards.

The child was immediately taken to Maimonides Medical Center for physical, emotional, and psychological evaluation. Terry and Valerie Collins are with him. Our team is investigating all leads, in association with the FBI.

END

PS

CHAPTER 10

Neal had trouble dismissing his newfound and unsettling suspicion. As an authority within the nation's foremost intelligence apparatus concerning both secrecy and deception, his own confidence had been greatly shaken. If this barn and these Mennonites were an illusion, then his compliments to the magician.

He was surely a master.

But...what if we are completely mistaken?

What if these people are who they claim to be?

A sudden announcement from a member of the second team broke Neal's introspection. "Sir? There appears to be a large metal object concealed beneath these hay wagons."

The casual grin on Brother James' face had not altered since his arrival. "Friends, that is just a metal plate covering an old cistern. This barn was built over it several years ago."

Ross moved towards this new area of interest. "Well, if it's just a cistern, then surely you won't mind if we take a little peak, will you?"

"Please," Brother James cried out, "do not lift that plate, Chief Ross."

Neal glanced up.

What? What did he just say?

Did he just say 'Chief Ross'?

But how...?

Complete silence overtook the barn as Ross pivoted about and studied the now-serious expression of Brother James. Schaeffer watched in fascination as the two men appeared to be locked in an unspoken combat of the wills. Ross was pokerfaced as he trained his gun directly at the suspect's head. "And how do you know my name? And don't tell me that a little angel just told you."

Brother James addressed him low and slow. "Chief Ross, I must insist. Lower. Your. Weapons."

"Why?" he asked, stepping closer. "Is it a sin to corrupt this holy place with our evil guns?"

"Of course not, friend," Brother James declared. "It's simply because we have you and your men hopelessly outnumbered and unquestionably outgunned."

Neal and Ross traded fast glances and then scanned the barn. "What the hell are you talking about, preacher?" Ross inquired skeptically.

Brother James attempted to move forward but two pairs of resolute arms restrained him. "Listen to me," he growled. "You need to turn around, right now, and go call your boss' boss. He will tell you that you are way outside of your damn jurisdiction here."

Ross shook his head and reached for his wallet. "Well, well. I guess you're no more a man of God than I am an agent of the FBI." He flipped his wallet open and displayed his credentials. "Howard Ross—*Chief* Howard Ross—with the Central Intelligence Agency. Oh, and your whole *boss' boss* thing? That would be the President."

"I know. He's my boss' boss, as well," the man countered. "That makes us even, I guess."

Ross swung his head around. "Uh, no. We're *not* even. For one, it certainly looks like I've got all the firepower." He redirected his attention towards a cluster of agents in the center of the building. "Get those damn wagons outta there and remove that metal plate!"

Brother James struggled afresh against his restrainers. "Do *not* move that plate!" he yelled. "You think that you've got all the firepower? Chief Ross…you know all too well that, in our business, looks can be deceiving. Contact your security detail outside. Go on. Contact them."

"How do you know about our security detail?"

"Raise them on your wireless. Try."

Ross stared him down for several seconds before snagging his radio. He pulled it close. "Charlie Hotel Romeo to Security Leader. Sitrep."

There was a pause.

An unacceptably long pause.

"Security Leader," an irritated Howard Ross repeated. "*Sit-rep.*"

Brother James rocked back and forth on his heels, staring at the floor. If he was concerned, Neal couldn't detect it.

Finally, a voice crackled through the walkie-talkie. "Oh, sorry. Security Leader can't talk right now. He'll probably be asleep for at least another hour or so." A bit of static followed. "But, even if he were conscious, he couldn't use his radio. His wrists and ankles are tied up. Over."

Ross' trademarked rage intensified as he quickly rattled off a few more code names into his wireless. Silence was its only response.

"As I said, Chief Ross, you need to lower your weapons. Turn around, and—"

"Get that damn plate up now! *Hendricks! Salvatore!* Guard that side door! Not a soul gets in or out!" Ross trained his gun on the source of his irritation. "If anything goes south in here, your blood runs first. I promise you." He looked around at his team. "Just remember what these dangerous sonofabitches did to us back at Dreamland, boys."

Brother James protested. "What are you talking—"

"Not. Another. Word," Ross snapped while four of the agents finished relocating the wagons. Another bent down, brushing away the loose debris with his bare hands.

"The plate is approximately…ten feet wide, and at least as long, sir," the agent called out. "It appears to be split down the middle. Looks…like…hinges…yes, hinges on either side."

"Pry it open, boys," Ross demanded. "And I want some serious heat on it. Watch for surprises. No telling what's down there. I doubt it's as friendly as a damn cistern full of water."

A handful of agents assumed heavily armed positions, as four others paired up on opposite sides to raise the heavy doors.

"On three," Ross bellowed. The four men dropped down and wedged their fingers in place. "One…two…*three.*"

The massive metal covers protested at first but eventually yielded to the strenuous effort. Their screeching rise resembled a thin drawbridge ascending out of the dirt floor. The armed guards inched closer, pivoting their nervous guns in all directions down into the much darker abyss.

"All clear," an agent signaled.

Ross wagged his finger at Brother James as he jogged over to the opening. "Keep a gun on him."

Neal clasped his flashlight tight against the side of his weapon as he studied the chasm. Something near the base of the right panel caught his eye and he flooded it with a pool of light. "Looks like a small control panel, Chief."

They knelt down together and studied the shoebox-sized metal casing. Two rows of five switches each ran down its length with a single key slot in the center.

Neal kept his voice low. "I've got a theory. I bet this panel activates a lift of some kind." He hunched over and dropped a chunk of debris into the gaping pit.

Nothing.

Ross rose up and pivoted to face Brother James. "Search him. Look for a set of keys."

A pair of agents patted him down thoroughly, yet he offered no real resistance. "Nothing, sir."

"What's that hanging around his damn neck?" Ross inquired. "I'm pretty sure Mennonites don't wear pretty jewelry. Specially the men."

One of the agents reached around and lifted the simple, braided necklace. An ornate cross with a pewter-like finish and irregular notches dangled from the end.

"Bring it," Ross ordered.

With a taut snap, the agent broke it away and flung it over. Ross only held onto it briefly. "What does this look like, Neal?"

Schaeffer took possession and shoved it into the slot. "It looks like…a solution." He grasped the end firmly and twisted a quarter-turn. They both leaned forward.

Looking.

Listening.

Nothing.

Neal flipped several of the switches and rotated the key back and forth.

"It's hopeless," Brother James offered. "There are well over a thousand possible combinations for those ten switches, Chief Ross."

Howard sauntered back towards him. "Your math is seriously flawed, pretend-preacher."

"Oh?"

"There are only *two* combinations."

"Two? Really? Please explain."

Ross smiled as he came to a stop inches from his captive. "You see…there is the wrong way." He positioned his gun beside James' left temple. "And then there is the way you're about to tell me." He leaned into his ear. "See? *Two ways*."

Brother James glanced down. "I need to make a call."

"To request reinforcements?"

"To request *permission*."

Ross lowered his gun and gestured wide. "Lead the way, preacher. I'll be your closest disciple. I gotta know what you've got at the bottom of that little well of secrets."

Brother James, with Ross in tow, trudged back in the direction of the dark corner from which he first appeared. He kicked at the bottom of a vertical strip of barn wood along the left wall. "Rotate that board outward. To the right."

Ross complied and raised his flashlight. A flat black telephone was nestled within the barn's framework about waist high. He snagged the receiver and shoved it against the ear of his reluctant guide. After the considerable difficulty imposed by his restraints, Brother James dialed a long series of numbers and waited.

"We cut your phone lines," Ross said.

"Not the underground cables."

Ross frowned.

"Greetings, my friend. This is Brother James. It looks like it will be a bumper crop this year." He hesitated and shuffled his feet. "Yes. And…yes. We need to inspect the cistern." Another pause. He bobbed his head. "Thank you, my friend. Goodbye." Brother James glanced up at Ross as he spun about and migrated back to the center of the barn. "Follow me."

Ross hung up the phone. "Wouldn't miss it for the world, preacher."

They reached the edge of the pit and Neal drew alongside. Brother James held up his arms which were locked in tandem. "This would be a whole lot easier, gentlemen, if my hands weren't connected like Siamese twins."

"Hendricks." Ross motioned. "Remove the good brother's cuffs, and keep a gun on him. Any sudden moves, send him to his Maker."

Five seconds later his hands were free and Brother James dropped to one knee before the control panel. He flicked an arrangement of switches and turned the key.

Now we're getting somewhere, Neal surmised as a significant vibration shot through his shoes. A few moments later he could actually detect the sound of the accompanying rumble. From the dark depths of the massive square shaft, a grinding hum began to echo as it steadily magnified in intensity. An indiscernible, faint glow drew closer, transforming into a luminescent square with a dull, metal bottom.

Neal nodded.

An elevator, he thought.

A huge, open lift.

Wow. And I thought we had big ones back at Dreamland.

The platform, rimmed on three sides with a series of long, white fluorescent tubes, hissed and decelerated to a smooth stop, nearly even with the barn's dirt floor.

Brother James boarded the platform, his every step reverberating with haunting echoes deep below. He spun around. "Gentlemen?"

Ross surveyed the room. "Like I said, boys…nobody in or out. We'll be back." He stared at Brother James while he and Neal advanced onto the lift. "And if we're not back within the hour…well…you know the protocols."

"Listen up, everyone," Neal admonished. "Keep your radios on. We'll be in touch with—"

"No you won't," Brother James interjected, shaking his bearded-head. "You *won't* be in touch. Once we reach the bottom of the cistern, that wireless will be a worthless chunk of steel. Courtesy of hundreds of feet of solid, Midwestern bedrock."

Neal shrugged. "Well…still…keep your radios on."

Brother James knelt beside the control panel once again and adjusted the switches before retrieving his key. The partial ring of fluorescent lights around the trio flashed five times, and after a slight delay, the massive platform descended into the precisely-carved earth.

Once they had sunk well-below the surface, Brother James faced his unwanted guests with a curious grin. He raised his voice to compensate for the continuous rumble bombarding them from all directions.

"Gentlemen…welcome to the Sandbox."

CHAPTER 11

Doc peered over at Denver and then placed his hand on Garrett's shoulder. "Would you also care to stay for our experiment, Mr. Frazier? As a craftsman who has supplied such indispensable aids to our research, it is only fitting you should observe the fruits of your labor."

Garrett scanned the other three faces now staring back at him. "It's getting late," he said.

"It will not take more than a few more minutes of your time," Doc cajoled.

"I don't know…Shep said it might be dangerous."

Doc squinted. "I can assure you, those particular dangers are but a memory. Mr. Collins here has observed a few. Please join us, I insist."

"Okay," he relented after a moment's hesitation. "But I'll just watch through that window in the door over there."

Ellen grinned and began distributing goggles. "As we all will, Mr. Frazier. You're safe. Trust me."

"Is the requisite marble in place, Miss Finegan?" Doc inquired as he began initializing a complex array of controls.

"Yes, sir. And the cord. It's ready to rock and roll." She donned her own pair of goggles. "But more roll than rock, I hope."

Denver made a face at her, pointing. "The headband on your goggles. It's kinda poofing your red hair out on the sides." He leaned closer. "You look pretty funny."

"Oh really?" she said playfully, continuing her own mechanical adjustments. "I look funny? Well, Mr. Collins…I will remember that the next time you want to take this gorgeous dolly to dinner."

He stretched the band out and slid his own goggles down. "Well, then again, now that I think about it…they do accentuate your beautiful eyes."

"That's what I thought," she replied.

Doc's commanding announcement grabbed their attention. "Activate the liquid nitrogen coolant and increase power to position two, Miss Finegan."

"Aye, aye, Captain Stonecroft."

Denver patted Garrett on the back as they inched up to the window. A deep and foreboding hum grew all around them. "It's time for the peep show."

Garrett felt another tap on his right shoulder as the spectacular blue visuals began their dance across his view. "Mr. Frazier?" Doc asked, holding up a string. "Would you be so kind as to give this an appropriate tug…on my command?"

"Uh, sure."

Stonecroft busied himself with some final motions and lifted his spectacles for a handful of readings. Ellen snuck up and joined the other two men at the window.

"Are you ready, Mr. Frazier?" Doc called out.

"Yeah."

"On three then. One…two…and *three*."

Garrett flicked his wrist and everyone crowded together to admire the tiny glass ball accelerating towards the portal. Denver, with vivid memories of his last visit coming to mind, braced for the worst.

Ellen noticed. "Relax, soldier."

A moment later, the marble reached the end of the rail and was swallowed by the pulsating surface of the portal.

It vanished.

"It's gone!" Ellen yelled out, jumping up and down. "It is gone!" She bounded over to Doc and nearly bowled him over. "That marble is history!"

"Or perhaps Miss Finegan," he added with a grin that looked like it would surely split his face apart, "the marble is *future*!"

Garrett pivoted around and seemed puzzled by the celebration. "Uh, so why is everybody dancing around? What just happened? Did I miss it?"

"Nothing!" Ellen said, ripping off her goggles. "Nothing…and everything! We did it. We did it." She shook Doc by the shoulders. "*You* did it!"

Denver was thrilled but held back from the party briefly. No doubt he alone noticed that the frenetic light show inside the portal had grown even more active.

He was also the only one who noticed something else.

"Uh, guys," he said. "*Guys!*"

Doc looked up. "Yes, Mr. Collins?"

"You might wanna see this."

The two researchers scurried closer as Denver backed away. Ellen noticed it as well. "Wait…what are those?"

Doc's nose was almost touching the thick glass. "To what are you referring, Miss Fin—"

"Those!" Ellen declared, jabbing her finger against the window. "Those little white things dropping from the portal."

A tiny object popped out of the colorful mist and bounced across the metal transom.

"What? Oh, yes," Doc responded. "Now I see." He pulled Ellen away. "Mr. Collins and Mr. Frazier? Please open the door, immediately."

"Ae you sure?" Denver asked.

"Yes, I am quite sure. *Hurry*."

Seconds later the door gave way and the four of them filed into the chamber. Garrett kept a cautious distance.

A continual surge of shiny objects materialized from various points in the portal and plummeted to the ground.

"It sounds like it's starting to hail," Ellen observed.

Denver took the lead. "That's not hail."

"No," Doc said as he came to a stop not quite three feet from the surface. Dozens of objects, perhaps hundreds of them, were now pushing through.

"Then what are they?" she asked.

Denver knelt down and snagged one as it bounced and danced along the metal mesh walkway. "It's…a marble."

Doc caught one himself and brought it close. "Fascinating," he whispered, lifting his glasses. "Simply fascinating."

The rate of the emerging glass balls multiplied exponentially, and the face of the temporal apparatus rippled like a strengthening waterfall. The spherical room became a high-pitched echo chamber as the roar from the device deepened.

"Marbles?" Ellen repeated, elevating her volume. "Like our marble?"

"Indeed," Doc yelled. "Exactly like our marble."

Before he even finished speaking the entire surface of the triangular portal morphed into a broiling sea of white bubbles, ejecting hundreds of thousands of identical marbles. Without delay, the group backed away and the convex floor far beneath them began filling with the massive invasion. The shrill noise resonating from the compounding racket grew beyond uncomfortable.

"Miss Finegan!" Doc bellowed out above the din. "Kill the power! *Kill the power!*"

"Already on it!" she screamed as she lunged for the control bar, slamming it down.

Denver whirled around just in time to witness the bizarre spectacle. He later told Doc that it was as if the fury of Niagara Falls was suddenly cut off, and the remaining water crashed to the rocks below. The unnatural silence was amplified by the intensity of the prior onslaught. A few straggling marbles pinged along the metal transom, but within seconds they merged with the remarkable stockpile down below.

Garrett spoke up with some trepidation as they all reconvened in the control room. "I take it that wasn't supposed to happen."

"To be honest," Ellen began, "I'm not even sure what just did happen."

"Well, whatever it was, it was incredible. Like something from a movie," Denver remarked.

Doc was already hunched over a microscope with a pair of marbles in his fingers. "*Incredible,* Mr. Collins, is perhaps far too inadequate to accurately describe the situation."

"Sir?"

"These two glass balls are perfectly identical," Doc elaborated. "They share matching flaws and imperfections, both within and without. In my estimation they would retain this degree of similarity down to the atomic level." He straightened up and approached the table. "In genetics, one would be inclined to employ the term *clone*."

"But how is that possible?" Ellen asked as she plopped down into her cushioned seat.

"My dear Miss Finegan, we forsook the rigid confines of terms such as *possible* or *impossible* the instant we arrived in Normal."

Ellen folded her arms. "I know all that, but doesn't this type of duplication violate some basic laws of nature or something?"

Doc sat as well. "Perhaps you are alluding to the First Law of Thermodynamics. In layman's terms, it has been expressed with the idea that matter and energy can neither be created nor destroyed."

"That's the one," she said. "That law."

"A universal law remains a universal law, Miss Finegan. We can rest assured that we have not broken any such thing, unless one wishes to claim the prerogative of the Almighty. Only the giver of natural law can interfere with its regularity."

Denver smiled as he strolled over to the table. "I don't know about the prerogatives of God Himself and laws and all that, but it sure seems like a few tons of marbles in that other room would beg to differ. If we didn't just create matter, then what happened?"

"The First Law remains unviolated, Mr. Collins. Your assertion that we have gained a sizable quantity of marbles is entirely correct. But your assumption that we have somehow created the necessary mass *ex nihilo* is unjustified."

Denver and Garrett each took a seat.

"Then where did the marbles come from?" Frazier asked.

"The proverbial short answer?" Doc replied. "*Energy.*"

"Marbles. Made out of energy?" Denver inquired.

"Precisely." Doc took his time and raised one of the marbles aloft. "The First Law forbids mere mortals from actually creating or destroying mass or energy. They cannot be made or unmade, but matter and energy can be readily exchanged. Matter can be converted into energy, and energy can be transformed into matter. In this respect, the sum total of all matter and energy in the Universe is a constant, as far as we know."

"I've always heard that matter and energy were two sides of the same coin." Denver proposed.

"Yes. In a basic sense," Doc responded. "Consider the atomic bomb. The physics underlying the tremendous explosive forces of nuclear technology illustrate the First Law in action. Even a minor amount of mass, if completely converted to energy, will necessarily result in an unimaginable release of power. This explains why a device weighing only hundreds of pounds can level an entire city, and kill hundreds of thousands. If not millions."

Ellen leaned forward with a self-satisfied grin. "I get it now. We did just the opposite. The portal converted the energy we were supplying *into* mass. The mass of all those marbles."

Doc sank back against his chair and tapped the glass ball on the table. "Perhaps."

"Is there a *second* option? Maybe a celestial marble factory?" she asked.

His face clouded. "There is another…but it is not a pleasant theory."

"We're all adults here, Doc," she said flippantly. "Lay it on us."

"To go from this…" Stonecroft aligned the two marbles between his thick fingers, creating the illusion of a single ball to his audience. A second later, he flicked his hand, spreading the two marbles apart as if by magic. "…to *this,* at the scale of what we witnessed next door, is beyond our capability."

"And where is the unpleasantness in your theory?" she pressed.

"Very well, Miss Finegan. My crude permutations concerning the total mass generated in the adjacent chamber leads to a serious physical inequity. By my estimation, it would have required—at minimum—a tenfold increase in our supply of electrical potential to account for our recent bounty."

"That was a lot of ten-dollar words," Denver lamented, "but I think I understood most of it. So, basically, there's no way we had enough power to make a mountain of marbles."

"Spot on, Mr. Collins," Doc said, regaining his composure. "We will fashion a fine research assistant out of you yet. Well done."

"Oh," Ellen mumbled, the remaining color leaching from her fair skin. "Okay. I think I am beginning to see what is so unpleasant."

"Care to share?" Denver asked.

"If I'm reading him right, I think that Doc's concerned that the mass to make those marbles…"

"Yes…?"

"It came from…somewhere else."

Garrett's interest seemed piqued. "Somewhere like where?"

Doc Stonecroft lowered his fist and rolled a single marble across the table. "Perhaps another place, Mr. Frazier." His face became stern. He released the second marble as well.

"Perhaps another *time*."

CHAPTER 12

In a word, Howard Ross was *uneasy*.

Of course, he would never admit it—even to himself—let alone allow his anxiety to manifest visibly. The tense visitor from the CIA gazed straight up. He felt considerably unnerved that the top of the rock-hewn shaft had vanished into the dark distance long before. Ross was no stranger to subterranean exploration. He had descended deep within the cavernous levels beneath Dreamland multiple times a day for years.

But even with the cold steel of his pistol pressed firmly against his sweaty palm, he had rarely felt so acutely disadvantaged. At the top of the shaft, Ross' assault team had outnumbered their opposition three-to-one. But the dangerous reality was that, in a mere matter of moments, his comforting inequity of force was sure to be reversed.

He had sought to pass the time by estimating the distance of their descent. "So, how far down are we?" he asked. "Three hundred feet? More?"

Brother James didn't seem interested in making eye contact. "That's classified."

Neal tried a little information-fishing as well. "When was all this built?"

Brother James shot him a silent smirk.

Neal smiled and looked away. "That's what I thought."

"You mentioned a location called Dreamland a few minutes ago," Brother James said. "Where is that located?"

Ross wasted no time and rather enjoyed his own response. "That's classified."

"Fair enough. Fair enough."

Without warning, the rim of fluorescent lights began flashing and Ross and Neal could both hear and feel the metal platform slowing.

"Stay close to me," Brother James demanded. "Touch nothing. Take nothing." He eyed both of them with disdain. "And put up your damn weapons. We may not be friends, gentlemen, but we're certainly not enemies."

Ross mulled over the frustrating request before gesturing silently over at Schaeffer. They stowed their firearms away.

"Here we go," their host warned.

A blast of new light broke through from below as the elevator passed beneath a rocky ceiling and eased to a gradual stop. Brother James debarked and motioned for them to accompany him. Ross ventured out and executed a cursory survey.

The roughly octagonal chamber was close to twenty-five yards across, a dozen feet high, and complemented with a polished concrete floor. He counted seven enormous metal doors, at least ten feet wide each, and spaced at regular intervals around the perimeter of the untreated rock walls. Large metal rings, each the circumference of a steering wheel, were protruding just off-center from the doors. To Ross, the spectacle reminded him of a series of massive, underground bank vaults.

Control panels, similar to the box they had seen topside, were mounted immediately to the right of each imposing entrance. The doors were identified from above with a single letter of the alphabet, in order from A through G.

A trio of colored bulbs, resembling a small traffic light, was positioned next to each letter. Ross noted that one doorway was green, two were red, and the rest were glowing yellow. He surmised they had traveled down to a central hub inside of what could be a massive complex.

Brother James grabbed a phone handset along the wall to their left and dialed a series of four numbers. "Attention, all departments," he announced as his low voice rang out through a series of overhead speakers. "Prepare for immediate cistern inspection. VISCON Four. Repeat, VISCON Four." He hung up.

"VISCON Four," Neal mumbled aloud. "*Visitor Condition* Four?"

"Now that—*that*—I can confirm, Agent Schaeffer."

"Can you confirm the purpose of this facility?" Ross inquired, pacing in a widening arc as he tested the limits of his invisible leash.

"*Purposes*, Chief Ross. But I have only been authorized to inform you about one aspect of our research."

Ross swung his head about, popped a cigarette out and laid it on his bottom lip. "Let me guess...your research has nothing to do with farming?"

"On the contrary, we actively farm over sixty acres of rich, Illinois soil."

"You know what I meant," Ross snapped as he lit his smoke.

"And I meant what I said. Right now we are working on Triticum aestivum."

"*Tritium?*" Neal erupted. "You're actually producing Hydrogen-3? So this is an atomic research facility?"

Brother James seemed genuinely amused. "Not Tritium...*Triticum*. More commonly known as winter wheat.

We planted the last week of September." He turned to his right and began advancing directly towards Door E. The trio of lights above it had just switched from yellow to green. "But producing wheat doesn't get the suits back at the Pentagon too excited. They're more interested in *killing* things, rather than growing things."

He blocked their direct view while manipulating a few switches on the control panel and inserted his specialized key. Two seconds later, the subtle hiss of high-pressure pneumatics indicated a significant internal release along the right seam of the doorway. Brother James took a few steps to the left and laid hold of the locking ring with both hands. After considerable effort, he completed three counterclockwise rotations and lifted a vertically-mounted handle.

The mammoth door broke loose and swung outward without so much as a whimper. An unmistakable wave of burnt oil and hot machinery was the first thing out. Brother James gestured for them to pass inside ahead of him. "This chamber is known by many names, but most of us regulars just call it *Forever South*. It is quite impressive."

For a man who had moved in and out of subterranean tunnels for nearly a decade, Howard Ross couldn't resist adopting his tour guide's assessment. "Impressive," he observed, blowing out a sustained stream of cigarette smoke. "Damn."

The rock ceiling looming high overhead with parallel rows of fluorescent lights captured Neal's attention. "Is the height of this cavern classified?" he asked.

"It varies somewhat," Brother James answered. "But the average is just under a hundred feet. And the width is about double that."

Ross concentrated on the gradual darkness that swallowed the opposite side of the chamber. He couldn't seem to detect the far wall. "What about the length?"

Brother James beamed and strolled towards a wall panel. "Ah, that. Well, gentlemen, you are facing directly south." He flipped a dozen switches. In a breathtaking linear fashion, hundreds of rows of lights rippled on and on into the indeterminate distance. "And now you know why we call it *Forever* South. The other end puts you just below the outskirts of northern Normal."

"Damn," Ross exhaled. "Beats anything at Dreamland all to hell."

"So, I gather that this Dreamland has at least one sublevel?"

Ross yanked his cigarette out and squinted for a handful of awkward seconds.

Brother James shrugged and waved his arms wide. "Hey…I showed you mine."

"If there were a location called Dreamland," Ross began, selecting each and every word with caution, "then there is a…*strong* likelihood that it would have a…significant underground component."

"Well, if Forever South had a length, then there is a strong likelihood that it would be…one mile long."

"A mile?!" Neal exclaimed. "What are you building down here…the Pentagon Motor Speedway?"

Brother James motioned to a loosely concealed area off to their right. A mixed cluster of technicians and construction workers scurried around multiple sheets of canvas tarps suspended from a wide expanse of scaffolding. Intense flashes from welding arcs cast oversized shadows along the irregular walls and towering ceiling.

"Our D-E-W," Brother James said.

They stared at him.

"A Directed Energy Weapon," he clarified.

Ross dropped his cigarette and mashed it. "I thought the War Department killed that initiative?" He folded his arms. "Even before the war ended."

"Energy weapon?" Neal repeated. "Invisible energy? Like microwaves?"

"Actually a particle beam," Brother James corrected. "And to your question, Chief Ross...*yes*. The War Department killed that proposal...albeit publicly. But you, of all people, should appreciate the difference between rhetoric and reality. I mean, at the end of the war, publicly, we were *friends* with Stalin. But I've devoted the last thirteen years producing weapons to neutralize any Soviet threat."

Ross ignited a new cigarette and pointed. "When do we start a tour behind the curtain over there?"

"I'm afraid this is as close as I can take you. Show and Tell is gonna have to be more tell than show."

"Does your...weapons program involve the production or manipulation of magnetic fields?" Neal asked.

Brother James seemed shocked by that inquiry. "Uh, as I said...we are creating a Directed—"

"Cut the polite bull, James," Ross demanded. "I have irrefutable evidence that this facility routinely generates powerful magnetic fields. Your signature is hard to miss. Magnetic fields powerful enough to disrupt space. Powerful enough to affect...*time*."

Brother James spun around and made for the door. "We're done here."

"No. We're just getting started," Ross countered.

Brother James halted and rested his left hand against the thick metal door frame.

"Chief Ross," he called without looking back, "you need to talk to the Pioneer."

August 9, 1983

SECURITY LEVEL: TOP SECRET

FOR: William Joseph Casey, Director, Central Intelligence
FROM: Lincoln D. Faurer, Director, NSA
SUBJECT: Person of Interest (NSSD 7-83)

Ongoing wiretapping and electronic surveillance efforts seeking the identification of the abductor of Denver Wayne Collins have isolated Dr. Henry K. Bodenschatz, psychological researcher with the Montauk Project, as a person of interest.

END

DCI/NSA/PS

CHAPTER 13

Neal Schaeffer was in the dark.

Literally.

His solitary comfort in the unsettling situation was that his boss was identically disadvantaged. He strained, listening for any indication that they weren't alone.

As far as he could tell…they were.

Leaning to the left in his folding chair, he kept his voice down. "Have you ever been blindfolded before?" It wasn't much of a stretch for him to imagine Ross' frustrated expression.

"Only in training with the OSS."

Neal nodded. "*Torture* training?"

"Sitting this damn close to you probably qualifies as torture." Howard hesitated. "So, what does your razor-sharp analytical mind have to say about this situation?"

Neal detected that the door to their small room was opening. "I have a theory about that," he whispered.

"Gentlemen," the familiar voice of Brother James called out as he navigated directly behind them. "I have brought our Director of Research to answer your specific questions about—"

"Here's my first specific question," Ross announced, showcasing his characteristic impatience, "why the damn blindfolds? It's not like we haven't already seen your facility."

"Chief Ross, you have only seen a portion of our facility. Though I have been authorized to confirm for you that

Forever South is the single largest section of our complex. By far. Regardless, I can assure both of you that our *unconventional* precautions, such as blindfolds, are completely justified."

"I doubt it."

A new voice—one much older and much softer—joined the conversation. "A former, dear friend of mine once said '*You can't depend on your eyes when your imagination is out of focus.*'"

"What the hell is that supposed to mean?" Ross asked.

"Mark Twain," Neal whispered, probably louder than he meant to.

"What?"

"Mark Twain, boss. His quote. It was from Mark Twain."

"I knew him as Mr. Clemens, Agent Schaeffer," the new voice added. "Even after four decades I still greatly miss our stimulating interactions."

"Who are we talking to?" Ross pressed.

Brother James intercepted the question. "He is known only as the Pioneer."

"Welcome to the Sandbox, Chief Ross," the elderly voice greeted. "I will endeavor to address your more pertinent questions, within the bureaucratic boundaries imposed upon me."

Neal wasted no time. "What experimentation is occurring here at the Sandbox that involves the creation of intense magnetic fields?"

The Pioneer paused. "I am not at liberty to discuss the precise nature of our important research. But I can confirm your assertion, Agent Schaeffer, that magnetic fields are part and parcel of our efforts."

"I don't care if I'm talking to the preacher, the Pioneer, or the damn President," Ross said. "The results of our evidence analysis is conclusive. Is this facility conducting temporal displacement research?"

"We are developing Directed Energy Weapons," the Pioneer responded.

"Yes," Neal said, "but could time distortion be…a side effect of your research?"

"With your level of clearance, I am fairly certain you are aware of what happened with the USS Eldridge in the latter half of 1943. In the Philadelphia Naval Shipyard."

Neal's head bobbed. "A bit before my time, sir. But yes, we are aware."

"We discovered, in October of that year, that magnetic fields are capable of producing a wide array of anomalies, Agent Schaeffer. Many…unintended. All fascinating."

"Are you sending or receiving people from the past or the future in this facility?" Ross demanded. "Does the name Denver Wayne Collins mean anything to you?!" He launched out of his chair, nearly knocking it over, and ripped off his blindfold. He removed Neal's as well.

Brother James threw his arms across the elderly man and spun him about, before shuffling him over to the door.

"Gentlemen, this conversation is over."

CHAPTER 14

In his haste, the edge of his immaculate desk served double-duty as a makeshift chair. Twenty minutes after his confrontational briefing with Howard Ross, Brother James flipped a lamp on and grabbed his phone before dialing a short number.

"It's me. Release them. All of Chief Ross' men." He decided to add a final order before slamming the phone down. "But keep a tail on him."

A meek voice rang out from a chair in a dark corner of the small office. "I'm leaving tomorrow for the holidays, Lawrence. We don't have much time to discuss this."

"I know."

"So…let's discuss Chief Howard Ross. Does he present a problem…or an opportunity?"

Brother James folded his arms and hung his bearded chin onto his chest. "His questions may be our answers."

"Perhaps," the Pioneer agreed. "But the disconcerting question is, how did a division of the CIA gain knowledge of the existence of the Sandbox?"

"To be honest, I'm surprised it took them this long. We all knew it was inevitable." Lawrence pushed off the desk. "Ross said something about our magnetic signature, and that it was '*hard to miss*'. Those were his words."

The Pioneer massaged the wealth of wrinkles on his forehead. "There are nearly four million square miles of land here in the United States of America. The probability that the

CIA *accidentally* discovered evidence of our research is infinitesimal. We may have a leak. A mole."

"I am not nearly as interested in the *how* as I am the *what*," Brother James admitted as he paced around the office. "They repeatedly spoke of temporal displacement. Of time travel."

The Pioneer's pale hands fidgeted with his cane, which was resting atop his narrow lap. "And of time displaced *persons*."

That observation attracted Lawrence's immediate attention. He shot a quick glance over at the Pioneer. "But despite your repeated assurances, and our best efforts, we have failed in that respect every time. Every time."

The old man matched his gaze. "Prior to a conversation we just had with two blindfolded men a few minutes ago, I would have wholeheartedly agreed with you."

"I just don't know what to make of it. If anything."

"Perhaps today's events place other recent events into sharp relief."

Lawrence frowned. "What?"

"Our last magnetic series at full power was four months ago. In August."

"The *tenth* of August."

The Pioneer nodded. "Yes, the tenth of August. Then, a short period of time later, we are notified that the FBI is conducting one of the most significant manhunts in US history. We are informed that apprehending this person is a matter of national security. This mysterious dragnet radiates from where? From Chicago down into our country."

"And?"

"And now, a few months later, the CIA arrives in full force, right at our very doorstep. And once again, we are confronted with that same name."

Brother James squinted with a thoughtful nod. "Denver Wayne Collins."

"Precisely. Mr. Denver Wayne Collins. The multiplied convergence of coincidences is growing hard to discount, Lawrence."

Brother James advanced closer. "But you've been at every single round of experimentation since '46. I've been at most of them. And I've studied all of the films. Lots of promise…but little progress. Are we missing something? We've never achieved measurable success. Never."

"Perhaps," the old man noted. "Perhaps *not*."

"But the only known side effects, besides the warping of the metal in the equipment due to the magnetic fields, has been the intense electrical discharges in the atmosphere above the Forever South terminus."

"Don't forget all the broken glass. And all the frightened people in Normal."

"But lightning and thunder and…*shattered windows* are not exactly the side effects we've been hoping for."

The Pioneer shrugged. "You speak of *known* side effects, Brother James…"

"Perhaps Chief Ross and his associate are on a manhunt for *unknown* side effects."

August 12, 1983

SECURITY LEVEL: TOP SECRET

FOR: William Webster, Director, FBI
FROM: Wm. Patrick Clark, Jr., National Security Advisor
SUBJECT: Detainment of Person of Interest

President Reagan has issued a directive authorizing the detainment of Dr. Henry K. Bodenschatz (researcher, Montauk Project) relating to activities impacting the national security of the United States.

Dr. Bodenschatz is to be arrested and relocated to Langley without delay. Notify my office upon his detainment.

END

DCI/FBI/WH/PS

CHAPTER 15

According to the map, it amounted to a total of only 6.4 miles.

But the fifteen minute drive back to the warehouse on the eastern reaches of Bloomington was the longest of Chief Ross' career.

No one risked speaking with him, including Neal Schaeffer, as Howard brooded in the backseat. Even radio communication, typically ablaze with coded information, fell uniquely silent while he burned through a half-dozen cigarettes.

As a long trail of ash flicked out his window, he concentrated on the row of box trucks just ahead of his sedan in the conspicuous convoy headed south. These transport vehicles, which should have been laden with high-value targets and confiscated technology, mocked his massive failure. The long procession, intended to be a parade filled with the spoils of conquest, was returning barren and uncelebrated.

The siege at the Sandbox had proved a curious and humiliating success.

The punishing reality emerged that Project SATURN had merely been allowed to execute their impotent assault. Every agent comprising their perimeter security detail had been neutralized in a coordinated counterstrike while Ross and Schaeffer floundered within. Their desperate Old West negotiations in the barn had netted them limited access, but only to an unlimited supply of perplexing new questions that begged to be answered.

Working within the upper echelons of the intelligence community provided a level of access to information that typically insulated Ross from surprises, but the Sandbox blindsided him. Even beyond that, the embarrassing encounter served as additional evidence to further erode his dwindling confidence in the leadership residing in Washington.

A tiny commotion broke out as Ross' sedan approached the main entrance to the warehouse. An agent jerked his door wide open even before the frame of Ross' car rocked to a full stop.

"Chief Ross," he said. "Director Dulles needs to speak with you immediately, sir. The DCI indicated that it was extremely urgent."

Ross pitched his new cigarette and crushed it into the rough asphalt as he stepped out. "I'm sure it is," he mumbled.

Neal scrambled out on the opposite side and arched over the roof of the vehicle. "You want me to join you?"

Ross refused to look back or answer.

An additional set of agents held the facility's doors open for him as the Chief trudged down a narrow hall towards his temporary office. He looked around and a scowl distorted his sullen face.

"Why the hell is it still so damn cold in here?!" he called out to everyone in general, yet no one in particular. "This isn't supposed to be a damn cryo-chamber! Get it done!"

He made a hard right and then pushed through the first gray metal door on his left. Moments later he connected with

Dulles' office. The brief but intense call required little interpretation.

Howard Ross was on a plane to DC less than three hours later.

August 13, 1983

SECURITY LEVEL: TOP SECRET

FOR: Wm. Patrick Clark, Jr., National Security Advisor
FROM: William Webster, Director, FBI
SUBJECT: Dr. Henry K. Bodenschatz

I regret to notify you that Dr. Henry K. Bodenschatz is deceased. According to our investigation, Dr. Bodenschatz was killed on Friday, August 12. His death was the result of a series of troubling research accidents that occurred at Montauk.

If you require detailed information regarding these accidents, you will have to contact DCI Casey. Jurisdiction for the investigation was transferred to the CIA earlier today. I must assume that this transfer originated with the White House.

END

DCI/FBI/WH

CHAPTER 16

The gentle slopes of Navy Hill intercepted the December sunrise over DC, engulfing the riverside fringes of Foggy Bottom in a chilling, wide shadow. Howard Ross could barely identify the dark expanse of the Potomac as his chauffer ferried him westward along E Street.

The dim morning view of the jumbled assortment of enormous stone government buildings lining the uneven acreage brought back years of memories in a single glance. A considerable portion of the OSS had been housed on this sacred soil, first thriving and then ultimately dying in a bureaucratic struggle before most people were even aware of its enigmatic existence. As the CIA ascended from its ashes, the disjointed campus of structures was quickly recommissioned to serve the nebulous purposes of American intelligence.

Ross grabbed his sleeve to wipe a circular hole in the condensation clouding his window. Something unexpected came into view at the end of a long row of chain-link fencing.

"Driver, stop here," he demanded.

A sign?

They put up a damn sign?

The iconic blue crest of the CIA, encircled with its full name, adorned the upper portion of the modest, beige marker. The official address completed the bottom third.

Central Intelligence Agency.

2430 E Street NW.

You gotta be kidding me.

To Ross, the entire spectacle defied reason.

He had labored for years concealing an unmarked and unnamed facility in an uninhabited stretch of the desert southwest, dozens of miles from even the smallest of paved roads. But here, on the northeastern reaches of the American empire, it appeared that caution had been thrown into the bureaucratic wind. For an intelligence operative entering his fifth decade of service in the necessary art of secrecy, the sign represented more than a location to Ross.

It signified a fundamental flaw within an agency in desperate need of his leadership.

He called out to the driver. "Let's go."

The sedan continued on its trek to the main entrance, not far off. Ross studied the area.

At least surveillance and protection are up to par.

Without much effort, he spotted two different vehicles with agents keeping watch. A couple more sentries had taken up key positions near the front of the complex. It appeared that the lack of secrecy was being compensated for by an abundance of security. Still, it seemed to be a bit much.

"Driver, stop here."

Well, that's a change.

As Ross topped the last of the stone stairs, an additional guard barred the way to the Director's office. Howard approached him. "I have an appointment with Director Dulles," he declared, either amused or annoyed by the formality.

He couldn't tell which.

The sentry shoved his hand out. "Identification?"

Ross obliged and displayed his golden badge. "Special Agent Ross. FBI."

"Just a moment, sir."

The guard snatched a phone and dialed. "I have a Special Agent Ross in the hall. Mr. Ross indicates he has an appointment." Pause. "Yes, sir." He lowered the phone handset into the cradle. "Right this way, Special Agent Ross."

The sentry led him a dozen feet further and opened a white door on the right. A voice that Ross typically dreaded speaking with every Monday afternoon resounded out.

"Come on in, Howard."

Ross pushed past the guard and stepped into the frugal office space. Director Dulles stood by his desk, surveying a handful of paperwork, surrounded by a thick and stable halo of pipe smoke. Another silhouette of a man, presumably more security, sat with his back to Howard before a large, bright window on the far side of the room. Through it, Ross could see the sun's first light was now beginning to gild the river with accents of gold.

"How was your flight?" Dulles inquired, lowering the paperwork and making his way across the room. "You look like hell." They shook hands. The Director briefly pulled out his pipe with a smile. "But, then again, you've always looked like hell."

"That's what life in the Nevada desert will do to a man," Ross countered. "The damn sun takes its toll. That reminds me about next year's budget request. I was gonna add another few grand to cover skin lotion for the staff."

Dulles lost his smile.

"We're not here to discuss your budget, Howard."

Ross lit up a cigarette and nodded. "Just why am I here, Director? Oh, and for the record…I don't like the sign out front."

Dulles turned away and ventured a few steps. "We're in the intelligence business, Howard. I think you know why you're here. I know that you know."

"The Sandbox?"

Dulles spun around. "You're damn right, the Sandbox!" He rushed back up to his subordinate and pulled out his pipe. "I'm not even going to ask how you just *happened upon* a government facility that even I didn't know about until nineteen hours ago." Dulles rubbed his forehead. "But…however you found it, and whatever you saw, and wherever you've been below ground there…forget it." He turned away once more. "Never happened. It was a bad dream. Maybe something induced by Dr. Gottlieb. A little MKUltra cocktail-induced hallucination. We probably need to haul your entire staff to DC for debriefing."

The Director slapped the side of his pipe several times and then wagged it in Ross' direction. "I've spent an almost sleepless night explaining to…*powerful* people why you are still the head of a division that most of them had never heard of before. Don't give me another reason to regret my painful defense. *Back down*. Don't make me transfer you to somewhere else, like the State Department. Headstrong-types like you don't sit well with my brother. You can trust me on that one."

Ross was silent.

That spoke volumes.

Dulles shook his head. "John's got enough problems dealing with all of the hostilities in Egypt right now. We'll be lucky to get the Brits and the French out of there by

Christmas. It's a helluva mess. And now all of this Sandbox business is happening."

Ross glared through the window at nothing at all, measuring his response. He yanked out his cigarette and pulled in a deep breath. "You're worried about...*Egypt?* And a little bit of diplomatic chess over at the State Department?! I've invested over forty damn years of my life into making sure this country stays strong and safe...and the last ten years chasing ghosts and technology so that we could have the...*luxury* of using time as a weapon. As leverage."

He could feel the heat of rage rising within. "But time and again, you enjoy tying my damn hands. Holding me back. Denying me my rights and privileges. And now that I'm, I'm on the threshold of completing my mission, you're doing it again!"

Ross leaned forward in his chair, tossed his cigarette on the floor and crushed it into the tile. "I guess I shouldn't be surprised. I was denied the DCI's chair ten years ago by the last administration. What's a little more rejection from the current one gonna hurt, right? Our last commander-in-chief got his job by default, and Eisenhower took the White House campaigning as a damn war hero. Hell, we both know Ike never saw a single day of combat. I guess I should be used to unqualified people pulling rank over me."

A gentle voice from across the room pierced through the heavy emotion. "I've also spent over forty years in public service, Mr. Ross. And last month, I just got my current job back for another four."

The silhouetted figure rose out of his chair and stepped into better light. "So, if you want to keep *yours*, I suggest that you follow Allen's salient advice, and drop it." The bald man hesitated, then pierced right through Ross with his unmistakable blue eyes. "And for the record, the sign out front was my idea."

Ross felt the fine hairs on the back of his neck stand at attention, and then he stood as well.

"Yes sir," Ross complied. "Whatever you say, Mr. President."

Research Log: Dr. Glen D. Stonecroft

DATE: December 14, 1956

A late start today.

Even with all available hands on deck, it is still occupying the greater part of the morning to excavate the enormous quantity of marbles from the lower extremities of the portal chamber. It is a shame that we do not possess a method to melt these balls into usable glass for our window factory upstairs.

I can only surmise that this physical phenomenon resulted from a type of feedback-anomaly due to either:
(1) a causal loop
(2) a temporal echo (for lack of a better descriptor).

I am still convinced that our solution is to be found in a phase adjustment, a polarity switch, or a combination of both. If there is time remaining this afternoon, I will seek to conduct a few more trials.

G.D.S.

****

UPDATE:

Success!

At 11:08 a.m. today, with Mr. Collins, Ellen and I present, two significant temporal milestones were realized. We were able to transfer no less than seven marbles into a sustained rift with no known adverse side effects, and soon thereafter, we achieved the ability to transmit and immediately receive seven additional marbles. This required a polarity switch in two of our three magnets. The phases are now 120 degrees apart.

One could only wish that the first batch of little spherical emissaries could send us a postcard. I am confident that their journey has been fascinating. Nevertheless, my heart is heavy knowing that my dear French colleague did not live to see this day. His joy would have been unspeakable.

I was concerned that our previous attempts to "see into the future" had been hampered by our recent modifications. Ellen and I ran a few successful tests. This ability appears to be in proper working order. Our next phase will necessitate organic transfer.

Our achievement in sending mass and receiving mass has signaled not only progress, but more importantly...hope.

G.D.S.

CHAPTER 17

The Pioneer's lips hadn't tasted a cigar in over seven decades, but the frigid mid-December air had transformed his shallow breaths into smoky plumes, now backlit by the afternoon sun. A Sandbox operative, clad in his traditional Mennonite work attire, held the side door of the barn open for him.

"Will you be returning this evening, sir?"

The Pioneer threw a black scarf around his thin and wrinkled neck and finished donning a pair of gloves. "No, brother. Definitely not this evening. I will return after the holidays. Just after the turn of the year."

"Have a nice trip, sir."

"Thank you, brother. And Merry Christmas."

"The same to you, sir."

The Pioneer, relying heavily on the assistance of a cane, ambled across the packed soil to a waiting vehicle. Another operative opened the car's back door at his arrival and nodded.

"Have a good day, sir," he called out above the dull roar of the running engine.

The Pioneer smiled broadly, tossed his cane in and settled into the backseat. Seconds later the door closed and the flat black Ford Customline eased down the dirt lane and made a sharp left onto the blacktop. The elderly passenger glanced out the window and squinted in his confusion. He snagged his cane and rapped on the back of the couch front seat.

"Driver? You've made a wrong turn." With a wiry finger he motioned back over his thin shoulder. "We are supposed to be heading *north*. Not south."

There seemed to be no visible reaction.

He smacked the seat again while gazing to the west. "*Driver?* Unless the solar system has significantly altered during my short tenure below ground, that afternoon sun should be on my left, not my right. Please turn around. This instant."

The unresponsive chauffeur continued due south. In fact, the car was accelerating.

The frustrated Pioneer prepared to poke the shoulder of his colleague with his cane, when the driver's right hand appeared just above the seat, clasping a white envelope.

The Pioneer tapped it with his cane. "What's this?"

No real explanation was expected.

He wasn't disappointed.

The driver rattled the envelope against the seat.

Though the situation was disconcerting and he was helplessly trapped, the old man couldn't deny that his interest was piqued. The Pioneer retrieved the parcel with understandable trepidation and slid out the enclosed letter. His fascination rose as his eyes worked their way down the document.

The wayward driver stole a furtive glance up into the rearview mirror.

And smiled.

CHAPTER 18

Denver couldn't resist making the easy joke.

"Leah just handed me this box full of little white rats." He trotted down the last three steps and slid the container onto the table in The Basement. "What're you guys doing down here now...performing a holiday version *Of Mice and Men*?"

Doc stepped out of the bathroom, wiping his hands on a towel. "I can assure you that Steinbeck could not have imagined the plans we have envisioned for these little travelers."

"From marbles to mice," Denver muttered. "Quite a switch."

Ellen sprang out of her chair and popped the lid open. "Oh! They are so cute." She snagged one, but it didn't appear to be as thrilled about the situation as she was. Ellen brought its tiny nose up to meet hers. "I will call you...*Sadie*."

Denver hunkered forward and peered inside as well. "Sadie?"

She rubbed the mouse against her cheek. "I had a pure white hamster named Sadie when I was about six. My one constant friend as a constantly-uprooted military brat."

Denver nodded. "A rat for a brat."

Ellen didn't seem phased. "Uh-huh."

"I can't believe you're touching that thing. I never met a woman who wasn't terrified of rats."

"Military kids are not regular people," Ellen reminded him. "And Sadie's an adorable mouse, not a rat."

Denver shrugged. "Looks like a box full of snake food if you ask me."

Ellen jerked it away. "Don't listen to him, Sadie. That bad, bad man was just joking."

Stonecroft closed the box with a chuckle. "These little mammals are not destined for a python, Mr. Collins, but for the *portal.*" He reached into a different box and fished out a small plastic ball. With a quick twist it popped apart into two identical halves. "And these hollow enclosures will bear our four-footed ambassadors into the future."

Denver froze.

Somebody's got to be joking.

Did Doc say mouse ambassadors?

He's finally lost it. I guess you can't stay sharp forever.

"I can discern from your expression, Mr. Collins, that our little enterprise seems a foolhardy measure."

"Well, I wasn't going to say it exactly like that."

Ellen hooked Denver's arm and continued to fuss over her new pet. "Now that we've been able to send and receive marbles through the portal, we need to test something a little more…alive. Like Sadie here."

"What're you worried about? A ball's a ball…what's the difference if there's something inside?"

"A marble is a relatively solid mass of silicon dioxide, my friend." Doc polished his glasses on the towel. "It is imperative that we conduct experimentation regarding soft tissue. Organic matter." After a brief inspection, he slid his spectacles back on. "We have proved the temporal rift can transmit mass, but we have not demonstrated that it transmits living cells without…shall we say…alteration."

"Alteration?"

Ellen covered the mouse's head and whispered quite loudly. "*Death.*"

"Oh." He pointed at the rodent in her hand. "You know, you shouldn't have named her. It just makes saying goodbye that much harder."

She let go of Denver and danced around the table with her new friend. "Forget he said that, Sadie. I will never tell you goodbye. We are best pals."

"What is the current level in our liquid nitrogen holding reservoir, Miss Finegan?"

Ellen scurried over to the shiny, metallic tank. She positioned the mouse near a small gauge then raised it beside her ear with a frown. "What's that Sadie? Seventy-four percent? Sadie said that liquid nitrogen levels are at seventy-four percent, Doc."

"Then the time for goggles is now," Stonecroft ordered as he overlooked an array of adjustments along the control console. "Mr. Collins, would be so kind as to select our first temporal candidate and load the creature within the first capsule?"

Denver opened both boxes and captured a mouse. "Uh, wait…won't it suffocate?"

"I had Mr. Frazier drill a number of holes in our canisters to aid in respiration," Doc explained.

Denver popped the ball open. "Yep, I see that now. Nice. Get inside there, little buddy. There ya go." He struggled to contain the excited creature. "Hey, wait…hold on now. Stay there. There. Got it." Denver slid a pair of goggles over his head and displayed his trophy aloft. "One time-traveling mouse in a bubble, sir."

"Excellent," Doc praised. "Engage our cooling system and power to level two, Miss Finegan."

"Hold on Sadie," she said, raising the bar incrementally. "This can sound kinda scary. But don't worry, I'm right here with you, baby."

Both rooms rumbled and roared before the predictable light show erupted in all of its splendor. "Level two, Captain Stonecroft!"

"Excellent," Doc praised. "Please escort our ambassador to the rails in the portal chamber, Mr. Collins. Ellen, could you assist Mr. Collins?"

"Sadie and I would be glad to," she replied. "Right this way, Mr. Animal *Not*-lover."

They progressed down the metal transom. "I like animals," Denver protested. "But bigger ones. Like dogs, horses, and…kangaroos. Those kinds."

Ellen smirked. "Sadie said she doesn't believe you."

"Well, your mouse is a terrible judge of character."

"I disagree…Sadie is very wise."

They slowed to a stop beside the track system. Denver studied the situation. "What do I need to do?"

"When Doc gives the signal, place our little friend on the rails and let it roll down the track and into the portal."

"Is it safe to be in here?"

She raised the mouse beside her ear. "Sadie says it is quite safe. It is Sadie Safety Certified."

"Wow. Gimme a break."

Ellen craned her neck and raised her voice. "Are we ready, Captain Stonecroft?"

Doc navigated around the door and stepped onto the suspended walkway. "Quite ready. Release the rolling rodent, Mr. Collins."

"Betty Larson would be proud of your alliteration there, Doc."

"Perhaps."

Denver lowered the capsule onto the track and encouraged it with the tiniest of shoves. The white ball careened in a lopsided fashion down the lane, wobbling all the way until the sphere was finally engulfed by the surface of the swirling temporal rift.

A rapid flash of light heralded the event just before the same ball materialized out of the mist and rolled a few inches back up the track. Doc jogged past Denver and snatched it off the rails. "Cut the power, Miss Finegan."

She obeyed and immediately raced back into the chamber. "Is our little buddy still alive?" she inquired, eyes wide.

With a quick flick of his wrist, Doc gave the ball a sudden shake. He raised his goggles as a strange smile crept along his face. "Perhaps it is a case of Schrödinger's cat, or rather Schrödinger's *mouse*."

"Schrödinger?" Denver mumbled.

Doc nodded. "Until we observe the outcome, the mouse could be both simultaneously alive…and dead. A conundrum of quantum proportions."

"I'm confused."

Ellen bent towards him. "Join the club. Sadie said she doesn't understand, either."

Doc twisted the ball apart as everyone arched forward and gazed down. A formless, green and gray moldy mass interspersed with tiny bones was firmly attached to the lower section.

Ellen jerked back. "Oh, disgusting! Don't look, Sadie."

Doc elevated the plastic shell with justified caution and wafted it just below his nose.

"What're you doing, Doc?" Denver cried out. "That things gonna be rank!"

The elderly researcher continued swirling the object. "On the contrary, Mr. Collins. I cannot detect even the faintest trace of foul odor. Interesting."

"Your nose must be broke, Doc. Look at that fuzzy mess! That mouse has got to smell. It just died."

"*Just* being both the operative and *falsifying* word, my friend."

"What? So, the mouse didn't *just* die? But, uh, it had to. One minute ago it was alive and rolling down that rail. I saw it. I was there. Or here."

With an uncharacteristically somber face, Doc pivoted towards the portal and studied it for a fast second. "Indeed," Doc agreed, "you did observe a living mouse rolling down that rail. But I submit that it was not one minute ago, Trailer Collins."

Stonecroft spun about and faced them.

"By the condition of these dehydrated remains, I would estimate this creature expired years ago…perhaps decades."

CHAPTER 19

We were humiliated at the Sandbox.

He had a horrible trip to Washington.

And now he's…tapping his foot.

An uneasy Neal Schaeffer studied his boss through the windshield.

And there's a pile of cigarette butts on the sidewalk. Speaking of butts…I'm gonna get mine chewed.

Neal veered the sedan up to the curb and brought it to a jolting stop. The heavy frame hadn't even quit oscillating when Ross flung the door open.

"Afternoon, boss. How was your trip—"

"It's 2:20, Mr. Schaeffer," Ross fairly yelled while sliding into the front seat. "Twenty-damn minutes late."

"I know, I was—"

Ross slammed the door. (On a lesser vehicle the window would've probably cracked.) He reeked with smoke, as always. "Is everyone assembled?"

"If by *everyone* you mean senior staff, then…yes. They are waiting at the Bloomington warehouse. We should've met at a hotel, though. The temperature this afternoon is—"

"I hate being late. And cold."

Neal hesitated. "You, uh, hate a lot of things."

"And I hate being late."

The agent-turned-chauffer shifted the car into drive and checked his side mirror for traffic.

Ross cleared his throat. "I already know what I'm gonna get you for Christmas."

Neal braced for the caustic punchline.

Ross snagged a fresh cigarette. "A damn watch."

"I already have a watch, boss."

"Then how about a new *job?*"

Schaeffer successfully navigated into the busy lane. He wagged his head with a slight shrug. "A little drastic for a few minutes of *justified* waiting, wouldn't you say? I think you're still bitter about your meeting with Dulles and Eisenhower this morning. And you're taking it out on me. Don't get me wrong…I can handle it."

Howard glared straight ahead with a stern poker face as he lit his smoke. "I hate waiting, Neal. You of all people know that I would rather gargle with a mouthful of blazin' hot razor blades, than wait. And I couldn't care less about my trip to DC. We have work to do, regardless of the idiocy occupying the capital."

Neal fought to suppress his giddy smile. "First off, don't gargle with razor blades. Hot or cold. Your tongue is already sharp enough."

"I'm not laughing."

"And second, forget about the wait. You're gonna thank me."

Ross folded his arms after a hard draw on his cigarette. "I doubt it."

The confined smoke began gathering overhead and Neal cracked his window a few inches. "Well, you may doubt it, but I don't," he declared. "I was on the phone with Corporal Jennings. He called right as I was leaving to come pick you up."

"There's a reason I left him back at Dreamland," Ross muttered. "I've got about as much use for that man as I do a second butthole."

"That *butthole* just hit pay dirt," Neal protested. "He may have discovered the name of the black mystery man we captured during Collins' break-in at Dreamland. And something—"

"What's the medical status of our mystery man?"

"Nothing new. Still in a coma."

Ross paused. "Continue."

Neal signaled and changed lanes. "A few days before Denver Collins raided Dreamland, a state cop was assaulted out on US 93. Near Pioche."

"Don't care."

"The cop said that he had pulled off the road to help a pair of men whose car had broken down." Neal hesitated and peered over at his boss. "A white male…and a black male. Both middle-aged."

"Starting to care."

Neal hit the brakes and eased to a shuddering stop at a red light. "The cop said the car was from out of state. He said it was from…*Illinois*."

Ross rolled his window down and flicked the cigarette out. "I'm close to being interested."

"Cop said that they were acting nervous…and loaded with cash. He ordered them to open their trunk. He found a rifle and other suspicious items. And that's when they knocked him out, and stuffed him into—"

"The light's green," Ross blurted out, gesturing loosely and pointing.

Neal punched the accelerator. "They knocked him out, then stuffed him back into his patrol car. Cop said that he woke up an hour later with a world-class headache and a flat tire."

"When does the damn part of this come in that'll make me thank you for making me wait for twenty minutes out on a cold sidewalk in Bloomington, Illinois, after a miserable flight?"

Neal tried to restrain his second grin in the past five minutes. "The black male's name was purportedly Terrance Groves or Graves. Something like that." He paused for maximum effect.

"The white male's name…was Denver. Denver *Jackson*."

CHAPTER 20

His present emotional state was a conflicted blend of grief and expectant hope.

Regardless of the enormity of his scientific success, the previous several weeks had witnessed some of the most extraordinary and difficult events of his temporal tenure in Normal. Doc paused for a moment as he ascended the concrete stairwell out of The Basement. The fact that he had potentially compromised the integrity of an expected future by recklessly intercepting his younger self at a roadside tavern was never far from his meditations.

For a man who had safeguarded the Four Accords with the burning fervor of a religious zealot, his own hypocrisy left him cold and distant at times. It was difficult to dismiss the notion that justified contempt smoldered behind every gaze from his associates, pleasant exteriors notwithstanding. He tried to suppress the feelings by occupying every moment with research.

And more research.

More marbles. More mice.

He prayed they could eventually forgive the one who seemed incapable of receiving a pardon from himself.

His thoughts descended into further guilt.

Emile.

Did I fail you somehow, my friend?

The clear image of a shallow, unmarked grave (which he had never seen) troubled his soul at inconvenient times. One who was a foreigner, on so many levels, had selflessly dedicated his time and talents to alleviating their misery, yet now his murdered corpse rotted as so much discarded garbage in a rural landfill.

The inequity of his demise, even offset by the wickedness of his betrayal, proved a distracting burden. But even under the full weight of the ramifications of the French researcher's less-than-noble passing, Stonecroft could not readily dismiss a deeper sense of optimism. His musings found expression in a verse by Emerson:

'Tis a brave master;
Let it have scope:
Follow it utterly
Hope beyond hope.

Doc sighed as he continued up the lonely steps towards the manufacturing floor. All of these impressions, of dark failures, and bright expectations, made a mockery of his late-afternoon concentration. But something else also added to the distressing mix.

He looked down at the folded document in his hand.

And then there is this letter.

The nondescript envelope had somehow found its way onto his kitchen counter one day prior. It was short on message but long on mystery. It spoke of a place and a time. It spoke of help and a title. He hadn't revealed its contents to anyone…not even Ellen.

As to its origin, he had considered a thousand scenarios. None of them were all that comforting in the final analysis. The FBI, CIA, or even the Soviets. But one name surfaced above most others…Bodenschatz.

Hank Bodenschatz.

As Doc traversed through the unusually quiet factory he avoided making eye-contact with anyone, especially Shep. He caught sight of the clock on the far wall.

4:25 p.m.

Minutes from now we shall discover if this be truth…or trap, you old fool.

"Leaving early today, Professor?"

He looked over to his far left as Leah rose up from behind her desk. Predictably, Tori continued reading, engrossed in her text. It took Stonecroft a moment to force a smile. "Oh, no, my dear. Just stepping out for a nice change of scenery." He peeled his coat off the rack. "The Basement is not a dungeon, but it can certainly imitate one from season to season."

Doc opened the door and the blast of chilling air almost caught him unawares. The warm, amber radiance of the soon-setting sun that had poured into the foyer was beautiful but deceptive. He buttoned his coat and checked his watch.

4:28 p.m.

And now I wait.

He didn't have to.

Doc studied with growing interest as a white, late model Chevrolet approached and slowed considerably along the asphalt. The vehicle's tires crunched across the gravel of the parking lot and eased to a gentle stop not quite ten feet from him. The scent of the hot engine met his nose as he struggled to see through the hazy glare across the windshield.

The driver hopped out and opened the rear passenger door on the far side. A frail gentleman, clad in a light gray overcoat, emerged after a short delay. The aged visitor ambled around the front of the vehicle, sporting a cane. And an envelope.

Heavens, Doc mused, *this fellow makes me feel a youth by comparison.*

To Doc's bewilderment, the driver slipped back into the car and raced out of the lot, throwing a fair amount of gravel in the process. The elderly guest seemed just as surprised at his own apparent abandonment. He rotated about and glared as the car and the drone of its motor faded into the distance. After a brief pause, he spun back around and approached Doc with deliberate steps.

There is something oddly familiar about him.

"Dr. Glen Stonecroft?" the man inquired with a squint which somehow added even more folds to his severely wrinkled face.

Doc smiled with a subtle bow. "Your servant, sir."

The visitor glanced down and pulled out a piece of paper, trembling. "I received a letter a few hours ago. A correspondence that included your name."

Stonecroft raised up his own document and adjusted his glasses. "As did I, my friend. Yesterday. It enjoined me to meet someone on this very day, at this very time. At this very location."

The other man nodded. "And here we are."

"But my letter did not reveal a name," Doc noted, rocking forward on his heels. "It only mentioned a title. And a most curious title at that."

"I have outlived nearly all those who have known me by name, Dr. Stonecroft. And since the war, I have only been known to a select few, and even then, as merely a title."

"*The Pioneer,*" Doc whispered.

"The Pioneer." The visitor pivoted on his heels and examined the parking lot. "It appears that we will be spending considerable time together, Dr. Stonecroft. My new chauffeur has been acting strangely. First, I was driven to a remote location and then it was insisted that I change my attire and we exchanged vehicles. And now, I have been deposited on your doorstep as a homeless stranger."

"I assure you that you are not homeless, my friend."

They both put their letters away and the visitor studied Stonecroft before speaking. "I have had plenty of time today to read and ponder something of your...*incredible* secret."

Doc was stunned and tried to restrain his fear. He must've failed.

"Do not be alarmed, Dr. Stonecroft...for I will share *my* incredible secret with you, as well."

"Certainly you cannot blame this poor mathematician for being far more than a little concerned," Doc said. "Our secret is a tremendous and most dangerous liability."

"You and your *associates* have nothing to fear from me, I can assure you." A thin smile grew across the man's gaunt face as he thrust out his hand. "Let me properly introduce myself," he said, leaning forward and taking a small step. The visitor whispered into Stonecroft's left ear.

Doc's knees almost gave way.

CHAPTER 21

The scene in the warehouse conference area certainly resembled the hope-filled initial planning session three days earlier.

The location, the same.

The players, the same.

Even the fruitless attempt at raising the temperature to a comfortable level…the same.

But beyond simple appearances and the familiar smell of burning kerosene, all similarities abruptly ceased.

Ross and Neal slipped in several minutes behind schedule with little fanfare and Schaeffer grabbed a seat. The minimal level of somber background conversations died an immediate and natural death.

Ross wasn't smoking.

And he wasn't smiling.

"About twenty-four hours ago," he began, "in a little barn, on a country road just north of Normal…we got our asses handed back to us on a silver platter, gentlemen." He took several nonchalant steps and studied the floor. "About nine hours ago, in a little town called DC, I got the extreme pleasure of having mine handed back to me for a second and then even a third damn time. By Dulles, and then by Eisenhower no less."

All eyes found something to look at. Anything other than Howard Ross.

"Where's Agent James?" he called out.

"Uh, right here. Sir."

Ross rested his palms against the table and locked his elbows. "I'm not even gonna ask you…how the hell we didn't know that we were under counter-surveillance? Nope. Or how our perimeter security personnel were all sacked like a damn third-string, junior varsity football squad? I sure won't. Nope. Wouldn't dream of it."

He straightened up without modifying his stone-cold stare. "And I won't ask *you*—Agents Mitchell and Durbin—about your abject failure in acquiring accurate intel on the handful of mock-Mennonites under your charge. Nope. Not at all."

With arms folded, he circled his prey. "And I could go all the way down the list. And trust me…it's a big list. I won't ask each and every one of you about the dozens and dozens of…miscalculations, and mischaracterizations, and mismanagement of this so-called intelligence operation."

A forced grin spread across his face as his hands went down to his hips. "The Pentagon—of all agencies—the *Pentagon* took us, took Project SATURN, behind the woodshed. Is anyone else bothered by that? Anyone? Even a little bit?"

No one attempted to take the bait in his rhetorical trap.

"No one is bothered?" he repeated. "Cause I am. And more than a little bit. But the DCI ordered me, he ordered *us*, to back off. To drop it. There was no such place as the Sandbox. Just…let it go. Let it go. But as the sun rose on the nation's capital this morning, something else dawned. It dawned on me."

A few pairs of eyes reluctantly began to watch him.

"I realized that Dulles' prohibition, his Mennonite-mandate, said nothing of abridging our efforts to apprehend Denver Wayne Collins. And just several minutes ago, we received convincing eye-witness testimony that Mr. Collins is now operating under the assumed name of one Denver *Jackson*." He paused. "He's here. Somewhere."

"Are we staying in Bloomington?" Agent Hargraves called out.

"The simple damn answer is yes and no. *Yes*, we are staying here. But *no*, not just in Bloomington. We are going to repurpose our mission, modify our focus, and realign our priorities."

He finally lit up a cigarette. "I don't accept, not for one damn minute, that there is some incredible coincidence between the existence of Phil Nelson, and the loss of Denver Wayne Collins' wallet a few miles from here, and a beyond-classified Pentagon research facility just down the street. Those Menno-*nots* were practically forced to admit that temporal experimentation was occurring at the bottom of their little well of secrets."

"What's the plan, boss?" Neal shouted out.

"The same damn plan we've had since I walked through the debris field on that ranch outside of Roswell in 1947," Ross replied. "It's time for us to mingle and blend in. It's time to mix with the population of these two towns. We're gonna keep a low-profile while searching for high-profile targets." He stepped back up to the table, flipped open a folder, and snatched a large photo.

"He's here. And we're gonna search every square-inch of this damn county until we apprehend Denver Wayne *Jackson*."

CHAPTER 22

I don't think I've ever seen Doc so nervous.

Or sweaty.

After locating an open seat in the lively upstairs conference room, Denver sank down next to Ellen. The grinning redhead was engaged in an excited exchange with Betty Larson off to her left. His quick survey revealed that every Jumper in town had convened for the hastily summoned special gathering. Even Tori and Grandma Martha were among the convocation.

The stately matriarch made casual eye contact with him and acknowledged his arrival. "Good evening, Mr. Collins."

"Ma'am."

Ellen shifted her chair sideways. "Well, lookie who decided to show up. At the last minute."

Denver shrugged. "End of the week rush hour traffic in downtown Normal was brutal. I got behind two bicycles and a John Deere."

"Should've taken the bypass," she teased.

Doc cleared his throat and rubbed his hands together. "First of all, I would like to thank everyone for assembling here today."

"Like we had a choice," Shep mumbled.

Doc continued, unaffected. "I had fancied beginning our meeting with a salient bit of poetry, but after careful introspection I determined that no verse could aptly capture the grandeur of the moment."

"I guess there's a first time for everything," Shep chuckled dryly.

Denver was relieved that no one else laughed.

"But if prose or poem will not suffice, then perhaps I may borrow from legends of antiquity. The mythical Phoenix rose out of the ashes of certain demise, only to ascend more powerful than before." His face beamed while he scanned the room. "My dear friends…just as the tale of that glorious beast embodies the truth that defeat may be the first necessary step before success, I stand before you today affirming the same. I stand with the firm conviction that our best days are yet before us."

Denver glanced over at Ellen and kept his voice down. "What's going on?"

She pressed closer with an infectious grin. "Just you wait and see."

Doc adjusted his spectacles. "I can enthusiastically confirm to one and all that truth is indeed stranger than fiction. To borrow a term from my friends in the world of athletic competition, we have experienced a '*game changer.*'"

"Spit it out, Doc," McCloud bellowed through cupped hands. "You're killin' us with suspense. I heard you got some good news. Bring it. Bring it."

"One may deem it Providence, as an answer to prayer, Chief McCloud. Or perhaps a coincidence of the highest order. Regardless of your estimation, I refuse to acknowledge it as anything short of a modern miracle." He motioned across the table. "Miss Finegan? Would you be so kind as to bring our guest?"

"It is my greatest honor," she replied, slipping out of her chair and disappearing through the doorway.

Denver's eyes tracked her movements with growing interest. *What's going on here?*

"Ms. Larson?" Doc called out. "You had inquired, just several days ago, concerning my estimation of how long it may require to perfect a working Temporal Portal. Do you recall my less-than-precise answer?"

Betty rested her elbows on the table. "I do. Let's just say it *didn't* stop the presses."

"Fair enough," Doc replied. "But today's announcement, in any other setting, would no doubt garner front page headlines on every paper. In every city. On every continent across our fair globe."

"You're overplaying your damn hand, Doctor Stonewall," Shep blurted out. "As usual."

"Not to contradict you, Mr. Sheppard," Doc countered, "but you are completely and totally incorrect. In every way possible."

Denver was pleasantly stunned.

Whoa, there, Doc! You're finally loosening up.

That was almost what that smug jerk deserved.

"Mr. Collins? At our last gathering, do you remember what you most confidently announced as our greatest need? You started quite the stimulating conversation with it."

Doc's penetrating and expectant eyes pierced right through him.

Crap, what did I say?

Think, Collins. Think.

We needed…was it hope?

No, not hope. Something else. We need…

"Help," Denver yelled, louder than he meant to. "We need help. Right?"

Doc agreed. "Indeed, that is what you said, my friend."

Denver was relieved.

"But we have needed far more than help. We have had enigmatic questions which have plagued us from the first day that Phillip Nelson landed here, having traversed the oceans of time. Questions revolving around our very existence in Normal. Why, of all the innumerable places across creation, why are we here? And with these great needs and great questions in mind," Doc proclaimed with a sweeping gesture worthy of a carnival barker, "I present to all of you today...*help*."

There was a flurry of commotion as chairs moved, necks craned, and all eyes strained on the entrance. A short pause only served to increase the tension.

What help? Denver wondered as he repeatedly glanced between Doc and the doorway.

Where's the help?

Help appeared.

Incrementally.

First, they saw his dark leather shoes.

Next, the tip of his cane.

Finally, his lanky figure shuffled into the conference room, flanked on his right side by a supportive Ellen Finegan. Gauging the looks on a majority of the faces present, the disparity between what they were expecting and what they were seeing must have been substantial.

And disappointing.

Denver sank back, struggling to conceal his skepticism.

Help is a...shriveled up, prune of a man?

Am I missing something here?

Ellen and the frail visitor came to a stop beside a thrilled Doc Stonecroft. Shep couldn't restrain himself. "So, when does the damn help arrive?"

The old man offered a modest wave as he gazed out at his unimpressed audience. He seemed to be lost in amazement, oblivious to their reaction. "You have no idea how incredible it is to meet you," he offered after a brief hesitation. His eyes glistened with rising tears. "If it weren't so undignified for a scientist, I would pinch myself…all over."

Denver could easily tell that a few of the others were trying to manufacture a more positive response. Their forced smiles were as shallow as his own guarded optimism. The elderly man's eyes landed and remained upon him. Denver squirmed.

"Denver Wayne Collins," the visitor said with childlike wonder.

Wait…how does he know me?

How does he know my name? Did Ellen tell him? Doc?

Who is this guy?

Betty reached over and patted Denver on the arm, seeking to get his attention. Denver snapped back. "Oh, yes. Yes, sir. I am…Denver Collins."

"Even without your beard, I could recognize you quite easily," the visitor observed. "You are quite popular in my circle of friends. I know of no other person which ranks so prominently to both the FBI and the CIA. You are the last of many miracles."

My beard?

The FBI and the CIA?

Miracles?

Who is this guy?!

"Can you get on with the show, Stonecroft?" Shep demanded.

"Of course. Of course," Doc complied. "Ladies and gentlemen, may I introduce to you the one person in the world whose credentials easily over-qualify him for such a time as this. Our help. *My* miracle."

Doc's entire face transformed into a smile.

"Dr. Nikola Tesla."

January 9, 1997

SECURITY LEVEL: TOP SECRET

FOR: Chief Neal Schaeffer, Project SATURN
FROM: Richard Forsythe, Northeast Section
SUBJECT: Caretaker Phase III Educational Update

We have intervened regarding all four colleges that Denver Wayne Collins has applied to for admittance and scholarships for the Fall of 1997. All aforementioned institutions have been successfully encouraged to reject his application.

Our Army recruiter has made initial contact and begun making appropriate overtures towards him.

END

PS

CHAPTER 23

"This is gonna sound a bit strange, and please don't take it the wrong way," Chief McCloud began, rising out of his chair, "but aren't you supposed to be...*dead?*"

Doc Stonecroft couldn't hide his embarrassment. "A million apologies, Dr. Tesla, but—"

"Not even a single apology is needed, Dr. Stonecroft," Tesla offered through a wrinkled grin. "But however thrilling our conversation may be, I can tell this is going to be a long and exhausting exchange. May I please take a seat?"

Doc rushed forward and pulled out a chair. Ellen guided Tesla into it. "At my advanced age, I cannot remain standing for extended periods." He deposited his cane onto the tabletop. "Nurse Finegan, could I get a small glass of water?"

"Absolutely, sir."

She raced off. He rested his spindly arms on the table. "Now, on to the important question raised by the patrolman there. It is my most sincere desire to avoid *obscurum per obscurius.*"

Doc moved into a chair beside him. "Dr. Tesla, this is our local police chief. James McCloud."

"Now it is my turn to apologize. *Police Chief* McCloud."

"Don't mention it," the Chief replied. "Rank and formalities mean very little in this group. We're all equals here."

"Theoretically," Shep mumbled.

"Thank you, Chief McCloud. I've read of you in the local newspaper several times."

"You mean *my* newspaper?" Betty Larson inquired.

Stonecroft gestured across the table. "Dr. Tesla, may I introduce Ms. Betty Larson. Editor of the prestigious *Normal Journal*."

Tesla nodded. "Ms. Larson. So, the newspaper editor and the police chief? Both in this one group? Don't tell me that the mayor is also among us?"

Betty smiled. "As far as we know, Dr. Tesla, Al Vorhees is a Local."

"A Local?"

Ellen returned with his requested drink. "A Local is a person who is *not* a Jumper. A person from here. Not just in place, but in time."

"Thank you for the water and the clarification, Nurse Finegan." He downed a quick drink. "So now, this Local will answer the original question. No, Chief McCloud…I am not dead. At least…not yet."

"But Doc," Denver protested, "you told us that he died. Back in the 1940s."

"I did," Stonecroft responded. "And he *didn't*."

"Let me guess," Denver said. "It's complicated?"

Tesla folded his hands in his lap. "Complicated, Mr. Collins. And classified. *Highly* classified." The newcomer seemed to stare off into the distance. "The year was 1942. The American Naval Base at Pearl Harbor had been decimated by the Japanese a few months prior. With the double threat of Hitler in Europe, followed by Hirohito in eastern Asia, Roosevelt approved a desperate initiative. Five years before, I had approached the War Department concerning the possibility of eliminating enemy forces through invisible, charged particle beams. Publicly, they rejected my proposal, but they immediately began secret preparations to implement my designs."

"A Directed Energy Weapon," Denver said.

"That is correct, Mr. Collins. In order to conceal this initiative, since my research and reputation were quite well-known, it was decided that I needed…to die." He paused. "My passing was meticulously planned. For nearly a year, the morgues of every major city in the States, and even a few overseas, were examined for a suitable body-double. In December of 1942, a remarkable substitute was found and rapidly treated to prevent decay. The gentleman had expired due to a coronary thrombosis."

Ellen jumped in. "Basically, a blood clot near the heart."

"Precisely. I left my residence at the New York Hotel for a final time on January 5th, 1943, and my deceased substitute was placed in my room. A hotel maid found the body on January 7th, and I was declared dead. Once deceased, I was free to pursue more…*important* objectives. Like helping to defeat fascism."

"Fascinating," Betty Larson commented with a fire in her eyes. "A reporter like me dreams of landing a juicy scoop like this. This kinda coverup makes Watergate look like a juvenile high school prank."

The Chief cleared his throat. "Uh, remember the Accords, Ms. Larson."

"Oh, yeah. Sorry," she said. "That one kind of slipped out."

Tesla grinned. "I would very much appreciate it, Ms. Larson, if you would avoid placing my little secret anywhere near page one."

"What secret?" she asked with a raised eyebrows.

"Thank you," he said.

"Anywho, Dr. Tesla," McCloud ventured, "why are you here, of all places?"

"The simple answer, Chief McCloud, is that *you* brought me here. The more complex answer is because I brought you here."

"Come again?"

"I am here, because I brought you here."

McCloud sat back down. "Yeah. Didn't help."

Doc Stonecroft removed his spectacles and polished them. "Dr. Tesla has revealed the answer to our most pressing and essential question."

"Why Normal," Ellen added.

"What?" asked Billy O'Connell.

"Why it is that everyone always jumps here. To Normal," she replied. "What is it about Normal that somehow draws all of us Jumpers here? Now we know."

"Over the years, our explanations have run a large spectrum," Doc began. "From geology, to meteorology, and beyond. But, in reality, the truth had nothing to do with Normal…*per se*."

"Then what?" the Chief implored.

"The Sandbox," Tesla replied.

"That…was…an answer?" McCloud responded.

Tesla raised his glass and enjoyed a long drink before picking up his cane. "Just over a mile north of town, you may have noticed a large barn. On a small farm, occupied by Mennonites. Simple people. Black clothing. Men with beards and so on."

"Those folks in the all-black cars," Denver said.

"Yes, Mr. Collins. They are known as the Black Bumper Mennonites. The central United States has quite a few communities of such Mennonites."

"I've noticed that they usually keep to themselves," Leah offered.

Tesla looked up at her. "Yes, we do."

McCloud squinted. "*We?*"

"I chose my pronoun very specifically, Chief McCloud. I said *we*."

"You're a Mennonite?"

"In one sense, Chief McCloud, yes. But this decision was not mine. It was made for me."

"By your parents?" Leah asked.

"By the *Pentagon*," he answered. "Actually, the War Department in those days."

Billy scrunched his face. "So, the government chose your religion?"

Tesla chuckled. "An interesting choice of words, young man. When one thinks of religion, certain words naturally spring to mind. Words such as meaning, purpose…truth." He hesitated. "*Truth*. But in my case, it wasn't about truth. Actually, quite the opposite. It was about—"

"Deception," Denver said.

Tesla offered a faint nod. "Deception."

"Deception?" Billy asked. "Is anyone else as lost as me?"

"It's a sham, Billy," Denver replied. "An illusion. Those Mennonites on that farm aren't really Mennonites. That's just a cover for something else. Something classified."

Billy leaned back. "Oh. Okay. I think."

Denver started laughing. "Men in Black. Literally. Wow. Now that…*that's* funny. You guys are the Men in Black."

Betty leaned towards him. "What?"

"Oh, forget it."

Tesla continued. "In 1942, construction began on an underground facility on that farm north of town. It was wartime, and everyone was so distracted with the war effort, that no one noticed a group of Mennonites setting up shop out in the country in the middle of the Midwest."

"A beautiful, simple and effective cover," Doc observed.

"It has endured undetected for almost fifteen years, so I am compelled to agree with you," Tesla replied. "Three hundred and fifty feet below that farm, carved out of solid rock. We call it the Sandbox."

"An interesting codename," Betty Larson noted, looking around at the group. "The term sandbox refers to a place of possibilities limited only by our creativity."

"An apt description, Ms. Larson," he said. "It wasn't until late in 1944 that real, substantive research and testing began here. Actually, my first major experiment was in the fall of 1943. Back in the Philadelphia Naval Shipyard."

Betty leaned forward. "What kind of testing?"

"In Philadelphia, we were exploring methods of military invisibility. Primarily through the manipulation of rotating magnetic fields. But here, in the Sandbox…charged particle beams. Directed Energy Weapons, if you will. But that was only part of the plan. The War Department was additionally interested in some of my lesser known areas of expertise. Temporal distortion. Time travel."

"Is it all starting to make sense now?" Ellen asked of the group. A few scattered nods met her hopeful stare.

Tesla nodded as well. "In late 1945, and into early 1946, we completed the initial prototype of a temporal device utilizing magnetic fields. Our first test at full power occurred on March 5th, 1946."

"Ring a bell anyone?" Ellen called out. "Anyone? It should. It was a red letter day."

Leah brightened up. "Nellie!" she cried out. "March 5th. That was the day that Phil Nelson jumped to Normal!"

Ellen beamed. "Bingo, girl! You accountant-types are good with numbers."

"Dr. Tesla gave us a list of dates on which the device was employed at full power," Doc Stonecroft explained. "Every single one of our jump dates was represented on that list. Every single one of them, without exception."

"You carry around a list like that?" Shep asked.

"In a manner of speaking…*yes*," Tesla replied.

"Dr. Tesla possesses what most would call a photographic memory, Mr. Sheppard," Doc said.

"Our last such experiment was on August 10th. Of this year," Tesla said. "That is *your* jump date, Mr. Collins, is it not?"

Denver started to respond when Shep hunkered over the table and motioned. "So this senior citizen is the damn reason we're stuck in this nightmare?!"

Tesla flinched but then composed himself. "The data is conclusive. In one respect, I am guilty as charged, sir. But in my defense, we did not intend this outcome. As far as we knew, every test was a failure. We knew of the lightning and the thunder, but until a few hours ago, we were not aware that any of you existed. With the exception, of course, of Mr. Collins."

Doc stood up. "Mr. Sheppard…Dr. Tesla and his staff are not responsible for our jump *per se*. But they are liable for our jump *here*. The electrical storm we each experienced, matched with a temporal rift caused by nuclear detonation, is or was the fundamental mechanism for time travel. Dr. Tesla's research merely drew us from the temporal stream to this place and this time. Heaven knows where or *when* we would have been displaced had it not been for the Sandbox."

"Hawaii would've been nice," Garrett Frazier growled.

"Far too much volcanic activity below ground and far too much Japanese activity above," Tesla replied. "But it was considered."

"Still," Garrett said, "it would've been nice."

Alexus raised her hand and waited for Doc to notice.

He did. "You have something to add, Miss Daniels?"

She rose to her feet as everyone turned to face her uncertain and shy stare. "This is all very interesting and informative, but I have only one question." She held up a single, trembling finger. "Just one."

Doc folded his arms. "Yes?"

She pointed her raised finger across the table. "Is he gonna help us get home?"

"He has pledged to assist us, Miss Daniels," Doc said. "After this meeting, all are invited as we demonstrate our temporal progress for him."

Dr. Tesla rested his hands on the table and attempted to lock eyes with her. "I will do everything within my power, young lady. I promise you that."

Shep didn't seem satisfied. "We've been disappointed before, so pardon my justified pessimism, Nick. And pardon my total lack of trust while you're at it. How do we know that you're not just distracting us while truckloads of men with less-than-noble intentions are surrounding the damn place?"

"That's enough. Back off, Sheppard," McCloud cautioned.

"Quit telling me what to do, patrolman Jimmy! Remember, what you said a minute ago? We're all *equals* here, right? So, while you're all so enamored with this dog-and-pony show, I've been thinking. And what I can't figure out is how a supposed high-level military scientist like this geriatric has ended up in the middle of our damn conference room? Something dangerous is brewing here, people. Can't you see it?! We're in trouble. It's probably already too late for us."

Ellen arched forward. "As usual, you don't know what you're talking about, Robert!"

"No. No. That's not the problem," Shep countered. "No. See the problem is that I *do know* what I'm talking about. And I think most everyone else in this damn room knows that as well." He glared across the table. "Choir-boy Collins over there heads to Area 51 and comes back with the goods. *Alone* I might add. And then we lose Pappy. But don't worry! As if by magic, a few days later, a savior from the government arrives. The magic man with all the answers. And we are all supposed to be happy and grateful."

Tesla ventured a quick glance over at Doc. "Area 51?"

"Later, my friend," Stonecroft whispered.

"Come on, people," Shep implored. "There's a very neat and predictable pattern here." He jabbed a finger out at Denver. "And a pattern with *him* at the center. Once again. Anyone surprised?"

Shep shoved up out of his chair and closed the distance between himself and Tesla. "And am I the only one that's concerned with the fact that our new best friend was already on a first name basis with old *Colorado* over there?" He wagged his head as he abandoned the room.

"Just let that little nugget sink in."

February 20, 1997

SECURITY LEVEL: TOP SECRET

FOR: Chief Neal Schaeffer, Project SATURN
FROM: Richard Forsythe, Northeast Section
SUBJECT: Caretaker Phase III Financial Update

Accounting has determined that the financial status of Terry and Valerie Collins exceeds the limits outlined in the Operation Caretaker Phase III Directives. This financial stability could jeopardize Denver's entry into the Armed Forces.

With your authorization, we are prepared to intervene utilizing both IRS audits and subsequent legal expenses to mitigate this threat. If unsuccessful, other measures including loss of employment are outlined in the Directives.

END

PS

CHAPTER 24

The descent took three minutes.

Denver estimated it at nearly twice that long.

This'll never work, he thought. *This guy's gonna need an elevator.*

And some oxygen.

"Only three more steps, Dr. Tesla," Doc encouraged as the small company guided their new elderly colleague down into The Basement. "I can assure you our presentation will be entirely gratifying."

Tesla forced a smile. "I am intrigued and exhausted, Dr. Stonecroft. I see you have an affinity for Central American stone architecture."

Ellen held his right arm firmly as they tackled another step. "Sir?"

"This steep stairwell," Tesla elaborated. "It must have been inspired by an Aztec temple of some fashion."

"In that case," Betty Larson called out from near the back of the convoy, "it's probably better to be coming down, rather than going up. You know what happened once they reached the top."

"Well," he offered, clearly out of breath, "I think either direction is life-threatening in my case." He smiled.

"Any day now," Shep grumbled.

"One more step," Stonecroft cautioned.

"And for that I am most thankful," Tesla replied as he completed the task. "In the Sandbox, it is all one level, once you go below ground. With a spacious elevator to the surface."

Denver circled around from behind. "Speaking of which, we might want to consider building an elevator for Dr. Tesla here."

"Nonsense, Mr. Collins," he replied. "I have spent most of my days for over the past ten years down in the Sandbox." He pointed his cane. "Erect a simple cot over there and allow me to work. An arduous climb back to ground level will be a rare event."

Ellen gestured to her left. "This is a bathroom right here. We even have a shower and everything."

"Then it is settled," Tesla offered as he rested both hands atop his cane. "Provided I have sustenance, an occasional change of clothing, and stimulating conversation, all will be well. My room at the New York Hotel was not appreciably larger. Better furnishings, and a few windows, but the space is comparable."

Ellen hurried to the far side of the room. "And our portal is just beyond this door."

"All in good time, Nurse Finegan. Just grant this old man a few moments to catch his breath. It has been a long day already."

"Of course," Doc said. "Saturate your lungs, my friend, with a deep breath. For what we are about to show you will surely take it away."

"You have yet to disappoint, Dr. Stonecroft," Tesla observed.

"Can we hurry this along?" Shep asked.

"When Dr. Tesla is ready," Ellen countered. "But…I can start the process." She jogged towards the control panel.

Denver couldn't help but notice that something seemed to be bothering Betty Larson as she strolled past. She rested against the table. "Dr. Tesla," she began, "I can't imagine that our government's foremost research scientist could disappear without some serious repercussions."

He motioned for a chair. Denver and Doc obliged. "Ms. Larson, I was scheduled to spend a few days at a house in Chicago. From there I was going to travel and spend the holidays in New Jersey. But I called and canceled my earlier engagement. That should buy us a few days until they will come looking for me. At least, that is my expectation."

She didn't seem convinced. "There's quite a few assumptions hidden in there."

"Yes there are," he agreed. "Even more of a reason for me to remain hidden here. Below ground. I would estimate once they discover my ruse, there will be a tremendous manhunt undertaken for me between the farm and Chicago. Dozens, if not hundreds, of agents. Everyone should be on their guard."

Ellen glanced up, then raced towards the phone. "I'll call the Chief and Billy and tell them about that."

"A wise move, Nurse Finegan. But do not use my name or even my codename. They will eventually be monitoring communications, no doubt. Might as well start being cautious now."

"Gotcha."

Tesla waved his hand. "Dr. Stonecroft?"

Doc scooted a chair beside him and sat. "Yes, sir?"

"Earlier someone mentioned a place unfamiliar to me. An Area 51?"

"Yes. Mr. Sheppard did allude to it."

"Would anyone care to elaborate?"

Doc hesitated and looked up at Denver. He peeled off his glasses and began cleaning them. "Ah, well, yes. Area 51 is a classified government facility just north of Las Vegas, Nevada. It is also a primarily subterranean complex. As far as we can determine, Area 51 is operated by the Central Intelligence Agency. And the Air Force."

Tesla leaned back as a subtle grin spread across his narrow face. "Dreamland," he mumbled.

"What's that, my friend?"

"Dreamland," Tesla repeated quietly. "Oh, it is of no consequence. It is just that I am finally connecting the dots on another conversation we had recently. With the CIA."

"One would presume you would have had those regularly?" Doc probed.

"Just once."

"Our own Mr. Collins has had the good fortune of traveling to Area 51," Doc announced. "He visited the facility in late November."

Tesla frowned at Denver and cocked his head somewhat. "By invitation?"

"Uh, no. Not even close. And I kinda doubt they would want me back. But it will be an experience I will never be able to forget. And unfortunately, an experience I probably won't be able to talk about."

"I believe I understand, Mr. Collins. I wish I could take you to see my little world at the Sandbox. I would be most interested in your...*professional* comparison."

"No offense, Mr. Tesla, but I would just like to get home. Maybe some other time."

"Indeed."

"As best as we can surmise," Doc said, "Area 51 was established in response to our failed temporal experimentation in the desert Southwest."

"The Southwest? Why in the world were you there, may I ask?"

Doc slipped his spectacles on. "It was a bit before my time, but in 1947 our group lacked the luxury of having sufficient power to energize the portal. So our resident theoretical physicist sought out the next best solution."

Tesla chuckled, or at least he appeared to chuckle. *"Lightning."*

A spate of laughter escaped Doc's lips. "I suppose it is a natural phenomenon with which you are most familiar. And famous for."

"Incidentally, Dr. Stonecroft, you might be interested to learn that I was born during an electrical storm of particular ferocity over Smiljan," Tesla offered, his voice growing stronger. "Some feared it as a bad omen. My lovely mother always disagreed."

"A wise woman," Doc added.

"The stories I could tell about electricity!" Tesla erupted. He looked around at the group with excitement as Ellen rejoined them. "I could entertain friends and family for hours on end," he shared. "Some fancied me as mad, others withheld judgment, but all were astonished. Of all my research of decades past, it is my work with the wonders of electricity that grants me the greatest satisfaction."

Betty folded her arms. "The fact that lightning is what brought all of us to you is certainly a bit of strange coincidence."

"A *marvelous* coincidence," Tesla corrected. "Dr. Stonecroft, what year did your group begin experimentation in the Southwest?"

"1947."

Tesla twirled his cane as he obviously contemplated this new information. "Come now…not just 1947," he said, squinting, "but *July* of 1947. On or about the 4th of July, specifically."

Doc seemed shocked. "You are correct, my friend."

"And not just the Southwest. But New Mexico."

"Correct, once again."

"I can still recall Major Marcel's report." Tesla brought a bony finger to his lips and bobbed his head. "Roswell," he whispered. "It was Roswell."

Shep migrated towards the portal door. "You sure seem to have a lot of damn information about us, being a complete stranger and all."

"Uh, Nurse Finegan?" Doc called out, rising from his seat. "I believe that it is the opportune time to make final preparations for our demonstration."

"Aye, aye, Captain Stonecroft."

"Are you sufficiently recuperated, Dr. Tesla?" Doc inquired.

"Quite. Though I will submit that this chair is rather comfortable."

Ellen smiled. "We can move that seat into the portal chamber for you. Front row seat."

Tesla shot her a glance. "Is that…*safe*, Nurse Finegan?"

"Absolutely. We've done this at least a dozen times."

April 17, 1997

SECURITY LEVEL: TOP SECRET

FOR: Chief Neal Schaeffer, Project SATURN
FROM: Richard Forsythe, Northeast Section
SUBJECT: Operation Caretaker Phase III Update

Army recruiters in Brooklyn reported that Denver Wayne Collins has officially enlisted with the Army as of 17 April. This event signals the successful completion of Phase III.

Awaiting your instructions regarding transition to Phase IV stateside and Phase V in Afghanistan.

END

PS

CHAPTER 25

Tesla was mesmerized.

He hadn't spoken audibly for nearly a minute.

Ellen ran her hand on the smooth support tube framing the left side of the portal and squinted at him. "I can't quite read your face, Dr. Tesla. Do you approve?"

More silence.

Shep strolled halfway down the transom and folded his arms. "Any chance we can get this started before the end of the 20th Century?"

Ellen held up her hand to shut him down before gazing at Tesla. His expression seemed a curious blend of childlike wonder spread across a face etched by years of intermittent success. And decades of disappointment.

She touched his shoulder ever-so-gently. "Well, what do you think of our little toy, Dr. Tesla?"

His wrinkled head turned gradually. "Regardless of its current or future capabilities, it has already transported me back in time, Nurse Finegan."

"Sir?"

He grinned while tapping on the device. "Your design is far more elegant than I could have dreamed. My heart feels renewed. As a young boy on Christmas morning."

She guided him back to his chair near the far end of the metal walkway. "Well, if this feels like Christmas, it's time to open your gift." She looked up after a few steps. "Ms. Larson? Could you assist me?"

Betty hurried over. "You bet."

Seconds later the aged newcomer was situated in his chair. Denver took up a position directly behind him, as Betty and Shep flanked Tesla on the left and the right.

Ellen circulated a box of safety goggles. "Just as a simple precaution," she warned. "We probably don't really need them anymore. Just force of habit. Now, we have calibrated the portal to allow us to see into the world of the 1960s. This will honor the Second Accord as well as we can. Specifically, the time frame that brought me into this wonderful mess."

"Fantastic! Absolutely fantastic." Dr. Tesla struggled to make his goggles fit his bony skull. "I feel as if my heart will race out of my thrilled chest."

Ellen exited as Betty knelt down and patted his hand. "Now just try and stay calm. It would be a disaster if tomorrow's headline read: '*Nikola Tesla dies again after witnessing the future.*'" She winked.

"No promises, Ms. Larson," he said. "I make no promises. And if it is so, then so be it. I have lived decades beyond my expected years. I can imagine no greater means exiting this world."

"Well," she said, "still…try to just enjoy the show. Alive."

Doc's excited voice, though muffled, echoed out. "Miss Finegan, engage the power."

"Here we go," Betty said.

The foreboding hum, though familiar to most, appeared to have caught Tesla off-guard. He squeezed Betty's hand. She leaned down. "Don't worry, sir. That sound is perfectly normal. Supposedly."

The first few flashes of spastic light erupted from the portal. He flinched again. "It'll get worse before it gets better," she explained. "Trust me."

The pulsating roar continued ramping up as the triangular face of the device swirled with cloudy, blue smoke. Tesla leaned forward.

Betty grinned. "Almost there."

But then, something new and unexpected caught her eye.

It was tiny, but she clearly saw it. Twice.

Um, what was that? Betty thought. *That was strange.*

She glanced over at Shep. He wasn't even paying attention.

Then it happened again.

The anomaly was followed by a distinct blast of white steam along the left edge of the portal. Several small arcs of electricity began dancing about the buzzing frame. They grew.

Shep finally noticed and jerked his head over his shoulder. "Uh, Ellen," he yelled. "Something's—"

But it was too late.

A jet of steam exploded with a shrieking hiss as an enormous bolt of electricity blasted from the center of the unstable portal. The long, white-hot arc burned a fist-sized hole through Shep's shaking torso, before lifting him off the ground and slamming him into the opposite wall. His lifeless form slid down the painted surface, leaving a bloody trail of ruptured flesh and burnt clothing in its wake.

Betty screamed in horror and lunged down in front of Dr. Tesla, as Denver struggled to drag the chair and it's occupant back towards the door. "Shut it off!" he yelled in vain. "Shut it down!"

But the portal's fury had yet to be satisfied. A fresh arc launched out and sliced a smoking path across the ceiling, before jumping erratically to the transom below. The surge in electricity raced up through Betty's hands and forearms, seizing her muscles, and jerking her flat against the metal walkway. Her body trembled and thrashed about under the massive and fatal electrical assault.

Two seconds later it was all over.

CHAPTER 26

They say it always come in threes, McCloud.

The Chief brought the dark car to a rocking stop in the icy gravel behind Nelson Manufacturing and threw it into park.

First Pappy…and now this.

Officer Billy spoke for the first time in several minutes. "Do we know what happened?"

McCloud dug his flask out of the glove compartment and sucked down a healthy swig. He twisted the cap back on. "It, uh, it was some kinda accident." After fidgeting with his hat for a few moments, he reached for the door. "Don't say anythin' to Leah or anyone who wasn't there. They may not have heard yet."

"Sure, Chief."

As they trudged through the factory, every solemn step made the burning knot in the Chief's stomach intensify. Being a city cop in Atlanta, McCloud had experienced the irregular horror of knocking on more than a few doors bearing the world's worst news. His face had felt both the blast of cold slamming doors as well as the hot tears of many mothers and fathers crushed beneath the burden of his emotional bombshell.

He could hear Ellen's sobbing the moment his heavy footfalls echoed down the staircase to The Basement. The painful lump in his gut jumped into his throat.

"Chief!" Ellen cried out as she rushed up to meet them. "They're dead. They're…they're dead. Both of them." Ellen threw her distressed arms around his neck as she collapsed against him. McCloud teetered backwards and almost crumbled under the weight. He struggled for a response. Any response.

"Are, uh, are you okay?"

She didn't look up and gulped in sporadic, shaking breaths. "No…no…no. I'm…not…okay. They're gone! I…I couldn't stop…it."

McCloud patted her heaving back. "It's not your fault, darlin'. It's not your fault. Accidents happen. Is everyone else okay?"

Denver bounded up a few of the steps. "Yeah, but we're all just more than a little shook up. I was worried about Dr. Tesla at first, but I think he'll be alright." He glanced back and lowered his volume considerably. "Doc's…well, he's pretty much in shock."

The Chief whispered in return. "What happened?"

Denver shook his head and leaned against the concrete wall. "It's hard to say. Apparently something went wrong with the cooling system, which—"

"A liquid nitrogen line ruptured," Ellen interjected. "Which…caused a thermal imbalance." She pushed away from the Chief's chest and wiped her hot face. "The, uh, the heat probably caused one of the…magnets to get out of sync." Ellen paused. "Then…then…"

"Some big bolts of electricity shot out of the portal," Denver explained. "It was pretty bad. And fast. At least…they didn't suffer."

Ellen began to crumple again and Billy rushed down to catch her. "Stay with Miss Finegan," McCloud instructed softly. "I need to talk to Mr. Collins for a few minutes."

"Yessir, Chief. I'm here for you, ma'am."

Ellen sank down and sat on the step, burying her face in her hands. "Thanks, Billy."

The Chief and Denver continued along the cold stairwell. As they reached the bottom, the Chief attempted to make eye contact with a stoic Doc Stonecroft on the far side. Tesla sat close by, with his thin right arm resting on the tabletop. McCloud worked his way over to them.

The Chief nodded. "Hey…listen. This wasn't your fault. It's not anyone's fault." He hesitated. "These things happen. We knew it wasn't gonna be easy. Nobody blames nobody. For any o' this."

He waited.

There was zero response.

The Chief glanced over at Denver and gestured towards the portal chamber. Denver bit his lip and bobbed his head. The pair backed away from the table and progressed into the doorway. A foul blast of cooked flesh and smoldering hair stopped McCloud cold. He reclined against the heavy door for a moment before venturing in.

Even his major-city law enforcement tenure hadn't prepared him for the unfamiliar tragedy that waited around the familiar corner.

Denver leaned close to the Chief's ear. "It's bad."

It was.

Betty's motionless body lay prostrate on the transom before him. The Chief finally found the strength to move in her direction. He had to look away once he caught sight of the white blisters that littered her exposed skin.

Lord, have mercy, he thought.

The blackened gash across the ceiling of the spherical white room distracted his silent attention for the moment. Denver cleared his throat and motioned down below.

It took a moment for McCloud's eyes to focus beyond the fine metal lattice of the platform. Shep's mangled remains were sprawled out like burnt human debris lining the bottom of the chamber. A glimpse of the scorched cavity that had been blasted through Shep's torso would probably haunt him the remainder of his days. The Chief glanced away only to discover the sickening bloody path from Shep's body up and along the wall.

Denver drew near. "Trust me. He never knew what hit him. It was over in a flash. Literally."

McCloud's cheeks flared crimson and his eyes flooded with tears. "Still…Mr. Collins. It's, uh…so violent. So sad. It's gonna kill the rest of the group."

"Yeah." Denver rested his hands on his hips and kept his voice down. "I know this is probably a bad time, but it needs to be said."

"It is a bad time. What is it?"

"Well, if Shep disappeared from the town, very few would even notice. But…Ms. Larson." Denver paused for a few moments. "Newspaper editor. Well-known in the community. An office manager. With employees. A woman like that can't just…*disappear*. With all the increased scrutiny surrounding Tesla and all, we don't need any more attention if you know what I mean."

McCloud let it sink in.

"I see. She needs to…simply die," the Chief muttered. "A more public and typical death."

"Exactly. But she was too young for it to have been a natural cause, like a heart attack. And Normal's too far from Chicago for something more violent. Like murder."

"No, not murder," McCloud replied, barely above a whisper.

"Then what?"

The Chief met eyes with him and then looked away. "I know what we need to do. I'll have Billy take Ellen and the other gals out o' the building. Get ahold of Garrett and tell him to helps us move the...bodies into the factory delivery truck. We can pull it inside."

"What's your plan?"

McCloud brought his hand to his chin. "I need you to follow me in Shep's truck."

"Follow you?" Denver asked.

"And fill up a gas can and put it in the back of the box truck...along with a cinder block."

CHAPTER 27

Denver was from Manhattan.

New Yorkers were somewhat accustomed to navigating through the snow in the winter. He grasped the steering wheel with both hands and struggled to maintain a straight course. This may have been winter, but this certainly wasn't snow.

"I would keep more distance between us and the delivery truck," Garrett cautioned. "Ice doesn't play by the regular rules of slippery driving. Zero traction."

Denver grimaced. "I am finding that out. It wasn't this bad this morning."

"Freezing rain hit after six o'clock."

A pair of glaring red lights shone out across the glassy asphalt.

"He's slowing down," Garrett announced, wagging his finger.

Yes, Mr. Frazier. I know what red taillights mean.

Fifty yards ahead, McCloud eased the box truck onto the soft shoulder and hopped out, waving his arms for them to stop. Denver did his level best to arrest their vehicle's motion without much sliding. He was successful, more or less, and cranked his window down.

McCloud jogged back towards them, his breath glowing bluish-white in the truck's headlights. The Chief, slightly winded and slipping somewhat, motioned off to their right. "Perfect spot. No houses for miles. There's a sharp bend just ahead. And a line of stout trees beyond that."

Garrett frowned. "Are you warning us to be careful?"

McCloud adopted a serious grin. "Uh, no. I want you to hit them. Hard."

"What?"

Denver pivoted to his right. "Don't worry, Mr. Frazier. I understand what the Chief has in mind. We need an accident...but...on purpose."

"What? Oh."

In less than two minutes the trio had taken steps to position the pickup a few hundred feet from the dangerous curve. McCloud secured the steering wheel in place with his own leather belt and checked and rechecked the angle. Denver hoisted a heavy cinder block out of the truck bed and slid it across the floorboard on the driver's side.

"Makin' any more sense now, Frazier?" the Chief inquired, zipping up his dark coat.

"Totally."

"I figgered you'd get it by now. Are we ready, Mr. Collins?"

Denver straightened up and crawled into the driver's seat. He examined the cinder block and the gas pedal. "It should work. I think."

"It'll work," the Chief reassured. "C'mon with me, Mr. Frazier." The pair trotted back to the delivery truck. "Let's get Denver's truck a rollin'. Won't be easy. This ice's like snot-covered glass."

With as gentle motions as the road conditions would allow, McCloud inched his vehicle forward and barely kissed the rear bumper of the pickup. He did his best to lean out the window. "Are we ready, Mr. Collins?" he bellowed.

An arm shot out on the driver's side with a single thumbs up.

McCloud leaned forward. "Here we go."

The Chief eased into the accelerator and the back axle of the delivery truck fishtailed at first. It took a few seconds, but forward momentum was gradually acquired.

McCloud studied the situation and rehearsed the plan. "He jumps left, we go right, pickup goes straight. Boom."

"In theory," Garrett added.

Their velocity increased steadily.

The Chief squinted. "Any time now, Mr. Collins. Any dang time."

The driver's door on Shep's truck popped open.

"Now that's more like it," the Chief observed with a satisfied nod.

The words had barely left his mouth when their headlights illuminated Denver's form leaping out and tumbling onto the grassy shoulder. McCloud cut his steering wheel to the right and removed his foot from the gas pedal. As planned, the pickup stayed true to course, continued to accelerate, and plunged with devastating force headlong into the grove of trees.

The Chief snagged a flashlight and aimed it out the window. "You alright back there?"

Denver wiped a few straggling clumps of dead grass off of his damp clothing. "Actually, I've been *in* a car when it wrecked and still lived to tell about it. And I've done my share of parachute landing falls, Chief. I think this Army vet'll be fine. That was kid's stuff."

McCloud killed the flashlight while his face grew somber in the pale moonlight. "Unfortunately, that was the easy part."

It was a grisly task.

Even Garrett had difficulty executing the plan.

The Chief noticed him cramped over beside the rear of the box truck. "Gonna be alright, Mr. Frazier?"

Garrett's whole body lurched forward as he vomited onto the icy grass. "Take yer time," McCloud consoled before cupping his hands around his mouth. "Mr. Collins? Could you give me a hand?"

A voice rang out from not too far distant. "On my way."

The Chief lowered a sympathetic hand down to Garrett's shoulder. "Why dontcha climb back into the front seat? We got this. Really."

There was a slight delay. "Yeah, okay." Garrett rose to his feet and leaned against the vehicle. "Thanks."

"No problem."

Denver appeared around the corner and McCloud slowed his advance, leaning into him. "Mr. Frazier is…havin' a hard time with this."

"We all are."

"This I know."

Denver glanced over at the bloody sheet that housed Shep's remains. The smell still gagged him. "Regardless of my opinion about his boss, Garrett worked with him in lockstep. For years. That's gotta be rough."

McCloud grabbed the covering and slid the corpse towards them. "Yep. Tryin' times indeed. Gimme a hand."

Relocating Shep's cadaver to the front seat of the pickup constituted a far greater challenge than they had experienced with Betty Larson. The earlier impact had crumpled the dash, shattered the windshield, and forced the steering wheel at least a foot further into the cab. Denver tried to avoid looking at the awful hole in Shep's chest while he pulled the sheet off the cold body.

"Don't forget to remove the cinder block," the Chief warned as he trudged back with a gas can swiveling from his right hand. "Did you toss Betty's purse in there?"

Denver rested his exhausted frame against the truck bed. "I did. And I did."

"Good. Then you might wanna head back to the delivery truck."

Denver wiped his moist brow and sauntered off. "Gladly."

The Chief hesitated for a few moments. "Cause I've got it all from here, Mr. Collins."

A faint hint of gasoline began to permeate the frigid night air during his short jaunt back. Denver arrived at the front of the vehicle and peered up at Garrett through the windshield.

He perceived a quick, rushing roar an instant before a dazzling fireball reflected off the glass in varying shades of brilliant orange.

June 25, 1997

SECURITY LEVEL: TOP SECRET

FOR: Senior Staff, Project SATURN
FROM: Chief Neal Schaeffer, Project SATURN
SUBJECT: Operation Caretaker Phase V

As we approach the new century at the outset of a new millennium, the geopolitical alignments and adversarial relationships of the Cold War are rapidly changing and/or dissipating. Over the past few decades, our anticipated need for a wide-scale military intervention in Afghanistan depended fully on the foregone conclusion of resisting Soviet expansion into the Middle East.

With the dissolution of the Soviet Empire, specifically the withdrawal of Soviet forces from Afghanistan nearly a decade ago in 1989, a clear future has become disturbingly murky. According to the intelligence obtained from the Collins' documentation, we anticipate a significant US military operation in Afghanistan within approximately four years, beginning no earlier than the Fall of 2001.

Unfortunately, the ascension of the Taliban to power last year in Afghanistan yields no clear and present threat to the USA. The recent alignment of the Taliban with radical, pro-Caliphate Islamic organizations may be worthy of consideration.

Regardless of the current scenario, it is imperative that Mr. Collins re-enlists for a second commitment with the Army in 2001. As we discussed at our April Strategic Outlook Session, I will be delivering a series of proposals to DCI Tenet next month regarding methods of influencing the current and following administration concerning combat operations in Afghanistan (Phase V). Please submit all updated recommendations no later than 5 July.

In addition to evaluating the future of geopolitical maneuverings, as the sunset of my long career looms on the not-so-distant horizon, I also am evaluating my own future usefulness to this organization. I have made no firm decisions as of yet, but the time of passing the baton draws nigh. I would expect to resign my appointment within the next twelve months.

END

PS/DCI

CHAPTER 28

"This menu beats anything we have back at Dreamland all to pieces," Neal remarked under his breath as he rose from the diner barstool to shed his coat.

Ross rubbed his forehead and flipped the coffee-stained, trifold document over. "That is one man's opinion, Mr. Schaeffer," he grumbled. "As usual, it does not happen to be mine or anyone else's. Not a single ribeye or New York Strip. I've checked. Twice."

Neal plopped back down. "We've been deep into the Midwest for almost a week. You need to start celebrating the differences. Enjoy a little culinary variety while we do a little sightseeing. You almost enjoyed the entrees underground at Cotton's Restaurant."

"Cotton's *Village Inn*."

"Whatever."

Ross grimaced. "Everything here is fried. Fried chicken, chicken fried steak, fried bacon, fried French fries. At least Cotton's had something grilled over an open flame."

"Welcome to true southern cooking, even if we're not really in the South," Neal beamed as a blonde waitress with bright red lips approached.

Ross noticed her. "The menu just improved."

"Welcome to Amanda's Diner, gentlemen," she said, flipping a small notepad open with a quick snap of her petit wrist. "A fast round of coffee to chase that mid-December chill away?"

"Black as you got it," Ross responded.

Neal studied her. "Same for me…*Katie*. Thanks. And where is your restroom?"

She motioned to their far right. "Just around the bend. I'll be right back with your coffee."

Neal leaned into Ross' ear as he jumped up. "Don't try to pick her up while I'm gone."

"No promises."

"Plus, she's probably…half your age."

"And half is *twice* the fun."

"You're sick."

Ross grabbed him and pulled Neal closer. "And just how much younger is your woman?"

"Oh, five years."

"Well," Ross began with uncharacteristic discretion, "if you were ten years old, she would be half your age, Mr. Sick."

Neal grinned and shoved off. "You're impossible."

"Thank you."

Neal shook his head and worked his way along the crowded bar as Ross lowered his menu, scanning the establishment. Most of the booths and several of the tables were occupied with happy couples or noisy families. He pulled his sleeve back to examine his watch.

5:15 p.m.

Must be the only restaurant open after the sun starts to go down in this one-horse town.

It wasn't actually dark, but to Ross it felt considerably later. Along with a host of other SATURN agents, he and Neal had been canvassing the modest pair of communities—primarily on foot—for three days running. The cold weather (combined with short days and long hours) gave rise to a certain physical weariness that was difficult to overcome by sheer enthusiasm alone.

But more than that, Ross had trouble focusing.

The initial thrill of the positive TDS Film results, offset by the humiliating power struggle in the Sandbox, and capped by bureaucratic bullying, had rendered Ross increasingly conflicted and bitter. What should have been a simple exercise, was now drifting higher and higher out of his impatient reach.

"Two cups of black," Katie announced as she returned with a steaming pot. "I'll be right back for your order. We're a little shorthanded today. Must be the rush of holiday shoppers."

He nodded and fumbled around with the menu for the third time, even less sure of his choice than the second. The waitress' distinctive voice rose above the chatter from four or five stools to his right.

"Haven't seen you in a while, Mr. Big Tipper."

Ross wasn't interested in the patron's response, but he couldn't help but be interested in hers.

"You want me to run that cow through the garden, Mr. Jackson?"

Wait…Jackson?

Jackson. Denver Jackson?

Ross attempted to be discreet and arched back.

Damn. Can't see the bastard.

He brushed his coffee out of the way and hunkered over the counter. One quick glance to the right revealed a partial face. His pulse quickened.

Katie returned. "Do you wanna wait for your friend to get back before you order?"

Ross didn't hear her, or at least he didn't care to respond. He growled something.

"What's that?" she asked, moving closer.

"I said *move over*." He pointed left more or less. "No, no. That way."

She obeyed as a puzzled look overtook her face. He studied the uneven reflections in the long mirror mounted horizontally on the wall a few feet behind her.

Collins?

Unbelievable. Hot-damn.

Gotcha.

Ross placed both trembling hands on the counter and rose to his feet. None of the busy patrons even bothered to look up as he incrementally closed the distance on his prey. His right hand slipped into his suit coat and then down to the pistol tucked away below his left arm.

The excitement and intensity of nearly a decade of disappointing pursuit grew with each and every careful step.

Four feet away he confirmed a positive ID.

Denver Wayne Collins.

The diner giveth...what the Sandbox taketh away.

He paused, hovering just behind Denver's left shoulder. Ross drew his weapon and pressed the short barrel into his seated victim's back. He kept his voice down as he bent lower. "You are under arrest, Mr. Jackson-*Collins*."

Denver raised off his stool in a gradual, measured response, his hands climbing higher and higher. He pivoted his head around and met the cold, determined eyes of Howard Ross.

There was a short look, a quick blur, and Ross woke up a minute later drenched with cold coffee in a shallow bed of fractured glass and porcelain.

Research Log: Dr. Glen D. Stonecroft

DATE: December 16, 1956

The crushing loss of Robert Sheppard and Betty Larson weighs heavily upon our best efforts to maintain appropriate focus in our endeavors. We have confirmed that a frayed supply line was the first responsible party in a cascading sequence of dangerous events.

That being said, the magnitude of the providential arrival of Dr. Nikola Tesla into the midst of our desperation cannot be overstated. It is poetically fitting that the eminent scientist who drew us forth shall be the eminent scientist who shall (by God's grace) send us hence. I cannot imagine that the supreme thrill of co-laboring alongside one of the greatest minds in all of history shall ever subside.

From my understanding, Dr. Tesla requires little sleep. By his own admission he remained up all throughout the last two nights reviewing these research notes and examining our apparatus. It appears that Miss Finegan and I will be adjusting our schedules of rest to alternate in shifts so that we may maximize our usefulness by keeping ourselves available to assist him at all hours. I may have to bring in a third assistant, perhaps Mr. Collins, if we are unable to accommodate Dr. Tesla's needs.

He seems most encouraged that we shall overcome our present difficulty with transporting organic matter. It is his opinion that our current system could inadvertently keep an object/person in the temporal limbo for up to many thousands of years.

Our labors yielded no success yesterday. All ten capsules returned with dead rodents in various states of advanced decay. Under Dr. Tesla's supervision, Ellen has been modifying the apparatus even since early this morning.

It is our intention to begin a new round of trials with our laboratory mice before midday.

G.D.S.

****

UPDATE:

Eleven mice were sacrificed on the altar of scientific inquiry today before we met with success this afternoon! Our lucky #23 rodent went into and out of the temporal rift at 2:57 pm. The mouse was functioning and appeared to be unharmed.

Dr. Tesla was still concerned about the passage of time within the temporal limbo and devised a most ingenious proposal. We inserted a fresh ice cube into the ball along with Mouse #24. When the creature returned from the rift, the cube had not melted beyond a few drops. Later we confirmed the instantaneous transport using my wristwatch. Mouse #25 returned with my timepiece in perfect synchronization with Miss Finegan's watch.

Building upon our success with receiving light from a specific time frame, we will now concentrate our triple efforts on sending organic mass into a specific time in the future. Through the physical and mathematical analysis of our TRS samples, confidence is high that we can extrapolate a system of temporal adjustment to allow for the selection of any moment in time. This should allow us the luxury of sending those Jumpers home from whom we did not receive a TRS sample. At least, to their correct time. Pinpointing a proper location will most likely remain impossible for all intents and purposes.

With temporal physics I am merely an acquaintance, but with temporal equations I rather fashion myself as one of the family.

G.D.S.

CHAPTER 29

The blast of cold ice water did more to rouse his anger than to arouse Howard Ross from his fist-induced slumber. That didn't prevent Neal Schaeffer from giving it a second round.

And enjoying it.

"C'mon, boss. Wake up," he implored. "Wake up."

Waitress Katie Long returned with an armload of clean, dry towels to continue mopping up the aftermath of Denver's frantic escape. Ross' barely conscious form was sprawled across the floor behind the bar, surrounded by the shattered remains of at least two plates, one coffee pot, and several cups and saucers.

Sixty seconds earlier, Neal had started to panic at the sight of a long trail of red that appeared to be gushing out of his boss' neck. His fear grew until Katie revealed a split ketchup bottle. A quick wipe of a towel proved that his only injury seemed to be a deepening contusion on his jaw.

And a deep blow to his pride.

"What happened?" Neal asked.

"There was a fight," Katie replied. "If you want to call it a fight. Kinda one-sided. It only lasted a few seconds."

"A fight?" Neal exclaimed. "With who?"

"With him," a groggy voice grumbled from down on the floor. Ross massaged his sore chin. "*He* was here."

"Who?" Neal asked.

"Mr. Jackson," Katie said, handing Ross a cold cloth. "Mr. Denver Jackson. I think he gets into a lot of fights. Today's one of the few times I've seen him without a bruise or a bandage or something. He's kinda mysterious."

Neal sat up but kept his eyes locked on Ross. "Denver was here? In this diner? Tonight?"

"You walked right by him on your merry way to the men's room, Mr. Schaeffer," Ross offered with a fair amount of unspoken accusation as he struggled to raise up. "What is killing my damn back?" He reached around and slid his gun out into the open. Katie practically screamed and lurched back against the counter. A small gathering of gawkers followed suit.

Two people actually ran out.

"Hey, hey everyone," Neal cautioned, "it's okay. It's okay. We're with the FBI." He fished a shiny gold badge out of his pocket and displayed it high. "We, uh, we've been looking for Mr. Jackson. He's a wanted man. A fugitive."

Katie blushed with a nervous chuckle. "I knew it. I knew it from the very first day."

"First day?" Neal repeated. "When was that very first day?"

She put her hands on her hips. "Goodness. It, uh, it was probably back in August. Right before school started back, I think. Early August. I knew he was trouble. Fake money and the robbery and all."

"He had fake money?" Neal inquired.

"And a fake name." Katie lowered her voice and stepped closer. "People think he is Denver Jackson. But, Ms. Larson told me his real name is *Collins*. Denver Collins."

Neal bent down to help Ross up to his unstable feet. "And who is this Ms. Larson?"

Katie grew somber, hesitating. "Um, she was the, uh, editor of our local newspaper."

"Was? Where is she now?"

"Ms. Larson—*Betty*—she was killed in an accident last week. It was horrible. Burned up. Just terrible."

Ross grabbed a dry towel and cleared the remnants of glass and porcelain off his suit coat. He pulled a pair of ice cubes out of his shirt pocket and shot Neal a stern look. "I need a damn cigarette." He felt all around and then inside his coat. "Wait. Wait. Back up. You just said robbery. What robbery?"

"Mr. Jackson, or Collins…he and some other people robbed Ms. Larson's newspaper office. And a few other places."

"How do you know he was involved?" Neal pressed, moving closer.

Katie's artfully crafted eyebrows shot up. "Cause they caught him. Red-handed. He spent over a month in jail, I think." She paused. "Small town crimes probably don't get the attention of the FBI. Are y'all from Chicago?"

Ross mopped his damp face and neck. "He went to jail? Where?"

"Well, *here*. Just a block over. At the Normal Police Station. The Chief's probably still there. Not sure. It is a Sunday. Weekends are hit and miss."

Neal grabbed Ross by the arm and they scrambled around the counter and towards the front door. He called back over his shoulder. "Don't leave town, Katie. We'll be back soon." Neal retreated to grab his coat. "And don't talk to anyone else. About anything."

"Wouldya like to fill out an accident report, gentlemen?" the Chief asked as the pair of suited strangers hurried into the station and slammed the door. "Cause I was just gettin' ready to lock up. Ain't no one in the slammer tonight to babysit."

"Accident report?" Neal asked.

McCloud shoved his chair under his desk, straightened a few stacks of paper and moseyed in their general direction. "Well, by the looks of your friend's clothes and jaw I'd say either an accident or a food fight." He smiled.

They didn't.

Ross flashed a badge. "FBI."

The door flung open and four more agents shuffled in and fanned out. The first two took up ominous positions not quite a dozen feet behind the Chief. One slid alongside Ross and whispered in his ear. Ross nodded. "Keep looking." He waved him out. The agent jogged back to the door and disappeared.

McCloud glanced back discreetly. "Do I need to throw on a pot of coffee, boys? Gonna be a long night? Sounds like a dragnet."

"Chief James McCloud?" Ross asked.

"Guilty as charged. What can I do for you?"

"We need information on a recent criminal that you had in custody."

"Gotcha. Well, that's a pretty short list in these parts." He furrowed his brow. "Unless you consider drunks as criminals."

Neal cracked open a thin folder and held up a photo.

McCloud nodded with a growing grin. "Good ole Denver Jackson."

Ross squinted. "So, you are familiar with our person of interest?"

"Familiar?" the Chief chuckled, as he backtracked and reclined against his desk. "I had to babysit that rascal for 'bout a month. Not a bad guy. Fell into the wrong crowd, I suspect."

Ross and Neal advanced closer. Neal spoke up. "When was Mister…*Jackson* in your custody?"

The Chief concentrated on the ceiling and stroked his rough chin. "Let's see, that woulda been about the month of…August…no, no…it was September. It was September. He was with me for thirty days. Breaking and entering. Theft. A little vandalism."

"Where is he now?" Ross demanded.

"Now that's a good question," McCloud offered with a subtle shrug. "He, uh, he worked down at the paper for a while. After that, he kinda fell off my radar."

"The paper?" Neal echoed. "The same newspaper he broke into?"

"That's the one. Yeah, I know it sounds strange, but it was what Judge Seyer ordered. It was a type of community service. It was awkward at first, but they warmed up to him. He did alright. At least, Betty never complained to me. Actually, I think she was sad to see 'em go."

"You are speaking of Betty *Larson*. The editor?" Neal asked.

"Yes sir. At least she was the editor. Betty—"

"Yes, we know that she was killed in a motor vehicle accident," Neal interrupted.

McCloud folded his arms. "Good gal. Been here 'bout three years. Worst part of my job, havin' to deal with traffic fatalities." He bit his bottom lip. "They, uh, hit a patch of ice…we think. On Friday night. Lost control. It was bad. Her and another guy. Might've been on a date."

Neal retrieved a notepad. "When and where did you see Mr. Jackson last?"

The Chief stalled, flitting his eyes around as if struggling to recall specific information. "Wow, let's see. He went back to the *Journal* last month. Doing something. Short term. Betty had to go outta town and they needed temporary help."

"What do you mean '*back at the Journal*'?"

"Oh. Well, I was pretty sure he had returned to Chicago after he served his time'n all. He was from there originally. Least that's what he said. But, here…he had an apartment for a while. I think it was over by the college. On the west end of town."

Ross dug around for a pack of cigarettes and forced one out. "Did you have any lengthy or detailed conversations with him?" He hung it on his bottom lip and ignited the tip.

"Lengthy?" McCloud snickered. "I can tell that you don't know him. Mr. Jackson wasn't much of a conversationalist. At least, not around me." The Chief paused. "Now, don't take me wrong. He wasn't rude or nothin'…just kinda tight-lipped. Me, on the other hand, well, see, I can just talk all—"

"What did he talk about?" Ross demanded, releasing a quick blast of smoke.

The Chief pushed off the desk and sauntered over to the cell. "Oh…he'd talk a little sports. A little chit-chat." He rested against the bars and pointed. "Anywho, he just sat there or laid there and looked at a small picture of his daughter. Janice…or Jezebel, or somethin' like that. I'm sure it wasn't Jezebel, but that's what comes to mind."

"Jasmine," Neal said.

"That's it, yep…Jasmine."

Ross continued the interrogation as Neal recorded various notes. "Did he have any visitors? Family? A wife? Any known associates?"

The Chief pivoted around until his back was pressed against the cell. "Uh, not that I recall. It was pretty much just him and me. Or sometimes my deputy. But not too much. Billy helped on weekends." McCloud shoved his hands into his pockets. "We never did catch the other fellas that helped him break into the paper. He said they were also from Chicago."

Neal glanced over from his notes. "What did they steal?"

"Not much. A little cash. Oh, and a safe."

"Tell us about the safe," Neal instructed without looking up.

"Okay. Well, Betty said it was a small office safe. I think there were some family heirlooms or other such keepsakes." He thought for a moment. "We never recovered it."

"Who else would have information about Mr. Jackson?" Neal asked.

"Well, Betty would've probably been the best one, but, uh, maybe James? James down at the paper. James *Cannon.* They worked together. I think he's been meeting with the owners all weekend to keep things going til they find a new editor. Sad deal. A shame."

Ross took a sizable pull on his cigarette and dangled it by his side. "You said Mr. Jackson was from Chicago. Where exactly in Chicago?"

The Chief pushed off the cell bars and wagged his head. "*He* said he was from Chicago. Not me. We never found anything to back that one up. He didn't have any ID on him the night of the burglary. But, then again, he never gave us any reason to doubt it neither." He paused. "Can't imagine why someone'd lie about where they were from."

Ross maintained a grave stare for several seconds before flicking his spent cigarette onto the concrete floor and obliterating it into a black smudge.

"People lie for all sorts of reasons, Chief McCloud."

January 12, 1998

SECURITY LEVEL: TOP SECRET

FOR: Senior Staff, Project SATURN
FROM: Chief Neal Schaeffer, Project SATURN
SUBJECT: Resignation

It has been with a heavy heart, yet with a satisfied conscience that I have formally announced my intention to step down from my appointment as the Director of Project SATURN. DCI Tenet has accepted my resignation, effective 30 January.

To have been able to serve this fine organization for over four decades has been my highest honor. I am looking forward to a seamless transition as Mr. Leonard Mueller migrates into this role. I will be retained in a reduced capacity for the foreseeable future.

Please notify all departments and personnel regarding these upcoming changes.

END

PS

CHAPTER 30

The trails of sweat he had restrained during his short but intense encounter with the FBI began to race down his hot and flustered face. McCloud plopped down into his desk chair as he cradled his phone handset.

He leaned back after dialing and stared out the window.

A female voice answered. "Hello?"

The Chief hunkered over his desk and massaged his wet forehead. "Leah, it's me. Grab a pen and a sheet of paper. I don't have a lot of time to explain, but I need you to do 'bout a thousand things in the next few hours. It's an emergency. About as bad as it gets."

"Um…sure, Chief. I'm ready."

He checked the window again and bit his lip.

"First, go through all the timesheets at the plant. I need you to make it look like Denver quit back before Thanksgiving."

"Okay," she responded with noticeable hesitation.

McCloud yanked a drawer open and drew out a small calendar. He scanned it. "The…six…teenth," he said. "Make his last day on that Friday." He tossed the calendar back into the drawer and dug out his liquor flask.

"Friday, November the sixteenth," she echoed. "Got it. What's going on, Chief?"

"A disaster," he replied. "A disaster's what's going on. The FBI's back in town. They tried to arrest Denver down at the diner. He knocked one of 'em out and then snuck down here to the alley behind the station."

"Oh my."

McCloud studied the window for the third time. "It's okay. I sent him to hide out over at Pappy's place for the time being. I need you to talk to everyone from the plant. *Everyone*. I would do it, but from this moment on, it's gonna be too risky. They'll probably have a tail on me for the next few days. And no more phone calls to the station or my house after tonight. They'll probably tap my phones." He paused. "And don't talk to any of the Jumpers using the office phone. Talk to everyone in person. Face to face. Privately."

"Yes. Whatever you say, Chief."

"I'm sorry to dump all this on ya, darlin', but my hands are tied. Tell Ellen and Doc that they need to move into The Basement with Dr. Tesla…*tonight*. At least until the FBI leaves town. You'll need to get them fresh clothes and food'n all. They have a bathroom down there. It won't be ideal, but this's an emergency situation. We need to keep the door to The Basement shut and hidden."

"Whatever. You got it. But they've already been sleeping down there the last few nights anyway."

He arched back as his chair groaned under the strain. "Is Ellen or Doc officially on the books at the plant?"

"No. Neither of them are."

"Good. What about Grandma Martha?"

"I'll check, but I don't think so."

He forced a weak smile. "Well, that's a few less headaches to worry about."

"What about Terrance?" she asked. "We have timesheets on him up until…Nevada."

"Yeah, well…let's say that he also quit. Picked up his final check and moved somewhere. Let's say he had family out west somewhere. And Denver…tell everyone Denver moved back up to Chicago after he quit. We don't know exactly where. He didn't talk much, except about his daughter. Put up a *Now Hiring* sign on the front door and put a stack of job applications on the counter first thing in the morning. Maybe before. You might wanna drop Tori off at Martha's for the next few days."

"Out west. Chicago. Daughter. Now hiring. Applications. Tori. Got it."

The Chief sucked in a deep breath and fought to subdue any indication of his rising concern. "Anywho, send Garrett over to Denver's place. Have him clear out everything except for the furniture. Empty the fridge and cabinets and all. Take the stuff out to Doc's place."

"Got it."

He hesitated for a few moments as dozens of potential problems and contingency plans fractured his ability to focus. McCloud continued. "And if anyone needs to tell me anything, have 'em tell Billy, and then he can tell me. I'm gonna stick to a very *visible* routine at the station and around town."

"I understand," Leah responded. "Are we…going to be alright, Chief?"

He took a quick hit on his flask and kept it close for several more the instant he hung up.

"I dunno, darlin'. This time…I really do not know."

CHAPTER 31

Two unfamiliar black sedans in the driveway were an unexpected greeting as he rounded the corner at a little past 9:45 p.m.

Okay, he thought. *That's odd.*

Guess I'll be parking on the street tonight.

The man killed the motor and hopped out, continuing to study the dark cars. Only the occasional weak reflection of a distant street light created any hint of their texture or sense of their overall shape. The moonless sky offered little if any help.

Who could it be? A little too early in the month for a holiday family visit.

The pair of nondescript vehicles wasn't the only thing that stirred his concern. He fumbled through his large set of keys and frowned as he ascended onto the small front porch.

Why in the world are all the lights on downstairs? It's Sunday night…they should've been in bed an hour ago.

Something's wrong.

As he unlocked and stepped through the front door, it was probably best that he didn't see the two agents who emerged from the darkness on either side of the house.

"This is James," a woman declared as she rose from the couch. "This is our son." The obviously distraught mother strolled over to the young man as he closed the front door.

James Cannon froze.

A pungent blast of cigarette smoke assaulted him.

His mother never allowed anyone to smoke in the house.

Four men in charcoal gray suits—two seated and two standing—locked eyes with him. They were as unfamiliar and lackluster as their sedans crowding the driveway.

One of the seated strangers rose up and crushed a fresh cigarette into a makeshift ashtray. "Mr. James Cannon," he said. "My name is Special Agent Ross. This is my associate Agent Schaeffer. We're with the FBI." He gestured towards the closest chair. "Please take a seat."

James glanced at his nervous mother, then over at his father occupying a large rocker by the fireplace. His dad was stoic, apparently paralyzed by fear. The tremble in his mother's voice coupled with her fake smile were almost embarrassing.

And alarming.

Ross gestured again. "Folks, we need to speak with your son. *Alone*. I must insist."

Mrs. Cannon hurried over to her husband and helped him up. "Yes. Yes sir, Mister, or…*Agent* Ross." They migrated towards the stairs and she rubbed James' hand just prior to ascending.

Agent Schaeffer stood out of courtesy. "Good night, Mr. and Mrs. Cannon. We just need to ask your son some questions. He is not in trouble in any way, I assure you. You can relax."

They hurried upstairs.

Ross made no attempt to conceal his disdain for his associate's reassurance. He glared at Neal. "Sit down, Mr. Cannon."

"Is this about Ms. Larson's car accident?"

"Sit down, son."

James obeyed silently and the other two agents proceeded to slide in behind him.

Ross shoved a handful of magazines onto the floor and plopped down onto the coffee table. The move allowed him to be nearly eye to eye and nose to nose with his victim. "Where have you been this weekend?"

James paused.

"Uh, I've been talking with the owners. Sir. The owners of the *Journal.*"

Ross was a statue. "Anyone else?"

"No. Sir."

Ross squinted. "Now, *James*...I need to know absolutely everything you know about Mr. Denver Jackson."

Schaeffer snapped opened a briefcase and retrieved a notepad and pen.

"What about him?" James asked.

Ross enunciated each and every syllable with force. "*Everything.*" He fished out a cigarette and a lighter from his breast pocket. "As in...not-one-damn-thing left out." The flame from his Zippo cast a deep crimson hue across his serious face.

James looked away. "Uh, not much to tell. I worked with him at the *Journal*. Denver helped me print our Friday paper." He dried his sweaty palms across his thighs. "He had been in some kind of...trouble...with the law. There were some break-ins...around town."

Ross narrowed his bloodshot eyes and allowed a double serpentine of smoke to drift out of his nostrils. "What else do you know?" He tapped on the young man's chest. "And don't even think about lying to me, boy. I can say the word and have you locked up for aiding an extremely dangerous fugitive."

"I'm not lying, Mr. Ross," James protested, beginning to tremble. "We didn't talk much. I'm not much of a talker. I just do my job."

"Denver and his associates stole a safe from your boss' office. What was in the safe?" Ross paused to take a long and deliberate pull on his cigarette. "What was she hiding? What were *you* hiding?"

James struggled with a response. "I, uh, I have no earthly idea of what Ms. Larson kept in her safe. Probably money or something."

Ross shook his head *no* with subtle motions. James squirmed. "Look, sir…I didn't even know she had a safe until the…burglary and all."

Agent Schaeffer cleared his throat and displayed a compassionate smile. "Thank you for your cooperation, Mr. Cannon. We really appreciate any help you can give us. This investigation is very important."

"I'm telling you all I know."

"Do you have any idea where Mr. Jackson went after he finished his…*employment* down at the newspaper?"

James rubbed his hands together and then rested his chin on his fist. "I, uh, I think, I mean, I know that he did a lot of work with Mr. Bodenschatz."

Ross jumped on it. "Who is he?"

"Well, sir, Mr. Bodenschatz is a carpenter. Local handyman. Mr. Jackson worked with him sometimes. Odd jobs. I'm not really sure about much more than that. Mr. Bodenschatz fixed the damage down at the *Journal*."

"I need a full name. And an address," Ross barked.

"It's, uh, Hank Bodenschatz. I'm not really sure where he lives. I think down by Division Street. Not too many with his last name in the area. Should be easy to find."

Ross made eye contact with one of the other agents and gestured. The man disappeared through the front door without making a sound.

Schaeffer tapped the pen to his notebook. "Can you tell us about any other people Mr. Jackson had contact with?"

James studied the floor. "Um, not too many people. Except Ms. Larson. And the police chief. His deputy. And Hank."

"Anyone else?" Ross asked.

The front door popped open and James flinched somewhat. Another agent brushed past his chair and delivered a small note to Ross. He examined it briefly and relayed it over to Schaeffer. "Begin surveillance," Ross muttered to the new arrival. "And TDS Film down at the paper. And the jail." The man exited.

"Answer the question, Mr. Cannon. Anyone else?"

"Sorry, I was startled. Uh, there was a young lady. A black girl."

"Black girl?"

"Yes sir. She helped down at the paper while Ms. Larson was out of town awhile back. Alexus. Alexus...*something*. I can't recall her last name."

Ross seemed interested. "What was her job?"

"Just a, uh, a temporary reporter. A stringer. It was only for a week or so. I only spoke to her once or twice. Just hello and goodbye. That sort of thing."

Ross' visible interest faded. He smothered his half-spent smoke and fired up another. "Have you ever heard anyone mention the last name *Collins* lately? Especially involving Denver?"

"Collins?"

Ross nodded without blinking.

"Uh, no sir," James responded. "Not that I can recall."

"Where did Mr. Jackson live?"

"I'm not sure. An apartment...I think. Toward the school."

Ross hesitated for several seconds before standing up. He exhaled a substantial trail of smoke. "What else would you like to add, Agent Schaeffer?"

A long silence ensued. Neal finally lowered his pen. "Mr. Cannon, after Denver left the newspaper, where did he go?"

James scrunched his face. "Do you mean…where did he go after work each day?"

"No, no, no," Schaeffer clarified. "I mean, after he finished his month working at the *Journal*. Besides helping Mr. Bodenschatz…did he have any other work or employment?"

"Oh, yes, of course. Sorry," James replied. "I misunderstood. Um, yeah. I remember him talking about getting a job at a factory in town."

"A factory," Schaeffer reiterated. "Do you know *which* factory?"

James smiled for the first time since his return home.

"Yes, sir. On the north side of town. They make windows."

September 8, 2001

SECURITY LEVEL: TOP SECRET

FOR: Senior Staff, Project SATURN
FROM: Chief Leonard Mueller, Project SATURN
SUBJECT: September 11 Vigilance

We are now only three days away from an event that will doubtless consume the foreign policy direction of the United States for years to come. We need to be prepared regarding the effect of the upcoming September 11 event and its effect upon Operation Caretaker.

Our best analysts have been unable to ascertain the exact nature of this threat after 45 years of research. I doubt that it will be cracked in the remaining 72 hours. Whatever it is and however it comes, the focus of the nation will turn upon Afghanistan in the immediate future.

The likelihood is high that this September 11 event will be a motivating factor for encouraging Denver Wayne Collins to re-enlist. Be prepared to discuss all potential impacts during our September Strategic Outlook Session which will be 8:00 a.m. on September 12 in Conference Room 2A.

END

PS

CHAPTER 32

The place looked ordinary.

With the exception of a half-dozen Project SATURN agents roaming about the yard clad in dark suits, the property looked like most of the other middle-class houses along the street.

But something was wrong.

And Neal Schaeffer knew it.

He stepped out of his sedan and into the cold glare of a rising sun as a pair of agents jogged over to him. "You guys sit on the place all night?" he asked.

They nodded. He paused and surveyed the neighborhood. "Anyone come or go? Anything moving inside?"

The taller of the two shook his head. "Nothing."

"You keep a low profile?"

"Two blocks away. Most of the time. A few drive-bys. Rainey got into the backyard. Looked around."

Neal glanced at the other agent. "See anything, Rainey?"

"I'll bet my next month's salary on the fact that Hank Bodenschatz is not in that house. Or at least, he's not *alive* in that house."

"What're the neighbors saying?" Schaeffer asked.

Rainey pulled out a notepad and pointed across the street. "The Huey's over there said they haven't seen anyone from the house since a few weeks back." He gestured off to the right. "And Mr. Greable said his wife and Mrs. Bodenschatz usually play Bridge with a few other ladies a couple of times a week. But she hasn't shown up, or answered the phone or door for quite a while."

Neal squinted. "Are they on vacation? It is getting close to Christmas."

Rainey shook his head again. "I already asked the Greable family about that. They said Hank Bodenschatz always asks them to keep an eye on the place when they're gonna be gone. Pick up their mail and newspaper and such. Always. They've been neighbors for over ten years."

The accelerating roar of an engine garnered Neal's attention as another four-door sped down the narrow lane and practically skidded to a stop along the curb. An agent toting a thick envelope burst out of the passenger seat and jogged up the grass.

"My search warrant, Agent Wilson?" Neal asked as the document changed hands.

"The ink from the judge's signature is probably still wet."

The judge's signature, Neal repeated to himself. *Now there's an uncommon sight for these agents. This group would've already been inside if Ross were here.*

He was probably right.

Neal returned the packet and cradled his hands on his hips, studying the two-story home. A small assembly of agents gathered and awaited his direction. "Lots of questions. Let's find some answers. I don't anticipate resistance. Keep your weapons hidden. No need upsetting the fine folks of this sleepy little street."

"Probably a bit late for that," an agent quipped.

Neal grinned and ventured a few steps up the broken concrete path toward the porch. "You're probably right. Well, let's go take a look around, boys."

After the formality of a courtesy knock, the deadbolt on the front door proved a minor nuisance for an agent sporting a specialized set of tools. He spun the handle and opened the door wide for Neal.

"Thank you, Agent Stone," Schaeffer offered with a subtle nod. "Always the professional. I do admire your work."

"It's why they call me Pick, sir."

The ordinary exterior gave way to an even more ordinary interior. It was comfortable, well-furnished, clean, and vacated.

"Hello?" Neal hollered without expecting or receiving a reply. "Alright, boys…fan out." He worked through the living room and moved into the kitchen. "Well, well," he mumbled as another agent stepped to his side. Neal reached down into the crowded sink and retrieved an unwashed plate. He pulled it closer for inspection. "I'm not sure if this is a dinner plate or a science fair project demonstrating the life cycle of mold and fungi." Neal raised his volume. "Where's Bollinger?"

A voice rang out from another room. "On my way."

Neal opened the refrigerator. It was well-stocked. He wasn't shocked.

A dark-headed man with glasses rushed in. "Whatcha need, boss?"

Neal handed him the plate. "How long has this been sitting here?"

The agent studied it, then the sink. "A lot of variables to weigh, including temperature, humidity, and quantity of food residue—"

"Spare me the *equation*, Agent Bollinger. I just need a ballpark answer."

Bollinger nodded and set the plate down. "Minimum of ten days."

Neal thanked him and migrated back into the living room as the rest of the team rejoined him from various directions. "Let's get a representative sample of current photos. Of Mr. and Mrs. Bodenschatz, and any children.

Look for address books, diaries, anything that may lead us to them or other family members."

He motioned towards the porch. "Confiscate their mail. And check every room and every closet and every drawer for anything—*anything*—that could be related to Denver Wayne Collins." He paused, contemplating, calculating. "You know, this is very odd. Hank Bodenschatz is missing. He is a primary witness who could provide us with key evidence concerning the whereabouts of Denver Wayne Collins, and he is missing."

Agent Bollinger spoke up. "Inconvenience…or contrivance?"

Neal Schaeffer folded his arms.

"I've got a theory about that."

CHAPTER 33

Despite the golf ball-sized patch of crimson inflammation, his stubble-pocked jaw looked far worse than it felt. Everyone at the breakfast table at the hotel noticed it.

No one asked about it.

He wouldn't have cared if they did.

To Howard Ross, the unsightly bulge was tangible proof that (after months of humiliating disappointment) he had touched the prize. As the streets, homes and businesses passed the car in an early morning blur, Ross caught another glimpse of his injury in the passenger window. He shielded his face from his driver and sought to suppress a rare smile.

The future had met him face to face, and now, the likely prospect of Ross' own ascendency in the halls of intelligentsia was merely a function of time and manpower. Denver Collins may have won a fight the night before, but Howard Ross was close to winning a war nearly a decade in the making.

He leaned forward and snatched the mic on the wireless. "Team Two, this is Charlie Hotel Romeo. What's your status?"

The speaker crackled alive. "On location at the residence."

Ross took another pull on his smoke. "Is November Sierra on location yet?"

Pause. "Roger that."

Ross allowed his cigarette smoke to slip out through pursed lips as he hung up the handset. "How long to this damn factory?"

One of the two agents in the backseat hunched forward. "Should be dead ahead on the right."

Ross discarded his cigarette out the window just as the driver pointed and slowed the vehicle. "There it is, Chief."

The plain metal siding and large foyer windows along the leading edge of the business came into view. Three cars, one delivery truck and a stray mutt dotted the gravel lot. Ross was almost disappointed.

Until he saw something through the spitting snow.

"Stop the car," he mumbled.

"What?"

"I said stop the damn car!"

The driver checked his rearview mirror and obeyed, almost thrusting the two agents in the backseat down into the floorboard.

"What is it, boss?" one of them asked.

Ross pointed at the sign perched just a few feet off beyond the blacktop. Everyone craned their necks.

"Nelson Manufacturing," he said. "*Nelson*. Hot-damn."

The dull roar proceeding from the maid's vacuum cleaner out in the hallway was only a mild inconvenience to the six men gathered in Ross' spacious hotel room. Ross actually enjoyed the background noise. It served to enhance their privacy. He jerked the curtains shut to block prying eyes and the glare of the late afternoon sun.

"What do we know about the factory? Give it to me. Everything."

Agent Bollinger adjusted his glasses and perused his notes. "Nelson Manufacturing. Building permit acquired in 1949. The business opened in 1950. In February of 1950. They manufacture residential windows for wholesalers and some local contractors. The founder, one Phillip Nelson."

"Unbelievable," Neal Schaeffer mumbled. "It all makes sense."

Ross paused. "You wanna add something, Mr. Schaeffer? Now's the time."

Neal straightened up. "On the morning we lost Collins at Dreamland, I told you these time travelers might be building some new version of a temporal device. Like their attempt at Roswell in 1947. Their desperation probably led to the recent break-in back in the desert."

"Thanks for reminding me of one of the most unpleasant Thanksgiving-weeks of my whole damn life. Continue."

"So, is it any coincidence that right after their initial failure in 1947, they would begin construction on a more permanent structure? A business. A factory. It would be a perfect cover."

Ross ignited a new cigarette and made no effort to contain his own enthusiasm for this theory. "I am beginning to like it. Talk to me about Nelson. Someone. Anyone?" He released a wide ribbon of smoke through an uncharacteristic smile.

Another agent joined in. "Phillip Nelson. Purchased a home on the north side of Normal in June of 1946. Previous address, unknown. Unmarried. Date of death, July—"

"Death?" Ross interjected. *"Nelson is dead, Hargraves!?"*

The agent bit his lip. "Uh, yes, sir. Mr. Nelson died in 1953. In July."

"Cause of death?"

"Apparent suicide, sir," the sandy-headed agent replied. "At his place of business...Nelson Manufacturing."

An awkward silence followed as Ross glared down at the floor. He yanked the cigarette out of his mouth and hunted for an ashtray. Someone shoved a coffee cup into his hands. "What else do we know about his business? *Bollinger?"*

"I spoke on the phone today with the receptionist. I asked for the manager. She said their manager had recently passed away."

Ross' head snapped up. "*Another* dead guy? You're kidding me?!"

"No, sir. His name was…Sheppard…a *Robert* Sheppard. Killed last week. In a car accident."

"I'm going out on a limb here, folks," Neal offered. "Let me guess…he was in a car with newspaper editor Betty Larson?"

Bollinger nodded. "Yes, sir. Both killed. In a truck."

Schaeffer shook his head. "So, not only is the founder and owner of Nelson Manufacturing dead…but the managers at both places Denver Wayne Collins was employed in Normal are also recently deceased?"

"Yes, sir."

Neal raised a finger. "And don't forget our mystery man at the funny farm, Mr. Gordon Thompson. He died recently as well. And his doctor. And an orderly. And lots of our people back at Dreamland. Life expectancy around Denver Wayne Collins seems to be pretty short. Goes against every actuarial table I've ever seen. Looks like the order of events is: meet Denver Wayne Collins, then you die."

"I didn't," Ross countered.

"Yet," Neal teased. "That cut on your jaw might develop a fatal infection."

"Any news on Hank Bodenschatz?" Ross blurted out.

"Nothing," Neal replied. "He and his wife vanished a few weeks ago. My team hit it hard all day but turned up nothing. I've notified the state police in Illinois, Indiana, Missouri, Iowa, Michigan, Kentucky and Wisconsin to be on the lookout for his vehicle. We can distribute photographs of him and his wife if you want."

"Not yet," Ross replied between pulls on his cigarette. "Not yet."

"We've identified relatives on both sides of the family. I've sent the FBI to question them."

All eyes turned back to Ross. "What new information do we know about Collins, boys? Talk to me. Mitchell?"

The youngest agent in the room sat up. "Yes, sir. According to Katie Long, a local waitress, Mr. Collins first arrived to Normal in early August. He paid with what was thought to be a counterfeit five-dollar bill. Mr. Collins was later arrested and connected with a series of local burglaries, including the office of the *Normal Journal*. He was charged and sentenced as Denver *Jackson*." He flipped a page of notes. "Denver Jackson was sentenced by a local judge to thirty days in jail and to provide restitution through community services. He was also placed on probation. He has worked at both the *Normal Journal* and Nelson Manufacturing."

"What about a residence on Denver Jackson-Collins?" Ross probed.

"Still working on it," Mitchell replied.

Ross squinted. "Work harder." He paused and released a quick blast of smoke. "Remind me, Neal…how did the waitress know his last name was Collins?"

"She said the newspaper editor lady told her. The one who died in the car accident. Betty Larson."

"And why would a newspaper editor share that sort of sensitive information with a cute little waitress from a two-bit diner?"

"That one's been bugging me all day, too, Chief," Neal admitted. "I *don't* have a theory on that one."

"Well, find a theory."

"I'll add it to my list."

"And just how did the damn newspaper editor even know what his real name was?" Ross asked.

"That's a good question, boss," Neal replied. "Even the police chief thought that Denver's last name was Jackson."

Ross paused before switching topics. "He could've been covering. What do we know about the police chief? What's his name?"

Agent Mitchell waved his hand. "McCloud, sir. James McCloud."

"Yeah, McCloud. What's his story?"

"I placed Hampton and Barrows on his tail since last night," Neal offered. "Nothing out of the ordinary on that front. He has one deputy, a William O'Connell. Or Billy."

Mitchell jumped back in. "James McCloud was appointed chief of police around May of 1952, by then-mayor Al Vorhees. He is unmarried. Lives on Willow Street. Previous address, Atlanta…according to the newspaper. He is fairly well-liked in the community. We've researched at both the *Normal Journal* and the *Pantagraph* here in Bloomington for all mentions of Chief McCloud. Plenty of references, nothing unusual."

"The only interesting fact we could dig up," Neal added, "was that Chief McCloud acted as coroner in the case of the Phillip Nelson suicide. Robert Sheppard was also mentioned in that article, but that would probably be expected, as plant manager."

Ross agreed. "That could be interesting."

Neal started tapping his pen rapidly. "Wait a minute," he said. "Wait a minute."

"We don't have a minute, Neal. Spill it."

Schaeffer turned to his left in excitement. "Mitchell…contact the FBI in Chicago. Get a list of all police departments contacted during our dragnet for Collins back in August."

"On it."

Ross started connecting the dots as the young agent raced out of the room. "Okay…okay. I see what you're getting at. If the FBI had a little visit with Chief McCloud—"

Neal's visible excitement was ratcheting up. "Not only a little visit, but a little visit with both a photograph and an artist's composite sketch of Denver Wayne *Collins*."

Pillars of smoke billowed out of Ross' flaring nostrils. "Well, well, well. If that's true, there is no damn way the good ole Chief would not have recognized who that thief was that he had to babysit for an entire month."

Schaeffer offered a rapid round of applause. "*Bravo*. You know, if you keep that level of analysis up…you'll be qualified for my job in no time."

Ross flipped him off as he pulled the cigarette from his lips. "McCloud just moved up our list. Now, what about that little weasel we interrogated last night?"

"James Cannon?" Neal responded.

Ross nodded.

"I had Randol keep tabs on him since last night. Nothing to report. He's about as boring as I figured he was. Dead end."

"Boring or not…stay on him."

"I'll add it to the list."

"And keep someone on that waitress."

"Way ahead of you, boss," Neal said. "Patterson."

Ross was stunned and stood up. "*Patterson?* You're joking, right?" He strolled over to the window.

"No joke. I sent Patterson."

"You remember what happened last time in—"

Neal's right hand went up. "I remember. He'll be fine. I talked to him."

"That doesn't make me feel any better."

"It should. I'm a good talker. I threatened him."

Ross squinted over at Neal. "You still have some reliable inside contacts within the Treasury Department?"

"Two or three. Why?"

"We need to get our hands on a few counterfeit plates they've confiscated. And several thousand bucks of their funny money."

Everyone but Ross glanced over at Neal in confusion.

"Did, uh, Dulles cut our funding, Chief?"

Ross wasn't smiling. "I need it by tomorrow. Here."

"You're serious?"

"I usually am. Is that a problem?"

"Wait…is *what* a problem?"

"The plates," Ross scolded. "And the money."

Neal responded slowly. "I will see what I can do. But, would you mind filling the rest of us mere mortals in on the rationale behind this odd little request from Mt. Olympus?"

Ross sauntered towards his second-in-command. "You're the high-paid, expert analyst, Mr. Schaeffer." He bent forward and released an expanding cloud of smoke directly into Neal's face. "Surely you can deduce the method to my madness."

Neal rose out of the irritating haze and began pacing. "Your request is highly specific. And it involves items which are highly illegal."

Ross sat down. "My third-grade niece could've figured that much out."

"Speaking of highly illegal items, Chief, what happened to all of the heroin we had in storage down at the warehouse?" Neal asked.

"It's back with the FBI in Chicago. Along with the cash."

"So," Neal continued, "we need to frame someone or a group of people, perhaps even indicting local law enforcement, for a robust counterfeiting operation."

"You just passed the ninth grade."

"And a significant counterfeiting ring would explain the necessity of a large contingency of FBI agents milling about the area, interrogating people." Neal smiled and nodded. "Not to mention, it works perfectly with the local suspicion that Mr. Collins passed a fake five-dollar bill at the diner a few months back."

Ross grabbed a piece of paper and rolled it up. He stretched it out towards Neal. "Well done. And here is your diploma, Mr. Schaeffer. Excellent work."

Neal started to take it, when Ross snapped it back. "But, you've missed one more potential connection, Mr. Analyst. A very important connection."

Neal resumed pacing in the congested space.

"It involves a female," Ross hinted.

"I already talked about the waitress—"

"Not her."

Neal stared up at the low ceiling. He spun around. "*Larson.* Betty Larson…the newspaper editor."

"Go on."

Neal strolled back over. "Who…better…to…implicate in a counterfeiting ring…than someone who *prints* for a living? Maybe she supplied the paper…or the ink? She is connected both to Collins and Nelson Manufacturing. And who knows, maybe the mob in Chicago put a hit out on her and the factory manager for taking a bite out of their action?"

Ross slapped the mock diploma into Neal's hand.

"Everyone in town already knows Collins spent a lot of damn time at the police station," Ross observed. "And we should have evidence shortly that local law enforcement was told to be on the lookout for a wanted counterfeiter. Hide a few thousand bucks of hush money over at the police chief's house, maybe even the deputy's place as well." He took a final hit on his cigarette. "To anyone on the outside, it all fits together perfectly. And it covers our asses."

Neal sat back down. "I hate to admit it…but it's brilliant. Absolutely brilliant. I've definitely been a good influence on you, Chief."

"Oh, you've been an influence, all right," Ross commented.

Neal smiled. "It even makes the suicide of Phillip Nelson seem more…*plausible.* A mob hit disguised as a suicide. People eat that kind of stuff up in the papers. Plus, I doubt he's actually dead."

Ross also smiled. "We're about to find out, boys."

"So, what's the new plan, boss?" Neal inquired.

Ross folded his arms and concentrated on the carpet. "Time to pull the noose in tighter. Continue round-the-clock surveillance on Nelson Manufacturing. Track every single man, woman, and child who comes and goes."

"We have. And then what?"

Ross jammed his expended cigarette into the coffee cup. "And then we round up these dangerous criminals, including the cop and his deputy…and we rip the factory apart. Let's see what or *who* they're hiding in there."

Neal frowned. "Now listen, I'm just throwing this out for consideration. But, uh, what if Nelson Manufacturing and the Sandbox are connected? What if it's all the same?"

"I don't give a damn if it's the same," Ross added.

"But Dulles said—"

"And I don't give a damn about Dulles."

Neal paused. "This could…*end* your career."

"If we don't get Collins, it's over anyway, Agent Schaeffer. Either way, I'm going for it."

"Well, if you go down…all of us will be going down, too. The prospects for future employment with Uncle Sam will not be great. Actually…zero. If we're not in prison."

Ross straightened up and leaned back with arms folded. "Probably. Anybody want to jump ship? Now's the time." He scanned their shocked faces.

Nobody spoke.

"Looks like curiosity is killing a roomful of cats," Ross offered with a thin smile.

"When do we make the bust?" Hargraves asked.

"How quick can you get me those plates?" Ross asked.

Neal rushed over to the phone. "I can pull some favors. They'll be here by tomorrow afternoon."

Ross grabbed a nearly empty pack and popped out another smoke.

"There's your answer, Agent Hargraves…we bust Nelson Manufacturing tomorrow afternoon."

October 8, 2001

SECURITY LEVEL: TOP SECRET

FOR: Chief Leonard Mueller, Project SATURN
FROM: Gavin Drew, Northeast Section
SUBJECT: Operation Caretaker Phase VI

Our Armed Forces liaison confirmed that Denver Wayne Collins signed for a second commitment with the Army on 8 October.

Preparations are already in place to assign Collins to the 5th Special Forces Group under Colonel John F. Mulholland, Jr.

Per your earlier request, I have notified my staff to begin transition to Operation Caretaker Phase VI.

END

PS

CHAPTER 34

"Excuse me…Mr. Ross?"

Howard glanced over at the female desk clerk off to his left as he trudged across the hotel lobby. She was waving a small, folded piece of yellow paper.

"Someone left a message for you. They said it was extremely urgent."

He jogged over, snatched the note and flipped it open privately. Ross yanked the smoldering cigarette out of his mouth.

Damn.

Seconds later he checked his watch before resting against the counter.

"I need a road map of Chicago."

The patchy veil of snow scattered across the rough concrete shifted and rolled like smoke in the fickle night breezes. Ross flipped up the collar on his overcoat and shoved his chapped hands into his pockets. He knew that large bodies of water typically moderated winter air temperatures, but Lake Calumet seemed powerless to provide him much comfort.

The plunging thermometer wasn't the only brute fact setting Ross ill at ease. He peered into the lakeside darkness, punctuated only by sporadic pools of light for a mile in either direction. The cluttered construction site for the new Port of Chicago was immense.

And empty.

Ross hadn't laid eyes on another person since departing the highway a quarter of an hour earlier. That isolation alone gave him pause. Over the years, nearly every drop-off specified by his blackmailer had been either crowded with people or conveniently situated near a phone.

Both were conspicuously absent.

He studied the area. This felt different.

Ross slid his hand under his coat and relocated his revolver to an exterior pocket. The ice-cold steel was the only thing that made him feel the least bit comfortable. He popped out a smoke and struggled against the intermittent gusts from the lake in a vain effort to light it.

An echoing voice that seemed to emanate from every direction shattered his silence. "O how the mighty are defeated, even by a fragile little breeze."

Ross flinched. He knew that voice.

It had been years.

Her haunting words called out again. "Been a long time, Howard."

His senses peaked as his eyes caught movement off to his right, about thirty yards out. A thin form seemed to coalesce out of the darkness and just stood there.

Ross continued to fumble around with his Zippo and eventually ignited his cigarette. "Not long enough," he said.

He could hear the smile rising in her voice. "Where's the hat I bought you, Howard? Perfect night for it."

Ross exhaled a lungful of smoke. "You died. Back in August."

She paused.

"Sorry to disappoint, Howard. It's me. Did you *like* the hat?"

It was his turn to hesitate.

"I'm very connected," he declared.

"Yes, yes, you already told me you were connected and in the information business. I hope you didn't sell my hat."

Ross ventured a few careful steps closer.

"I saw the police report," he called out. "And the coroner's report. You're dead."

"Really?" she responded, rubbing her arms. "No kidding. This isn't what I expected death to feel like. Though I did hate losing that car. I loved that car. I don't like the desert, but I did love that car."

He took another hit on his cigarette. "What do you want? I doubt you need money. Or that you've *ever* needed the money."

The dark female form sauntered closer. "What do I want? Now that's a good question, Howard. Go ahead, ask me what I want for Christmas. Ask me."

He refused to humor her and blew out a trail of smoke instead.

"Fine," she said. "I will tell you what I want for Christmas, Director Ross. I want you…to leave those people alone."

"You've been busy," he offered. "Now *Roswell*…Roswell. That was pretty damn clever."

"I can neither confirm nor deny my involvement, Mr. Director, sir. But I'm glad you liked it. Got you out of town, didn't it? Couldn't have Mr. Collins and you in the same place at the same time."

He grinned and wagged his cigarette in her direction, leaving tiny accents of smoke hanging in the air. A small breeze erased them from sight moments later. "And the accident down in the Cryo-lab. Impressive."

"Why don't you come closer so I can see if your eyebrows have grown back, Howard."

"Oh…I think I'll keep my distance, thank you."

"Pity. I remember the days when you wanted to be closer," she taunted. "Much, much closer."

"I got what I wanted."

"So did I," she retorted.

A long blast of a ship's horn reverberating in the distance punctuated the tense silence.

"So, why now?" he asked as the mournful sound faded away. "After all this time?"

She advanced closer, each footfall accompanied by a hollow echo. "Before…it was business. Now it's getting personal. Leave them alone."

"I don't care about them," he snapped.

"Oh, I know, Howard. It's never been about them. It's been about you. It's always been about you."

He pulled the mostly-spent cigarette away from his lips and flicked it away. It bounced and scattered glowing embers along the dark concrete before the wind rolled it out of sight. "Intelligence isn't about knowing. It's about going," he observed.

"And just where are you going, Howard?"

He blew into his cold hands and stuffed them away into his pockets. Ross forced a smile and kicked at the ground. "Oh, don't worry your pretty little head about where I'm going," he remarked. "I doubt you'll be able to see it from hell."

She laughed out loud. "My, my…that's pretty harsh, Howard…even for— "

BAM!

She clutched her left side and crumpled to the ground as the echo of his gunshot reverberated wildly among the partially completed steel superstructures crowding the lakefront.

Ross prepared to snap off a second round, but a trio of bullets plowing into his chest and abdomen in rapid succession ended his chances for a violent encore performance. His body lurched and flung backward, while the shock of the impact ripped the gun out of his hand, sending it skidding along the pavement.

Ross gasped spastically, fighting to catch a breath as blood began to saturate his lungs. He could feel the cold, hard ground beneath his back, but had lost all sensation below the waist. There was no doubt in his mind that at least one of the rounds had passed all the way through, severing his spine. He coughed and thrashed about, staring straight up into the starless sky.

Something came into view.

Staring down at him.

It was *her*.

Darkstar studied the pitiful sight for several seconds before kneeling beside him. She grimaced and rubbed her side. "I just really don't know what to think about you, Howard Ross. First you try to pick me up at a bar, and now…now you try to knock me off at a dock." She forced an unconvincing grin. "Talk about sending a gal mixed signals."

He gurgled a few vain attempts at a nasty comeback, but she ignored it and rummaged around inside her purse. "I've heard it's frightfully hard to blackmail a dead guy." She opened her fist and released a cascade of photographs that tumbled down across his bleeding chest.

"So…I figured it wouldn't hurt to let you have these." She retrieved one that seemed to interest her and examined it, as his blood ran down and dripped off the lowest corner. "My, my…I forgot how much I liked my hair like that."

Echoing footsteps sounded out in the distance.

She rose quickly and scanned the darkness off to the west.

Three, maybe four people were approaching.

Fast.

Darkstar glanced down at him and released the last photo. It bounced off his shoulder and tumbled to the concrete just beside his unconscious head.

"You've paid enough for them over the years…you might as well enjoy them before you die."

CHAPTER 35

The lake air was cold.

Death was much colder.

He lowered to one knee beside the well-dressed but motionless corpse. The weak incandescent lights overhead transformed the massive pools of blood covering Ross' torso into sickening black blotches that drained into dark puddles under each of his arms.

Neal Schaeffer refused to suppress the flood of tears unleashed by the loss of a boss, a mentor, a friend. His rush of raw emotion was exacerbated by the burning knowledge that the murderer responsible might even be watching his grief from afar.

Perhaps even reveling in it.

Neal wasn't known for vulgarity or profanity, but uncontrolled volleys of both ran amok within his thoughts.

He studied Ross' colorless face, etched not only by recent pain, but by a lifetime of bitter experiences. In many ways, his boss didn't appear all that different from the self-assured, martini-toting hothead that lured Neal away from the Secret Service almost exactly seven years earlier. His tortured mind recalled Ross' stunning job offer on the fringes of a presidentially-sanctioned sand volleyball game in 1949.

The warm beaches of Key West, bathed in the soft glow of window lights from Truman's Little White House, though, couldn't have been more removed from the horrific scene splayed out below him along the cold, hard concrete of south Chicago.

It doesn't seem possible.

Ross had been the quintessential survivor.

Two world wars and scores of domestic and bureaucratic battles overcrowded his resume. People had gunned for his job and even for his very life on multiple occasions. It appeared that even a decade of barren research and fruitless manhunts (on the taxpayer's dime) couldn't topple Howard Ross.

But now, the man untouchable had fallen.

Neal wiped his own hot face, blinking several times. "What…uh, was the time of death?"

A nearby agent responded with reverence. "Around 8:45. Give or take a few minutes, sir." He hesitated. "When we arrived on scene…there was…nothing we could do."

Neal looked up. "The shooter or shooters?"

"Barrows and Hampton pursued a single assailant. They said she appeared to be wounded and—"

"She?"

"Yes, sir. *She*. The female assailant escaped. On a motorcycle." The agent raised up and dangled a pistol. "The Chief's firearm had discharged one round. It was over ten feet from his body. We heard a total of four shots."

Neal's eyes returned Ross' bloodied form. He donned a pair of thin gloves and carefully retrieved one of the photographs littering his chest. A long silence ensued as he studied the beautiful face caught up in Ross' passionate embrace.

The other agent ventured closer and knelt down. "What do we do now, sir? Where do we go from here?"

Schaeffer rose to his feet, dusted off his knees and scanned the area. A half-dozen agents were milling about, taking photographs and collecting evidence. "Contact Glenview," he said. "Get a plane ready…"

"…I wanna be headed to Washington before midnight."

October 11, 2001

SECURITY LEVEL: TOP SECRET

FOR: General Tommy Franks, Commander CENTCOM
FROM: George Tenet, DCI
SUBJECT: SPC Denver Wayne Collins (NSPD 7)

It is imperative that I meet with you regarding the involvement of Army Specialist Denver Wayne Collins/5th Special Forces Group at your earliest convenience.

This involves NATIONAL SECURITY PRESIDENTIAL DIRECTIVE-7.

END

DCI/WH/CC

CHAPTER 36

Over the past seven years, he had spoken by phone with CIA Director Allen Dulles on countless occasions. Their actual face-to-face meetings numbered upwards of a dozen, if not more. But this was only the second time that Neal Schaeffer had sat in the DCI's office.

And both uncomfortable encounters were because of Howard Ross. And both briefings revolved around the issue of the blackmailer.

"A female?" Dulles muttered between quick puffs on his pipe.

A bleary-eyed Neal Schaeffer straightened up in his high-backed chair. "Uh, yes, sir. It would seem that Ross was able to wound her before she fled. On motorcycle. From our examination of his gun, it looks like he was able to fire one shot."

Dulles leaned back and squinted. "A wounded female fleeing on a motorcycle. Has a familiar ring to it, Mr. Schaeffer, wouldn't you say?"

"I've been thinking the exact same thing, Director. I ran through a thousand different scenarios during the flight here." Neal arched forward, resting his elbows onto Dulles' desk. "I would say the likelihood is extremely high that Ross' blackmailer is the same woman who helped Denver Collins escape from Dreamland."

Dulles lowered his pipe into a glass ashtray. He selected a handful of photographs and studied them briefly. "And now the photographs that Howard was so intent on keeping off my desk are suddenly *on* my desk. A little late perhaps."

Neal nodded in agreement and picked up one of them. "Debbie Sullivan."

"You've already identified the woman in these photos? Well done, Neal."

Neal flipped his picture over and held it up for the Director to see. "Don't give me too much credit. It wasn't that hard. Written in red for the whole world to see. Debbie Sullivan."

Dulles frowned and rubbed his forehead. "But Mr. Schaeffer, you and I both know Howard's…*romantic* exploits were anything but secret. Ross with a young, pretty blonde in his arms is hardly scandalous. Some in this town might even consider it commendable at his age."

"I've got a theory about that."

"Well, until my breakfast briefing with Eisenhower, I'm all ears," Dulles quipped. "So you've got at least three hours. Wait…make that *two*. I need a shower."

Neal pushed up out of his seat and sauntered over to the window. There wasn't anything to see in the pre-dawn darkness, but he preferred to move around during analysis. "In my estimation, all three women are one and the same woman."

"All *three* women?"

"Yes, sir. All three. The wounded blackmailer, the girl in those photographs, and the mystery woman who helped Mr. Collins break out of Dreamland."

Dulles retrieved his pipe again and sat back. "And let me guess, her name isn't *Debbie*?"

Neal spun his head around. "I would say that Tatiana…or Natalia is far more likely. Statistically speaking."

The Director exhaled more than spoke. "KGB."

"By the looks of Ross in those photos…his hair, his clothes, I would say most of those were taken in the late 1940s. Maybe '48 or '49. See any connection?"

"Not yet."

"That's right about the same time when the boys over at Arlington Hall first caught a mention of Project SATURN in Soviet communiques."

Dulles slid his pipe out and wagged it towards Neal. "Ah, yes. The famous *purge*. That was during...*Hillenkoetter's* watch, I believe. A mole is bad enough, but mole hunts are a nasty business. Nearly all the senior and midlevel staff got the axe. I've seen the reports."

Neal shrugged. "Axes may be nasty, but they are very efficient at creating openings. No pun intended."

Dulles almost laughed. "Well, I suppose you would be the resident expert on that subject, Mr. Schaeffer. Didn't you come on board in '49?"

"Officially? 1950. January."

Dulles grabbed his steaming coffee cup and cradled it in his lap. "So, in order to save the game, Howard Ross clears the bench, leaving perhaps the only player responsible for his losing predicament. *Himself*."

Neal strolled back over to the desk. "That is one possible scenario, sir. She could've gained actionable intelligence from him in any number of ways. Access to his house in Vegas, his car, his house phone. Everything could be bugged. Locating and infiltrating Dreamland would've been the next logical step."

Dulles took a slow sip of coffee. "That would explain quite a bit. Including the recent explosion on the Cryogenics. She almost killed him then and there."

"With all due respect, I don't believe killing Ross was her goal."

"Oh?"

Neal chose his words carefully. "As a compromised point of access, Ross was far more valuable to her *alive* than dead. Far more."

"But he's dead *now*," Dulles replied. "So why now? After all these years?"

"I…don't…know." Neal slumped down into his chair and stared into his lap. "And the guilt from that is going to haunt me forever."

The Director rose up with some urgency and set his coffee down. "Hey, listen, Neal...hell, that wasn't your fault. You did all you could."

Schaeffer was lost in introspection. "I thought I had him. Or her. In Chicago. *Twice*. And in Vegas a few weeks ago with that prostitute. I was so close. We were so close. I had people tailing Ross, day and night."

Dulles circled around. "And now the evidence is piling up that we are probably dealing with a highly trained Soviet agent. Maybe more than one. You can't beat yourself up over that. In this game, the offense always has the advantage."

He took a few hits on his pipe before sitting on the front edge of his desk. "I put you on this mission, and as the Director of Central Intelligence, it is my professional opinion that you did absolutely everything within your power to fulfill that mission."

Schaeffer glanced up. "No offense, Director, but words like that may sound wonderfully satisfying at the end of a report. But they really don't do anything to satisfy the conscience."

The Director paused. "Well, you're just going to have to come to terms with that in your own time, and in your own way. But I'm telling you that Chief Ross could not've had a better man at his right hand."

Neal managed to mumble his reply just above a whisper. "Thank you, sir,"

It was Dulles' turn to take a short trip over to the window. "Merciful heavens…if I were a betting man, I would predict that Howard's murder will push Eisenhower over the edge."

Neal cleared his throat. "Sir?"

"Oh, it all started with this whole Suez Canal nonsense. Then Eisenhower's stress level shot through the roof when you discovered the *Sandbox*. Your little rural adventure has sent a bitter shockwave from the Defense Department to the White House, and at a very volatile time. I don't know why they've kept the DCI in the dark about it over the years, but whatever they're doing on, or below, that farm…it's big."

He tapped his smoldering pipe against the glass. "When I tell the President that the head of the most secret division with the CIA has been murdered by a Commie assassin while investigating the most secret project in the Pentagon, there'll be hell to pay. And maybe an opening for the position of DCI. You might want to drop off a resume at the White House."

"But we weren't investigating the Sandbox," Neal protested. "We were close to getting Collins."

"That's the whole point, Neal," Dulles fairly shouted. He marched back over to his desk. "The Sandbox. Collins. It just might all be the same damn thing! Who knows? We don't know. I don't know." He hesitated. "Do you think it's just some fantastic coincidence that Collins shows up in the backyard of a beyond-top-secret, experimental, underground research lab?"

"That's it," Neal muttered. "Maybe that's it."

"What's it?"

"The Sandbox. And Collins. And Dreamland. All of it."

Dulles frowned. "Pretend I don't understand."

"Maybe…and just *maybe* Collins is working for the Sandbox...or for the Pentagon. Whatever. Maybe Collins was sent on a mission to Dreamland to get the one material that they still needed for their research. Several pounds of a high-temperature superconductor. Then we showed up and started getting too close to them and they cried foul. Maybe what's good for the Pentagon's gander, doesn't seem to be appropriate for the CIA's goose."

Dulles opened a pouch to restock his pipe. "Regardless of cute analogies, getting too close was the problem, or *is* the problem. I thought I made it clear to Ross when he was sitting right there, in that same chair, to back off. I guess I should've told him to go home."

"He felt it was best to stay in—"

"He felt *wrong*." Dulles reignited his tobacco. "And now it has cost him his life, and maybe my job. Maybe yours, too. Who knows? We all may end up casualties of the Second Great Purge."

Neal sensed it was time to slow down. He allowed several tense seconds to pass by in silence.

Dulles changed the subject.

In the worst way possible.

"Tell me, Neal…how did you find the Sandbox?"

The ramifications of that simple question petrified Neal.

"Spit it out, Schaeffer," Dulles demanded as he sat back down.

"Um, can I plead the Fifth?"

"You may not."

"You want the truth?"

"I'd be surprised with anything else, especially coming from you."

Neal spent a moment enjoying the sweet aroma of Dulles' pipe smoke before selecting a precisely vague response. He found it. "Imaging," he said.

"Imaging?"

"Imaging."

"Care to elaborate?"

"No, sir."

"Do it anyway."

Neal took too long. Dulles squinted. "*Aerial* imaging, Mr. Schaeffer? Aerial imaging involving a certain fleet of U-2 aircraft? Did SATURN utilize a high-altitude reconnaissance spy plane that has been specifically prohibited by presidential fiat from engaging in any type of domestic surveillance?"

A shy grin spread across Neal's embarrassed face. "That was a big string of long words, Mr. Director."

"And I just need a few short ones, Mr. Schaeffer. Either a *yes* or a *no* will do."

Neal's political response was both brilliant and damning. "No *and* yes," he offered.

"You're not running for office, Mr. Schaeffer. And if you are, this voter's not impressed."

"Well, *no*…I didn't know about it until after the fact. And *yes*. Yes, it was aerial imaging."

"*Dammit*." Dulles slapped the top of his desk. "Dammit. This makes…*complicated* things even worse." He locked eyes with him. "How many people know about this?"

"Well," Neal began, "about five seconds ago that number pretty much doubled."

Dulles almost smiled. "So…me, you, the pilot, and an analyst?"

Neal felt it best to just nod.

"Four. I can live with four," Dulles said. "In the intelligence business with a chain of command, that's about as close as you can get to zero, anyway."

Neal took his first real breath in over two minutes. "If you're happy…I'm happy."

"I'm *not* happy," Dulles clarified. "But I am less unhappy."

More tense silence.

"Where do we go from here?" Neal inquired.

"*We?* I don't know about *we*, Mr. Schaeffer. But *me*...*I* am going to a briefing with the President. And *you*...I want you to return to Dreamland. And take everyone else with you. Suspend all Project SATURN activities related to your current investigation...effective immediately. Get out of Illinois. For *now*."

"But we have developed some incredible leads. Leads involving Phillip Nelson...sort of."

Dulles remained firm. "And I have developed some incredible headaches. And the wrath of a President. And the Pentagon. You need to pack up."

"But...what of Denver Wayne Collins?"

"Is there a question in there that would supersede my last order?"

Neal hesitated. "I...suppose...not."

Dulles folded his arms. "Don't worry, Neal. From what Howard chose to share with me, I don't think this is the last time you will cross paths with Mr. Collins."

"Sir?"

The Director leaned forward. "I will be awaiting your plans for *Operation Caretaker* with great interest. The possibilities are staggering. And regardless of the present...difficulties, we still need to keep eyes and ears on the Soviet temporal research program."

Neal brightened up. "Oh, yes, sir. I understand. Uh...thank you...sir." His voice trailed off.

"Besides the obvious, what else is bothering you, Mr. Schaeffer?"

"Oh. Well, uh, what...about the Chief's remains?"

Dulles grew solemn. "Oh...yes. Thank you for reminding me. Yes, have Howard's body transported here to DC. I will make all the proper funeral arrangements." He opened a drawer and fished out some stationery and a pen. "I will leave it at your discretion for any type of memorial service that you would like to host back at Dreamland with your staff."

Dulles drafted a quick letter and planted a large and hasty signature along the bottom.

Neal was taken aback. "*My* staff, sir?"

The Director spun the document around for his surprised guest to read.

"Yes. *Your* staff…*Chief* Schaeffer. Promotion effective immediately."

CHAPTER 37

What is that sound?

Denver tilted his groggy head back and cracked an eye open. His level of debilitating darkness did not change.

There it is again.

The unfamiliar jingle of Pappy's phone, muffled by the acoustics of the narrow hall, filtered through a partially-opened bedroom door. Denver struggled to peel the covers back and groped his way into the living room. He snatched the handset in mid-ring.

"Hello?"

"Is that all I get? A *'hello'*? The last time we spoke you called me a hero."

Denver pinched the bridge of his nose. "Uh, what? Who is this? Ellen?"

"*Ellen?* Have you been cheating on me with that ginger-haired hussy, Mr. Denver Wayne Collins? I really thought we had something going on. Being trapped together in an elevator was quite…sensuous."

That voice.

It continued. "Anyway, my unfaithful friend…go back to sleep and rest easy. The immediate threat in Normal is temporarily past. You have a window of opportunity to move about freely. Use it. I cannot guarantee it for very long."

CLICK.

Denver gazed into the darkness, imagining he could make out the phone handset in his palm. His wandering mind then visualized something else that he couldn't see.

Oksana.

October 14, 2001

SECURITY LEVEL: TOP SECRET

FOR: Chief Leonard Mueller, Project SATURN
FROM: George Tenet, DCI
SUBJECT: SPC Denver Wayne Collins (NSPD 7)

I met with General Franks on 13 October at the Pentagon concerning NSPD 7. We outlined and signed off on a comprehensive set of protocols to safeguard SPC Collins during combat operations within Task Force Dagger in Afghanistan.

We spoke with Colonel Mulholland by video conference and received explicit assurances that SPC Collins would be appointed to a highly decorated and experienced unit. Colonel Mulholland has been ordered to prevent this unit from exposure to high-risk combat operations.

You may initiate the transfer of all necessary Operation Caretaker Phase VI personnel and equipment to the Middle East at your discretion.

END

DCI/PS

CHAPTER 38

Everyone was quiet.

And everyone in The Basement appeared to be fascinated with their own watches.

Garrett halted in the threshold of the portal chamber and shot a curious glance as Denver stepped alongside. Frazier's unspoken question was perfectly understood. The answer materialized as a simple shrug and the quiet shaking of Denver's head.

Doc noticed their entry and peered over his rims. "Good early morning, gentlemen. It may be that your timely arrival coincides with the advent of yet another. And it is so good to see you again, Mr. Collins."

"It's only been four days, Doc. But thanks for—"

"Thirty seconds!" Ellen called out with a polite wave.

Denver eased forward along the mesh ramp. "Is this a portal experiment?"

Tesla nodded.

"But, the portal isn't even…on," Denver protested, loosely gesturing across the room.

"Precisely," Doc agreed with an abundance of enthusiasm.

Denver came to a stop near the end of the empty rail system. "But, it's usually glowing all blue and everything when you're experimenting with—"

"Twenty seconds!"

"When…you're experimenting with time travel and things like that."

"We have been anticipating this paramount event for…fifty-nine minutes, and…forty-*six* seconds, Mr. Collins," Doc said.

"Because—?"

"Ten seconds!"

The three researchers rotated towards the inactive portal in unison.

Doc smiled while maintaining constant concentration on his watch. "Because, Mr. Collins, we eagerly await a temporally displaced individual."

"Who?"

"Shhh!" Ellen scolded playfully. *"Five seconds!"*

"Four."

"Three."

"Two."

"One."

Denver couldn't help but squint as he pivoted away from the predictable explosion of light and sound that he knew would erupt from the portal.

He got neither.

Ellen squealed.

He opened his eyes. The lab-coated researchers were huddled near the opposite end of the rails like a shifting, solid white mass with three heads. Doc was bobbing up and down with delight. "Magnificent!" he cried out. "Magnificent!"

Garrett and Denver jockeyed for positions on the narrow walkway to land a better view. "Care to share the magnificence, folks?" Denver inquired.

"Hello there, girl," Ellen offered in a sweet, soothing whisper.

Denver finally gained a functional vantage point and gawked. Doc was cradling the two halves of an empty ball as

Ellen massaged a jittery white mouse back and forth against her right cheek.

"Welcome to the future, Sadie," she mumbled.

"What's the fuss?" Garrett asked.

Tesla began clapping. Doc seemed hardly able to contain himself. "The fuss, Mr. Frazier? *The fuss?!*" He lowered the parts of the ball onto the rails and clutched Garrett's shoulders.

"The fuss, my dear Mr. Frazier, is that we are moving from mice to men!"

Research Log: Dr. Glen D. Stonecroft

DATE: December 18, 1956

After prolonged years of prayerful and careful research, on Tuesday, December 18, 1956, we transported a living organism one hour into the future!

The mouse (christened Sadie by Miss Ellen Finegan) entered the temporal rift at 6:26 am and resurfaced at the same location exactly one hour later at 7:26 am. Present for this auspicious event: Dr. Nikola Tesla, Miss Ellen Finegan, Denver Collins, Garrett Frazier, and Dr. Glen D. Stonecroft.

G.D.S.

****

UPDATE:

A second and third mouse have now both completed their temporal journeys. The former jumped one hour with no ill effects, the latter double that interval. We convened a small conference and shared our findings with the group at 11:30 am. Most were present.

We expressed the urgent need for our first human trial. Mr. Denver Wayne Collins volunteered for a one hour temporal displacement experiment.

G.D.S.

****

UPDATE:

Success! Our first human time traveler!

Mr. Denver Collins stepped into the portal at 12:21 pm on Tuesday, December 18, 1956, and precisely one hour later reappeared in the chamber at 1:21 pm the same day! Miss Finegan performed a thorough medical evaluation with satisfactory findings. To all present, the space of one hour elapsed. According to Mr. Collins, the ordeal was instantaneous. A watch that he carried objectively confirmed his subjective experience.

He has now volunteered to undergo our second human trial. A 24-hour trial. Our current plans are for Mr. Collins to step into the temporal rift at 3:30 pm this afternoon. If the trial is successful, he should return at 3:30 pm tomorrow (Wednesday, December 19, 1956).

We continue to investigate methods of selecting proper geographical locations for our non-TRS sample Jumpers. At present, if our on-going experiment with Mr. Collins is a success, then we should gain the ability to transport a Jumper to any point in time, but, unfortunately, not any point in space. A worst-case scenario would only allow us to transport Jumpers to this exact underground location. Those Jumpers would then have to navigate back to their home from Normal.

This would necessitate that this subterranean laboratory would have to remain, intact, until our final non-TRS sample Jumper. This model, while not ideal on many fronts, is tenable.

G.D.S.

CHAPTER 39

The best thing about a business foyer lined with massive windows was the sheer amount of light.

It also tended to be the worst thing.

At times.

And to an exhausted Leah Swan, it was one of those times. The golden glare, which cut a distracting swath across her receptionist's desk at 10:25 on a Wednesday morning, was an on-going nuisance.

Historically, her solution had been the careful and continual manipulation of product posters taped to any one of three windows clustered near the center of the long row of glass. The temporary blockage typically provided relief for a few weeks, and then the seasonal game required her to shift the pieces once again.

But the rays of the late-morning sun were merely an excuse to get up and moving. Even though she was wrung out from a sleepless night, Leah needed to stay occupied. She glanced at the clock for the sixth time in the last ten minutes.

Five more hours.

Five more hours until he gets back.

But…what if Denver doesn't come back?

Whoa. Stop thinking like that, Swan.

Do something.

Anything.

Leah jumped out of her seat and circled around her desk. She pivoted about. "Did you enjoy spending the last few days with Martha?"

Tori nodded.

"Well, I'm glad to have you back." Leah studied the brilliant gleam peaking around the worn edge of the poster along the window. "Tori, dear?"

The focused teen looked up from her writing assignment. "Yes? Ma'am."

"Open the top, left drawer and find me the clear tape holder. It's black."

"Okay." Tori lowered her pencil and slid a drawer out. She stared for a few seconds.

Leah gestured to the other side. "The *left* drawer."

"Okay." Tori eventually located the tape dispenser and held it aloft.

"Thank you, Tori," Leah offered as she retrieved it.

The young girl returned to her studies.

"Tori? I said *thank you*."

No response.

"What do we say, Tori, when someone tells us *thank you*?"

"You are welcome. Ma'am."

Leah peeled away and moseyed towards the offending window. "That's better, Tori. Much, much better. Always remember, thank you and you're welcome. Thank you and you are welcome."

She reached the dusty glass and examined the situation. "Well, *no thank you*, Mr. Sun," she mumbled while peeling the poster back. "You are *not welcome* here. Not welcome…at…all." Leah relocated the promo piece about five inches to the left and added a couple fresh strips of tape. She started to admire her simple success when a new annoying glare ruined the moment.

And this annoying glare was moving.

She slid over to the next window.

Oh, a car windshield. That makes sense.

The vehicle crunched to a stop about fifteen feet away, roughly parallel with the foyer. A door opened. A man of medium build, wrapped in a dark, full-length coat with matching hat stepped out on the passenger side and made for the entrance. The gray sedan left, in more than an obvious hurry.

"Keep working on your studies, Tori," she called out while the door flung open. "We've got a customer I need to talk to."

The visitor raised his head and tossed his hat onto the rack. "Not just a customer, Mrs. Leah Swan," he said, unbuttoning his overcoat. "But a *friend*. I need a job. I saw your sign on the door. *Now Hiring*. Sounded promising."

Leah grew unstable on her feet. "It…it…can't be," she whispered before dropping the tape dispenser.

The man cupped his hand to his mouth. "Hello over there, Tori! You are looking beautiful as ever. I believe *I* still owe *you* a trip to the zoo."

The studious girl rose out of her seat and smiled.

"Hello. Mr. Nelson."

CHAPTER 40

The trickle began around three o'clock.

Billy slipped in and shuffled below ground without much fanfare. Alexus trailed not quite five minutes later, followed by a bored yet curious Garrett Frazier. Then the Chief. By 3:20, Leah had secured the front door and abandoned the front office.

Her trek across the deserted production floor was slowed by an understandable merger of both physical and emotional exhaustion. Denver's uncertain departure and Phil's sudden arrival had exacted a heavy toll on her conflicted system. Intermittent fear tormented her joy in a rollercoaster fashion.

Leah was both thrilled and flattered that Phil had dedicated his first three hours back in Normal making up for lost time with her and Tori. The Chief and Doc finally tore him away for a ninety-minute private debriefing in the upstairs conference room before escorting him down below just before two o'clock. In his characteristic kindness, Phil insisted that Tori accompany him, arm in arm. Leah was relieved that though his body may have shown signs of neglect, his compassionate heart was demonstrably intact.

Leah locked the upper door behind her and navigated along the stairs.

I have so many questions.

Her mixed thoughts tended to return to the same subject.

Chief James McCloud.

He owes us a lot of answers.

He owes me a lot of answers.

She reached the last step.

And you better make it back, Denver Wayne Collins.

I owe you something.

A lot of apologies.

"You doing okay, Tori?"

The teen glanced up from her tabletop art project. "Yes. Ma'am."

Leah circled around and patted her shoulders. "It's nice to have Mr. Nelson back, isn't it?"

Tori nodded.

"It's almost time, Ms. Swan," an excited Officer O'Connell announced while jogging across the room. "Come on. Everyone's heading into the portal chamber."

Leah smiled and fought back a nervous yawn. "Oh, sure. Thanks Billy."

He guided her past the table and they slipped up behind the cluster of spectators clogging the doorway. Phil pivoted to his left and wrapped his arm around her.

"You know, Mrs. Swan, for ten extra bucks I can get you a front row seat for the big show." He winked.

"I would pay a thousand just to know that he's gonna be alright." Her voice trailed off.

Phil faced her. "This Collins must be a pretty good guy. I've heard quite a bit about him already. Especially from Doc."

Ellen raised up on her tippy-toes and shot Phil a hard stare over the top of the Chief's thinning hair. "And from me, too," she interjected.

"Yes, Miss Finegan," Phil laughed. "And from you. In fact, from all the adult females. Except for Martha that is." He scanned in all directions. "Speaking of Mrs. Tomlin…where is our beloved grandmother?"

Leah found her voice again. "She, uh, she's at home working on your *welcome home* dinner party for tonight. I've got to go help her after work."

The Chief whirled about. "Oh, yeah…thanks for reminding me, Mrs. Swan. I promised to pick her up some veggies and drop 'em off in a bit. I can taste it all right now."

Billy reached over and patted him on the belly. "Looks like you've tasted enough already, Chief."

McCloud frowned and cradled his own protruding gut. "Ah…the pitfalls of a cop with an easy-goin' desk job."

"No, don't blame your job, Chief," Phil countered. "You've got the same problem my father had. You're too friendly," He paused for effect as several heads turned. "You and my dad just never met a food that you didn't like."

"That ain't true, Phil. Cooked cabbage. I hate it with a passion. Can't even stand the smell."

"That makes two of us," Garrett echoed.

Ellen ventured out onto the walkway and faced the group. *"One minute!"*

Leah tensed up, so much so that she almost scared herself.

What if he doesn't return? she mused.

Then I'll never be able to make things right.

"Are you feeling well, Miss Daniels?" Billy asked, snapping Leah's attention over to the table. Alexus settled into a chair and covered her mouth with her right hand. She thrust the other one out in protest.

"I'm okay," she said as Leah drew alongside. "Just a little nauseous all of a sudden."

"See?" the Chief called out, pointing. "I just mention cooked cabbage and *wham!*"

"Or it could just be the excitement," Leah added.

Ellen studied her watch. *"Thirty seconds!"*

Alexus sank back and took a deep breath. "I'll be fine, Mrs. Swan. Really. Thank you." She gestured. "Don't…uh, don't miss the big moment because of my upset stomach."

"You sure?" Leah asked.

"Yes, ma'am. It'll pass. Always does."

Leah patted her arm. "I'll be back to check on you."

"Thanks."

"Tori, dear? Keep an eye on Lexi for me, okay?"

The young lady kept drawing. "Okay."

"Ten seconds!"

Leah found a slim opening between Garrett and Billy and wedged herself within. Her limited view of the portal was partially obstructed by Dr. Tesla's lanky left side.

Ellen nodded with a growing grin.
"Five…four…three…two…and *one*."

Leah held her breath as Denver Wayne Collins seemed to materialize in the center of an empty portal.

Right on schedule.

Applause and grins broke out.

Doc ripped his glasses off as tears welled up.

Tesla tapped his cane in satisfaction.

But despite the celebration, something was wrong.

Denver suddenly froze and his eyes darted around in panic. He opened his mouth, as if struggling to speak, but total silence was the eerie result.

"Denver!" Ellen screamed out, rushing towards him. "What's wrong?"

His right arm shot up as if cautioning her to stay back. He rocked and wobbled in place, before completely collapsing face down onto the metal mesh a few seconds later. Ellen lunged forward and dropped beside his motionless form. Denver appeared to be convulsing as she grabbed his arm and rolled him over.

"Is our dear friend in a state of traumatic shock?" Doc called out.

The crowd inched closer.

"Wait a minute," Ellen declared, leaning in and hovering just above his chest. "These aren't convulsions."

Denver opened one eye and smiled.

"You're *laughing!*" she said.

"Laughing?" Doc asked.

"I—I—am...so, so sorry," Denver managed to eke out. "But...but I couldn't resist...a little fun."

Ellen punched his shoulder. "That wasn't funny."

Leah shook her head. "Inappropriate, Denver."

Phil Nelson rubbed his chin and squinted.

"I like this guy already."

March 15, 2002

SECURITY LEVEL: TOP SECRET

FOR: Chief Leonard Mueller, Project SATURN
FROM: George Tenet, DCI
SUBJECT: SPC Collins Injury

I have received notification through CENTCOM that SPC Collins was injured on 27 January in a massive offensive in the Shahi-Kot Valley, located within the Paktia Province, Afghanistan. Collins' injuries were non-life-threatening and he was airlifted to Bagram Air Base for treatment and recovery.

Current information suggests that his wounds were sustained from shrapnel associated with an IED blast. He is expected to make a full recovery and return to active combat.

END

DCI/PS

CHAPTER 41

The festive, holiday atmosphere throughout Mrs. Tomlin's place bordered on euphoric. Clusters of people were scattered throughout her living room and well-stocked dining area as Martha floated seamlessly between and among them all. Her penchant for reading was perhaps only superseded by her passion for highly-cultured entertaining.

No one remained a stranger once they crossed her hospitable threshold.

Especially when that stranger was an old friend.

The man finished an intense and heartfelt visit with Doc Stonecroft, and capped it with a lengthy hug. He leaned back, wiped away a series of tears, and started to pass by Denver.

"Besides your little joke…that was quite a brave thing you did today, Mr. Collins. Or yesterday," the man said, reaching out. "And I want to thank you."

Denver blushed and shook his hand. "Funny how that works. If a crazy stunt ends well, they call you brave. If things go south…well, then you're a fool. But I appreciate the thought, Mr. Nelson. I'm curious, do you remember meeting me before today?"

Phil retained a firm grip and drew him closer. "First off, like I said earlier today…it's *Phil*. And second, you'll have to forgive me, Mr. Collins, but the last few years are pretty hazy."

"I completely understand. We, uh—*you and I*—we met at the hospital several weeks ago. In Chicago. Before they ran me out. And when we came back to get you, someone had moved you."

Phil released his hand and raised his eyebrows as they both sat down in a pair of living room recliners. "I will have to take your word for it. I wish I could fill in the blanks…but for the most part, they're still…*blanks*."

McCloud meandered up behind them toting a chair from the dining room and straddled it. "What do ya think about our newest Trailer here, Phil? Hell…Collins may not look like much on the outside, but he ain't too bad in a pinch. He's a pretty good thief. And he's pretty good at gettin' into trouble. With the FBI no less."

Phil frowned. "Not the typical compliments one would expect, especially coming from a cop."

"It's complicated," Denver explained as Ellen strolled over and occupied the closest end of the blue sectional sofa.

"I know all about complicated," Phil remarked, his eyes glazing over. "Especially the last month or so."

"If you don't mind a total stranger asking, what happened after you left the hospital?" Denver pressed. "You did leave the hospital, didn't you?"

"I don't know *how*, and I don't really know *when*, but yes, I did leave that state-sponsored nightmare. Things don't start clearing up for me until about the second week of November. That's when the blanks stop being just blanks."

"Where did you go, Phil?" Ellen asked.

"I was in a small house. Out in the middle of nowhere. Farmland as far as the eye could see. I couldn't even tell you what state. And there were two women. But one of them didn't start showing up until the last ten days or so, so mainly just one woman. The other was hit and miss."

An enthralled Denver rested his elbows on his knees and bent closer. "What did they want from you? What did they do to you?"

"Do? They…*fixed* me, Mr. Collins. Helped me recuperate. I remember getting quite a few shots. And exercise. And food. Lots of food. I should be as big as a house. But, I was pretty sick the first week or so. I threw up a lot. And I do mean a lot."

Ellen lifted and assessed each of his arms. "And you still have a long way to go." She spun her head to the left and craned her neck to see into the dining area. "Mr. O'Connell? *Billy!* Could you bring another plate of snacks for Mr. Nelson? Lots of meat. Thank you, sweetie." She looked Phil up and down. "You're at least twenty pounds under ideal body weight, young man. So eat."

He gestured towards her on the sofa. "When I left, Ellen there was like a daughter to me. Now, it looks like she's gonna be more like my mother."

"How about weight coach?" she offered playfully.

Phil donned a guilty grin. "Our retired hostess has already informed me that she will be handling my rapid caloric intake. At least, that's what Doc called it."

"Sounds like you've got a great problem, Mr. Nelson. Mrs. Tomlin is an amazing cook," Denver offered.

"Now, I do remember that," Phil asserted. "In my opinion, her skills with food are legendary. But then again, I am about three years behind the data."

"There ain't nothin' wrong with your data," McCloud chuckled.

"The Finegan women are also legendary," Ellen added, feigning insult. "But we know when we're beat. Martha's the champ in these parts."

"I have missed two culinary delights," Phil announced. "*Anything* by Mrs. Tomlin, and believe it or not…movie theater popcorn."

Ellen brightened up. "Me too! Hey! *Around the World in 80 Days* is showing down at the Normal Theater."

"One of my favorites, but I doubt that many of us will have the luxury of very much free time," Phil lamented.

"Plus, I don't think I should suddenly reappear in downtown Normal."

"Did you know Frank Sinatra has a quick cameo in the film?" Ellen asked.

"Uh-huh. He's the...*piano player* in the saloon on the Barbary Coast," Phil answered.

"I forgot that you were Mr. Movie Trivia," Ellen teased and they all chuckled.

Denver capitalized on the levity in the conversation to study his newest acquaintance.

That skin...Phil could use a few days out in the sun.

Make that a week.

At the beach.

His eyes...so tired...yet so kind.

He looks older than he probably is.

Denver's mind flashed uncontrollably to their first encounter within an isolated cell at Dunning. The bleak recollection of the haggard shell of a forgotten man threw him off-balance. He blinked hard and tried to rush back to the present festivities. The obvious contrasts challenged credulity.

Phil's rusty wheelchair had been exchanged for a cushioned recliner.

A barren chamber in a distant mental ward yielded to a living room occupied by close friends with an enviable buffet only a few steps away.

A frazzled and broken stranger was supplanted by a vibrant, affable and commanding presence.

"What'd you and the two ladies talk about?" McCloud asked.

Phil swallowed and wiped his mouth. "Just small talk. Current events. Chit chat. The first one identified herself as Barbara, the other was Debbie. Just Barbara and Debbie." He grabbed a quick bite from a chicken drumstick. "Good old Barb and Deb."

Ellen set her glass on the coffee table. "Did they ask you any questions?"

"Nothing more than '*How are you feeling?*' Or, '*What sounds good for supper?*'"

The Chief couldn't repress his approval. "Sounds like a pair o' perfect dames, if you ask me. I mean, as long as they were lookers, too."

Ellen almost lifted off the sofa to smack his shoulder. "I see that chauvinism is alive and kicking by the end of the 20th Century, Chief. When I jump back, I just can't wait to see what other cultural revolutions await the modern woman in the 1990s."

"For Pete's sake! I'm no chauvinist, Miss Finegan," McCloud protested. He tapped Phil's arm and restricted his volume to a breathy whisper. "Did they have nice figures?"

Ellen pushed off the sectional. "Oh yeah…did Phil also tell you that one of them didn't own a pair of shoes and the other was pregnant?" She snagged her drink and waltzed off, pointing at Doc over by the window. "Oh look! A *rich* senior citizen. My, my…he looks so lonely." She paused and glanced back over her shoulder. "Finish that plate, Phil. I'll have Billy bring you another one. And drink plenty of water. Eight full glasses a day."

"Redheads are so dang cute when they pretend to be offended," McCloud noted.

"She's definitely a handful," Denver said.

"I had forgotten how entertaining Ellen can be," Phil quipped. "I may be out of the hospital, but it looks like I'm right back in the care of an overbearing nurse. Albeit an adorable one."

"Speaking of being back," Denver said. "How did you get here? To Normal?"

"Well…Barb woke me this morning. Early. About sunrise. They fed me breakfast and gave me these fancy new threads. And a new coat and hat." He tossed a pair of grapes into his mouth. "Next thing I know, I'm in the backseat of a car, blindfolded for the first thirty minutes or so. And three hours later, Debbie drops me off in my old stomping grounds in Normal. Right out front at the factory. She never said a word the whole trip. Just music."

Denver was intrigued but reserved. "An incredible story. But that's…that's not the incredible story that I am actually interested in."

Phil brought a glass of water to his lips. "Oh?"

Denver lowered his voice and scooted closer. McCloud followed suit. "What happened in July of 1953, Mr. Nelson? How did you end up in that mental hospital?"

The Chief laid an uncomfortably firm hand on Denver's forearm and squeezed.

"You know what, Phil? Denver and I need to take you on a tour o' the police station…we've made a lot of improvements."

CHAPTER 42

"You're right," Phil agreed, "I absolutely love what you've done with the place, Chief. At least the parts I can see in this darkness." He glanced towards the desk, followed by a quick perusal of the jail cell. "The police station looks *exactly* like it did the day I left."

McCloud snickered as he circled around and secured the rear entrance behind Denver. "And that's where you're wrong, my friend." He hustled over to his desk and gestured. "I can't believe you didn't notice. I have a new chair. The other one was black. And it didn't rock as well as this one."

"You got me there. I must be totally blind."

"Speakin' of blinds," McCloud said. "I probably need to shut those over there. Can't have anyone see Phil Nelson livin' and breathin' in Normal."

Denver took the initiative. "Without the lights on, I doubt anyone could even see Phil in here. But I'll take care of the windows anyway."

"Mr. Collins is pretty handy to have around, Phil. He's pretty familiar with the place. Spent 'bout a month here in the clink. He's a regular…regular."

"Sounds like I'm not the only one with an interesting story, Mr. Collins."

The blinds dropped down. "It's complicated."

"Pull up those chairs, gentlemen," the Chief invited, after flipping on a small hallway light. "Let's have a pow-wow. I been waitin' three years to get to the bottom o' this mess. It's given my ulcers ulcers. I'm sick of the lies and…and the fraud I helped to create."

Denver was stunned. "Fraud? What're you talking about? You had something to do with it, Chief?!"

"Let's let Nellie— "

"You were working with Shep?!"

The Chief waved his hand, unflustered. "Shep was workin' with Pappy." He locked eyes with Phil. "But now that recent…*unfortunate* events have brought some kinda justice to those two men, we can all speak freely. At least here. We can figger out later how to tell everything to the others."

"I already shared quite a bit of my story with Leah and Doc," Phil said. "You can't expect people to not have a million questions. Including me."

McCloud pursed his lips. "It just needs to be handled right."

The soft glow of the distant incandescent bulb showed that Phil's face had drained of expression. He planted his elbows on the cluttered desk. "Leah told me about what happened. To Shep and Pappy. They may have become my enemies, but I wouldn't have wished their tragic deaths…on anyone. Ever." He hesitated. "It seems that you and I are both lucky to be alive, Mr. Collins."

Denver rested against the desk and rubbed his hands together. "Afghanistan wasn't nearly as dangerous as the Midwest in 1956."

"Perhaps you can explain that Afghanistan reference to me if we manage to get back home. I doubt the Second Accord would smile too favorably on that information."

Denver looked away.

September 11th, 2001.

World Trade Centers.

Osama bin Laden.

Taliban.

Afghanistan.

He nodded. "You're right. It wouldn't."

"I don't think I ever met the newspaper lady who passed away," Phil mused.

"*Betty*. Betty Larson," the Chief replied. "Good gal."

"Yes, Ms. Larson. How in the world did we miss her? When did she jump?"

"1952," Denver answered. "I think it was February. I know it was cold."

"You know," Phil began, "it sure makes one wonder. You think about just how many others might be out there. Somewhere. We've had some who came and left. Like the Forrester kid. We woke up one day and he had skipped town. Any news on that front, Chief?"

"Nope. Not a peep."

"What's the head count?" Phil asked.

The Chief squinted. "Of Jumpers?"

Phil nodded.

"One shy of a dozen."

Phil stared into his lap. "Leah told me that we're not really sure about Terrance."

Denver struggled with a satisfying answer. "Tee was with me. In the raid on Area 51 in Nevada. He, uh, never showed up at the rendezvous point. The fact that the government hasn't captured us yet tends to suggest…"

"Unfortunately, it suggests that he *didn't* survive," Phil said.

"I'm sure they would've found some means to torture our location out of him. I've been in the military. Uncle Sam has his ways."

"Then let's pray his death was fast and painless," Phil offered.

"Amen," McCloud whispered.

"I've been thinking about all the people we've lost, like Ken…and Larry. And Michael," Phil rehearsed with a grave stare. "If and when we ever get home, I worry about the rest of us. Have you heard of survivor's guilt?"

"I have," Denver volunteered. "They talk about it in combat zones. After an attack, some of the survivors can feel a false guilt about not dying like their friends did."

"It happens with cops, too," McCloud added.

"That's right," Phil agreed. "Now we may need to add Jumpers, right alongside soldiers and cops. Those who make it back home might fall under that same condition."

Denver didn't seem concerned. "Considering all the pitfalls and problems caused by a bunch of people from the future screwing with the past, I would say that survivor's guilt is the least of our worries."

Phil nodded. "I can't argue with that."

"Speaking of guilt, are we ever gonna get back to discussing what happened to you in 1953?"

"Well, Mr. Collins, to stick it in a neat little nutshell, it was like you said…a bunch of futuristic people screwing with the past. Or, at least two people trying to screw with it."

"Shep and Dr. Papineau?"

The Chief rose up and wandered about the polished concrete floor. "Yep."

"There was a period of several weeks, starting around May, when I noticed things," Phil said. "Little things. Fragments of conversations, when there shouldn't have been any conversations because of the language barrier. Or I would catch them together at odd times. Or in odd places. Late night meetings and so forth. And, like an idiot…I kept it to myself. I was in denial. I try to look for the good in people."

"Shoulda told someone," McCloud scolded from the far side of the station.

"I know, James. I know. And then it kinda came to a head during the first week of July. I overheard Shep on the telephone. It was late, after hours. He was talking about exploiting our technology, and somehow using it for their personal gain."

"Breaking the Third Accord," Denver quipped.

"You bet. In the worst way possible. A dangerous proposition. It could lead to terrible repercussions. I put two and two together. I figured out that Shep had to be talking to Dr. Papineau. Which made no sense at the time."

"I had me a similar experience with that little French weasel," McCloud hollered out. "But unlike you, Phil, *I* told someone. I told Billy. That private investigation saved Denver's skin. And earned me a painful scar."

Denver piped up, "Thanks again, Chief."

"All in a day's work, Mr. Collins. I'm a public servant. And dontcha worry 'bout my wound, I'll probably carry it to my grave. I'll think 'bout ya every time I take my shirt off."

"Please don't." Denver hunched forward and folded his arms on the top of the desk. "So, Mr. Nelson, let me guess. You confronted Shep, right on the spot?"

"I actually waited until Sunday. After the holiday. I thought I could persuade them through common sense...by appealing to reason. I scheduled a meeting and confronted both of them at the factory. Shep being, well...*Shep,* he flew off the handle and threatened me."

"Imagine that."

Phil straightened up and rubbed his chin. "Wait, wait, hold on...let me back up. *First,* he offered me a part of the action. I flatly refused. It was *then* he went ballistic and started threatening me. I told them that if they didn't change their ways, then they were leaving me with no alternative but to tell the group about it."

The Chief leaned down directly between them. "That was your second bad idea."

Phil shoved him out of the way. "Yes, James. Once again you're right, and I was foolish. There's a reason why you're in law enforcement, and I'm a school teacher."

"Amen to that."

Denver squinted. "So you delivered your ultimatum. Then what?"

"Well, after that, Shep overpowered me, tied me up, and brought me out to his house. Two days later, he hauled me to Chicago and turned me over to a large, heavyset psychiatrist. I think his name was Monte...Mont-something. *Montgomery*. They shot me up with a bunch of drugs, and the last three years passed by like a blurry, surrealistic dream. I don't have any specific memories after the second or third day there. Nothing I would trust, anyway. I know it's been three years, but it seems like three weeks."

Denver paused. "He died."

Phil leaned forward. "What? Who died?"

"The psychiatrist doctor guy."

"Dr. Montgomery is dead?"

"Yep. Car accident. Several weeks ago. Right after *you* died."

"Me? After I died?"

"Yep. When Leah and I went to get you, the clerk told me that you had died. She even said you had been cremated. I never told Leah that. It would've tore her to even tinier pieces."

McCloud reclined against the desk and studied Phil with a skeptical grin. "Even in the dark you look pretty dang good for a pile of ashes."

Phil traced a finger across his lower lip. "I'm not entirely sure if that's a compliment."

"Actually, you've died *twice* in the past three years, Mr. Nelson," Denver noted. "Don't forget your apparent suicide at the factory in July of 1953."

"The Chief and Leah filled me in on that this afternoon. But I can assure you the last time I pointed a gun at something, it wasn't my head. It was probably a soda can. And I probably missed." His fleeting smile vanished. "The Chief showed me a newspaper clipping about my death. It gave me chills."

Denver readjusted in his seat and peered up at McCloud. "I've also read that same article in the archives down at *The Journal*. It said that the police chief was the acting coroner, and that *you* confirmed the death as being from a self-inflicted gunshot wound."

"That it did, Mr. Collins. That it did." The Chief returned to his chair and plopped down hard. The springs squealed as the seat almost rocked back to the tipping point. "In spite of all of his…*charms*, Robert Sheppard knew how to stack the deck. In his favor. If you woulda asked me two weeks ago if I thought Shep was capable of murder, I probably would've said *no*. But in 1953, I wasn't so sure. And with Phil gone, someone had to step up and keep things together for the group."

"What does that have to do with lying about Phil's disappearance?"

"Shep showed up on my porch and said he and Phil had a severe fallin' out, and that he had to put him away somewhere for safe keepin'. I found out later it was Chicago."

Denver nodded. "And I bet he told you if you didn't go along with his story about a supposed suicide, then he would kill Mr. Nelson?"

"He never went that far. Shep's pretty smart. He just danced all around that possibility."

"I should never have appointed him as factory manager," Phil mourned. "A few people warned me not to do it. I thought I knew best."

"This may sound naïve," Denver began, "but why didn't you just arrest him, Chief?"

McCloud placed his hands behind his head and stretched with a nervous laugh. "Oh, don't think for one minute that I didn't dream about lockin' his arrogant ass up. But he'd thought that one through, too. He warned me if I didn't play ball, he and his allies would spread a truckload of rumors 'bout Phil that'd rip the group to smithereens. Shep was an expert at gettin' Peter to hate Paul, if ya know what I mean."

"I do," Denver said. A moment later he raised his eyebrows. "You could've shot him."

McCloud lowered his voice. "Off the record, that little option seemed appealing. From time to time. Sometimes daily. But even if I'd done that, I still didn't know where Phil was. Or even if he was alive. Or who the supposed *allies* were that Shep spoke of. As you always say, Mr. Collins…it was *complicated*. Very complicated."

Denver collapsed back against his chair and rubbed both sides of his surprised face. "Wow. Hello hard place, meet rock."

"You got it, son. I wasn't 'bout to let Phil's accomplishments and legacy get pulled apart like cotton candy. Too many people were countin' on me for a sense of stability. And leadership. Once Shep got rid o' Phil, he tried to steal the reins at every turn."

"I noticed. I think everyone noticed."

"He never did care that much for any of the Accords," Phil said.

The Chief cradled his thick arms on the desk and wagged his head. "I'm just glad that I had Doc and Ellen on my side. At least most of the time with Ellen. She and Shep had an up'n down relationship. I tell ya, Shep had me over a barrel at times, but that can hardly excuse my recent behavior, Mr. Collins."

"I'm not following you, Chief."

McCloud toyed with a pencil. "It was when you came back from Chicago. On the day that Frazier almost snuffed Betty out. Shep pressured me into smearin' your good name. He came to the station all hot-n-bothered and started throwin' around all manner of threats and promises. I caved. And that is unforgivable."

"It's not only forgivable…it's understandable," Denver countered. He studied the jail cell, now that his eyes had adjusted to the lack of light. "I can still clearly picture Shep standing near those bars over there and threatening to sink my body to the bottom of Lake Bloomington. No…you don't need my forgiveness, Chief. Not by a longshot. And even if you did, I think saving my ass from Hank makes us even."

Phil reached over and tapped Denver's left arm. "This may sound strange, Mr. Collins, but I almost wish that you had jumped here several years ago."

"Oh?"

"Uh-huh. Doc feels like they're on the verge of getting us all home. I wish you and I had had more time to become better friends."

"Well, look me up when you get home."

Phil withdrew his arm. "When were you born?"

"1979."

"Well, Mr. Collins, I could visit you, but you wouldn't even be a teenager yet when I got back to Colorado."

Denver nodded with a slight chuckle. "I guess that's right. Hadn't really thought about the, uh, time difference and all."

Phil sunk back. "What year did you jump from?"

"2014."

A distant and bemused expression spread across Phil's exhausted face. "It is such a bizarre fact of this whole time travel business."

"What's bizarre?"

"I was just thinking. If I were to walk up to you on the street, even five seconds before you jumped here to Normal, you wouldn't know me from Adam. But five seconds later, after you jumped back, we would practically be family."

Denver frowned. "Now that is bizarre."

"So, from my perspective…once we get home, I will have to wait about twenty-five years before you will even know who I am, Mr. Collins."

CHAPTER 43

A grandfather clock down the narrow hall erupted in a chorus of chimes that echoed throughout the modest cottage.

Eleven bells, Collins.

Denver clamped his eyes shut while his head sank back against the stiff couch. He struggled as he adjusted in fine, wiggling motions, seeking to get comfortable in the darkness. Pappy's furniture wasn't nearly as broke-in as the used set Denver had purchased for his own abandoned apartment on the west side.

He stroked the textured cushions on either side.

I bet Pappy never even sat on this couch.

He didn't really strike me as the 'couch' type of guy.

But me…gimme a couch, a remote, and a few NFL games, and I am right at home. Right at home.

He forced a smile.

Home.

There was no doubt that he had made a valiant effort to adopt his new place.

But he couldn't seem to make it feel like home.

Denver hadn't felt at home since waking up in a musty motel four months before on the rural outskirts of Normal in the wrong decade. In more honest moments, he would have to admit that nowhere had felt like home for at least a year before that.

Four years stationed with the Army domestically, and four more in the Middle East, had imparted to him the capability of adapting to new quarters at will. But once he had returned stateside and wed Jennifer, the notion of home was radically altered.

Once his daughter was born, it was forever settled.

I may get back to 2014, he thought.

But I may never get back home.

As the evening's whirlwind of hope-filled emotions and the revelation of Phil's near-resurrection began to wane, his thoughts, as always, returned to Jasmine. In an instinctive move, he reached around and fished out his wallet.

He sighed.

Nice move, Collins.

The comical picture of his six-year-old wasn't there.

His single physical connection to her had been confiscated by the CIA at Area 51. Once or twice Denver had entertained the reckless notion of re-invading the underground fortress to retrieve his only worldly treasure. That glossy piece of print was worth far more to him than a rucksack stuffed with a priceless superconductor.

But, if Doc's prognostications were even close to correct, he wouldn't be relying on a two-dimensional representation much longer.

What's this?

A brief flash of light penetrated his eyelids.

Headlights?

Denver sat up and shoved his wallet into his back pocket. It was headlights. A car was barreling up the short driveway.

Friend or foe?

He scrambled for the bedroom, snatched a pistol from the nightstand, and stole his quiet way back towards the living room window. With a flick of his wrist, he flung the thin curtain back. The dark vehicle was stopped and the motor was silent.

A figure stepped out.

A female figure.

Oh...it's Leah.

Leah?

It was Leah.

Denver released the drapes and fell against the wall. Of all the wounds he had endured since arriving to 1956, the abrupt demise of his only true friendship seemed destined to remain raw and bleeding. He couldn't even recall their last civil conversation, but he had often relived the last time she had chilled him with a piercing glare born of betrayal.

And now she's here.

He opened the door just as her fist attempted to knock. Leah lurched back.

"Sorry," he said, opening it wider. "Didn't mean to scare you. I was just trying to be polite. Guess it backfired."

"Oh, uh, no, no," she mumbled. "You're fine. Can, uh, can I come in for a minute?"

He motioned inward. "My house is your house. Actually, *Pappy's house* is now my house, which is now your house."

She breezed by, her head down. "I won't stay long."

Denver closed the door without making a sound, then flicked on the lights. "Stay as long as you want. I have some coffee. It might be cold."

"No…no. Thanks."

He circled around towards the sofa. "You wanna sit down? The furniture's not very—"

"I'm sorry," she blurted out.

"What?"

Huge tears raced down her almond cheeks. "I'm…sorry. For everything."

"And just what do you have to be—"

"I should have believed you. I should have known that you wouldn't lie to me." Leah folded down into a chair, sobbing. "I should've done a lot of things, and I didn't."

He stepped over and knelt before her. "Whoa, there, missie. With everything that's been happening, who can blame anyone for what they do or don't believe? I don't even think that *I* would've believed me. And I'm pretty trusting."

"Stop it! Quit making excuses for me, Denver!" She jerked her head up and he spotted the dark trails of smeared eyeliner streaking towards her jawline. "You were trying to tell me what was happening and I, I was too…too blinded by my own stupid—"

"Hey! Listen to me! You were a normal human being who had been lied to and disappointed more times than you could handle. It shut you down. That kinda pain and disillusionment would shut anyone down."

"You deserved better."

He waved his hand. "I don't deserve anything. None of us deserved any of this. It just…happened." He brushed a few strands of hair out of her hot face. "So forget about apologies or explanations or whatever. Okay?"

Leah grabbed his arm. "You told me! You told me he was alive. And then…then…"

"And you got your hopes up and then he wasn't there. And then another part of you died, Leah. You've been through a lot. Everyone—*anyone*—would have reacted the same way. So, congratulations. You're *human*."

"I didn't treat you like a human."

He lifted her wet chin and locked eyes with her. "You forget I was in the Army. They quit treating you like a human the moment a grunt hits formation at boot camp. I don't get to reapply for human status until I turn forty."

She chuckled as she slid the back of her hand across both cheeks. "Quit trying to make me laugh when I'm mad at myself."

"Is this what you look like when you're mad?" He pointed. "Puffy red eyes…black stripes running down your face? A little smeared lipstick. It's a good look. Different. But a good different. I could see this style of makeup really catching on with the young girls."

She straightened up and sucked in a deep breath. "I wish you would yell at me or something." Her shoulders dropped. "Or act hateful."

Denver scooted along the floor to the sofa and rested his back against it. "Oh, so now I know what this is all about." He yanked his knees up and laid his arms across them. "You are already starting to miss Shep."

Leah frowned with a vicious squint.

"Too soon?" he asked.

"Maybe. Maybe not." Leah slumped out of her own chair and snuggled up beside him on the floor. She matched his posture exactly. "I don't know what to think anymore. When Nellie walked into the foyer today, I thought I was dreaming. I felt like laughing and crying…and *vomiting* all at the same time. Actually, I think I did."

They laughed together.

"I didn't hardly sleep last night," she mumbled.

"Oh?"

"I was afraid. Afraid you wouldn't come back. I kept thinking that you and Phil had both…killed yourselves. Just in different ways. It was horrible. Tossed and turned."

"And now, Phil and I are still here. You lost all that good sleep for nothing."

She couldn't hide a tiny smile. "Yeah."

"Yeah."

Leah picked at a thread on her skirt. "You know, we're always so worried about all these threats and dangers…from the government and from interfering with the time stream and blah blah blah." She glanced over at him. "Who knew that our real enemies walked by us every day? Ate with us every day. *Lied to us*…every day."

Denver leaned into her. "You know that the Chief didn't really have a choice, right? Shep had him boxed in."

She flattened her legs out and rubbed her thighs. "My head learned that a few hours ago. My heart hasn't really caught up yet. It was all just so hard...and I know you weren't there, but I can still picture the Chief telling us all about Phil's body and the gun. And then the casket, and the funeral, and everything that was said there. And now, three years later, you find out it was all a lie?!"

"Well, if he hadn't played along according to Shep's rules, there's a good chance that Phil would never have walked into that foyer today."

"I know, I know. But do you know how many times I went to visit the grave of someone...who wasn't even there?" She looked over at him. "Don't get me wrong, I'm glad he wasn't, but just the thought is so...humiliating and painful."

"It makes you feel betrayed. It makes you wonder about who else may be lying to you."

"Yeah. That's the worst part. The death of trust."

He hesitated thoughtfully. "You know, looking back, I'm kinda glad you didn't see Phil when we went to that mental hospital."

Her tears had finally abated. "Why?"

"He didn't look anything like he did today. Today he looked good. It was a mental image you didn't need. Trust me."

She lowered her head to his left shoulder and embraced his arm. "Thank you."

"For what? Having incredible biceps?"

"For having an incredibly patient and understanding spirit."

Denver blushed. "Be careful with talk like that, Mrs. Swan?"

"Oh?"

"Yeah…I've got quite a reputation with the CIA and the FBI. Don't spoil it."

CHAPTER 44

Neal stared at the bare, beige walls.

It's like a blank slate.

The staff had done a commendable job in removing almost every trace of Howard Ross from the primary administrative office in Dreamland. Even before Schaeffer's C-47 had touched down on the desert tarmac, they had relocated Neal's desk and most of his personal effects to their new home down the hall.

His first twenty-four hours after returning to Nevada had been furiously busy, but strangely quiet. Either out of respect for Chief Ross' passing or in acknowledgement of the heavy burden that had now befallen him, most of the senior staff had kept a wide berth around Neal. Pressing matters that usually found their way to his desk were intercepted.

Phone calls were deflected.

Conversations were minimized.

Everyone knew that the transition would be hard enough. There was no need to make it more difficult.

He bent over and dug through a jumbled box.

And there it is.

Neal only had three photographs of himself with Ross, and this was by far his favorite. The candid picture had been snapped by a member of the press on the same weekend Ross had recruited Neal within the shadow of the Little White House in Key West.

He lowered it to the desk and spoke out loud. "And you, my friend, are going to stay right here. You will always be with me."

Chief Howard Ross.

Neal arched back in his office chair and studied the picture. Ross would always be *Chief* Ross. Even in death. It was the only way Neal had known him, and it would continue to be the only way he remembered him.

Chief.

Neal had been stunned about the effect of that one little word and the enormity of what it entailed. Just the mention of it had caught him totally off-guard when his Douglass Skytrain began its descent on his return flight. The copilot had gently rocked him awake.

"Wheels down in five, Chief Schaeffer."

Chief Schaeffer.

Chief Schaeffer?

It sounded wrong. Almost offensive.

He had seen the uncomfortable title on a handful of memos and had been addressed as such over a dozen times since returning to Dreamland. In every occurrence it was a surreal reminder of a reality he had never fully contemplated.

In most respects over the years, Schaeffer had been the de facto head of Project SATURN. He had carefully and methodically lifted the reins from the tight hands of his micromanaging boss on so many occasions that Ross never even sensed the loss of control. But unlike his predecessor, it wasn't about ego with Neal, it was always about results and efficiency.

In a very real sense he had been the boss.

But now he had both the title and the responsibility.

And he hated it.

With both the demise of Ross and the rise of a new mandate from Director Dulles, Neal was abruptly thrust into an uncertain transitional period in the lifecycle of Project SATURN. As he prepared to sail across the turbulent, brackish waters of shifting operational directives, his analytical and managerial confidence was weak in the knees. The horizon was hazy and he knew the political winds that drove policy were often fickle at best.

Neal slid his top-left drawer open and fished out a modest dossier labeled *Operation Caretaker*. He flipped the cover and focused on the color reproduction of a driver's license that was paper-clipped to the corner.

Denver Wayne Collins.

To Neal, the absolute contrast in mission objectives was staggering. For nearly a decade, Project SATURN had been dedicated to the hunt for temporally displaced persons. But now, armed with the knowledge of their target's sure arrival, in a sense they had already caught him…twenty-three years early.

Denver's future arrival would be among history's longest of pregnancies, as it were. Project SATURN's expectation of his birth would precede his actual conception by nearly a quarter-century. Neal, like the shortsighted mutt fixated on chasing cars, found himself in the awkward position of theoretically having succeeded.

It was difficult for him to comprehend the sublime realization that the most productive parts of his redirected career would not even begin until he was in his mid-sixties. Even more sobering was the undeniable possibility he might not even live to see Operation Caretaker's fruition in the second decade of the twenty-first century.

He pulled the photo even closer.

What year are you from Mr. Collins?

2014?

2015?

Later?

The clamoring of his black desk telephone brought a sudden close to his temporal deliberations. He snatched the handset and lowered the photo.

"This is Schaeffer."

The distinctive voice of the DCI shook him to full attention. "Neal, it's Dulles."

"Uh, yes, sir. What can I do for—"

"What you can do is gimme a straight answer."

"Yes, sir?"

Dulles grew quiet. Neal imagined him taking a hit on his pipe. "Have you ceased any and all Project SATURN operations in Central Illinois, Chief Schaeffer?"

"Yes, sir. Except for a small team handling financials and a cleanup crew, we have cleared out. Per your instructions."

"Did you detain, or are you detaining any individuals connected with your recent investigation?"

"No, sir."

"I need a straight answer."

Neal rubbed his forehead. "It was, sir."

There was a lull in the conversation. Neal seized it with some trepidation. "May I ask concerning the nature of the call, Director?"

"No you may not…but I'm gonna tell you anyway."

"Thank you, sir."

"You never heard this from me."

Neal nodded. "I understand, sir."

"In the past several days, a high-level Pentagon military scientist has disappeared. And when I say high-level, I mean so-damn high that I can't even get authorization to know his name. All we have is a codename."

Schaeffer gazed up at the ceiling.

A Pentagon scientist.

It's got to be him.

Neal almost whispered into the handset, "The Pioneer."

It sounded like Dulles fumbled his phone. "How in the hell did you know that?! Did SATURN have something to do with it, Neal?!"

"Oh, no, sir." Neal selected his words with great care. "Chief Ross and I met him, sir. Down in the Sandbox. At least, we *spoke* with him. We were blindfolded. For the most part."

"And now, a short time after that whole debacle and he's vanished!" Dulles retorted. "You're the analyst…what're the odds of that, Neal?"

"I can assure you, sir, that it is a curious and unrelated coincidence."

"You swear?!"

"On a stack of Bibles from here to the Moon."

"That's not enough," Dulles grumbled.

"It's the truth," Neal replied.

"I don't need truth, I need *answers* dammit," Dulles demanded. "You got any idea how much heat the agency is taking right now?"

Something occurred to Neal. "They…could be…related."

"Who could be related?"

"Chief Ross and the Pioneer."

Dulles hesitated. "Explain."

"It could be her." Neal rested his elbows upon his desk. "It might be the woman."

"Woman? What woman? Today's not a great day for games, Neal."

"What if the woman who executed Ross really is a KGB assassin? A Soviet operative sent to eliminate high-level targets in our temporal research divisions? The Sandbox practically confessed to engaging in temporal activities."

"Then the Pioneer isn't *missing,*" Dulles quipped.

"No, sir," Neal began.

"He's dead."

Research Log: Dr. Glen D. Stonecroft

DATE: December 20, 1956

Our final (and substantial) obstacle in this temporal enterprise has been tentatively conquered. Dr. Tesla first postulated then demonstrated that the three magnets, while primarily responsible for initiating a temporal rift, are also accountable for determining positioning within an X, Y, Z coordinate system.

The portal is, by default, the origin at 0, 0, 0. By placing the rift into a "Receive Light" only mode, Dr. Tesla varied the relative rotational velocities of each of our three magnets. This allowed us, in real-time, to observe both the temporal and geospatial results.

As his models predicted, we could maneuver the portal's destination position up to several miles in any physical direction. We had to recalibrate our rotational potentiometers to allow for greater discretion in spatial targeting.

At 1:19 pm this afternoon, we targeted the gravel lot behind Nelson Manufacturing for a one-hour jump utilizing one of our laboratory mice. At 2:19 pm, the test was concluded with positive results.

G.D.S.

****

UPDATE:

We conducted five additional spatial tests at varying times and varying locations on the property, with flawless results. Within the hour we will initiate a final 24-hour temporal transport experiment. Based upon previous tests and mathematical models, I cannot foresee any impediments to success.

We are going home.

G.D.S.

CHAPTER 45

Friday, December 21, 1956

Denver struggled to concoct a word worthy of capturing the moment.

A barrage of intense emotions surged through him; an indefinable blend of excitement, fear, hope, and nostalgia were piled atop a layer of intense sadness.

He glanced at the medley of faces assembled in the upstairs conference room. All of the Jumpers were present. Even Tesla had attended what everyone had hoped would be their final official meeting.

Smiles were everywhere.

But strange sorts of smiles.

He studied them.

Without exception, each elated face still retained traces of the visible aftermath of their group's horrific losses. Garrett Frazier slid back in his chair, allowing Denver to catch sight of Phil Nelson engaged in a private exchange with a beaming Leah Swan.

It's so good to see her smile again.

And talking with her best pal Nellie.

Beautiful.

Denver concentrated on Phil. His well-dressed and well-shaven appearance couldn't have been more removed from the pathetic patient Denver had discovered just weeks before. Phil turned his head.

And there's that triangular birthmark.

He chuckled quietly.

Nellie's personal portal.

Denver leaned forward and squinted. *I've only been here for less than five months, but it's been over ten years for him. Wow. Can't imagine the awkward conversations he'll have back in Colorado.*

When he gets back home.

That thought paralyzed him for a moment.

Back home.

But not everyone is going back home.

McCloud rose out of his seat, as if somehow responding to Denver's somber introspections. "Ladies and gentlemen. If y'all could take a seat and quiet down for a moment, I'd appreciate it."

The joyous room fell silent and still.

"Within a couple o' days, by the grace of God and the wisdom of our friends, each of us…will be going home."

A spontaneous round of applause erupted, and the Chief eventually joined in with tear-filled eyes. Several people began gesturing over at Doc, Ellen and Tesla. The researchers were embarrassed, yet celebrated with as much vigor as the rest. Doc, in his characteristic humility, finally waved them off.

"That's right," McCloud called out. "That's right. They deserve it. Doc and Ellen. And now Dr. Tesla. Years of late and sleepless nights. Years of blood, sweat, and lately…tears. Lots o' tears."

The clapping died down.

"Lots of tears," the Chief mumbled. He cleared his throat and retrieved his notebook. "And, uh, in memory of those that'll *not* be goin' home…I would like for us to observe a few moments of silence as I read aloud each name."

He paused.

"Kenneth Miller."

Phil Nelson unfolded a handkerchief and brought it up to his pained face.

"Lawrence Etherington."

Leah scooted against Phil and wrapped her arms around him. She buried her head on his shoulder.

McCloud continued.

"Michael Ritenour."

The Chief hesitated. "Terrance…" his voice cracked and broke. "Terrance…Gaines."

Alexus sobbed out loud and smothered her wet face in her trembling hands. Martha sought to reach out and console her. The Chief waited respectfully.

"Robert…*Shep*…Sheppard." McCloud raised his eyes to the ceiling and inhaled deeply a few times. He composed himself and peered back down at his notes.

"And…uh, Beatrice Larson. *Betty*. Larson."

Billy O'Connell leaned onto the table. "Betty," he whispered.

The Chief closed his notebook in silence.

Few people moved.

No one made a sound for quite some time.

Doc Stonecroft rose from his seat and most faces turned towards him in expectation. "If I may be so bold, I would enjoin us to add another name to that somber society." He was obviously collecting his thoughts. "Regardless of his—final *indiscretions*—I submit that, without his tireless service, we would still be languishing with precious little or even no hope of return. My colleague…Dr. Emile Papineau."

"*Pappy,*" Ellen mumbled through fresh streams of tears.

"Pappy," Phil echoed softly.

Doc folded his hands together before gazing down at the floor. "And may we continue our memorial as we pause to reflect on those, who, for whatever reasons, departed from our warm association of their own accord. And for those dear people, who perhaps were never discovered and thus never welcomed into our fine community and finer family."

He paused, allowing time for individual meditation, while adjusting his spectacles. "May God above grant each of them passage home by whatever means. Or may He bless them with a life of peace and prosperity in their new home, in this time and in this place."

Denver looked over at Grandma Martha. Her thin lips offered several silent *Amens*.

Denver added a few of his own.

Doc sank back into his chair and McCloud nodded. "Yes. Beautiful. Thank you, Doc. Well said. Well said. As always. What would any meeting be without your words o' wisdom? And now…your words of *comfort*. So, thank you." He lowered his notebook to the table. "As we travel back home, each of us carries special thoughts of these special folks. Cherish those memories. Heck, think of them often. Remember their friendship. Or…their kindness. And, uh, some…their *sacrifice*."

The Chief glanced off to his left. "Are you ready, Mr. Nelson?"

Phil sat up straight and nodded.

McCloud dropped down into his own seat. "Mr. Nelson would like to discuss some other important matters."

"Thank you, Chief McCloud," Phil said as he stood and strolled closer to the table. He spent some time surveying their faces. "Over ten years ago, a very scared, and a very average man from Colorado found himself relocated to this town in a moment of time…in a split second. In a flash."

He concentrated on the floor.

"And since March of 1946, through trial and error…and in fear and doubt and hopelessness and now hope reborn, we have, uh, *endured*. You know, words would fail for me to express my absolute respect and the gratitude that I feel towards each of you. You have indulged my crazy vision. Most of you have at least *memorized* the Four Accords, and some of you were even foolish enough to try and put them into practice."

A few rumblings of laughter broke out in the conference room.

He smiled and his eyes flared red. "I won't make anyone recite them right now, but as a school teacher…I need to warn you that there will be a pop quiz later."

"Ain't happenin', teacher," McCloud teased.

"I agree," Denver added. "I'm not a natural test taker. I crack under pressure. Ask Leah. She knows."

Phil shrugged. "Well, maybe you two gentlemen can do something worthy of extra credit."

McCloud jabbed a stubby finger at the badge on his chest. "Uh, been there, done that. Police chief for several years now. A model public servant."

Denver thrust his hand high like an overachieving, middle-school student. "Okay, how about infiltrating a top secret *and* highly-dangerous underground government facility in the middle of the desert? That's gotta be worth something."

Phil's eyes flicked back and forth between the two men. "I'll think about it. Chief, can I have the notebook, please?"

McCloud slid it across the tabletop.

Phil snatched it and spent a moment locating a certain page. "After meeting with Doc, and the Chief, and Mrs. Tomlin, there are several important loose ends to tie up, and questions to answer. Obviously, if all of us suddenly disappeared from Normal, it would rouse a lot of suspicion. Especially someone in the public eye, like Chief McCloud. Or Mr. O'Connell."

Denver folded his arms and leaned back. *Hmmm…I hadn't thought about that one. That could be bad.*

Phil cleared his throat. "As most of you may have heard, Officer Billy officially put in his two-week notice at the police department recently. Once our researchers proved that the portal was functioning, we thought it would be wise to start a process to minimize suspicion. Billy was step one. The Chief met with the mayor late yesterday to resign. He cited a family crisis back in Georgia. His resignation was effective immediately. That's step two."

Alexus raised her hand. "What about the factory?"

"An important question, Miss Daniels," Phil commented. "And one that I was just getting to. I guess this is as good a time as any for our biggest announcement of the night. A very big announcement." He rotated to his right and motioned. "Mrs. Tomlin?"

Denver sat up. *What's this? Grandma Tomlin? A big announcement?*

"Thank you, Mr. Nelson," she offered in her genteel style. "After careful and prayerful consideration, I have elected to remain behind here in Normal."

What? Denver thought. *Remain behind?*

"What do you mean, Mrs. Tomlin?" Leah blurted out.

"What she means," McCloud replied, "is that she's not gonna be using the portal like the rest of us. Martha's planning on remaining here in Normal. In *this* time."

"But why?" Alexus asked.

Martha placed her pale hands on the table. "My sweet child, this decision was mine, and mine alone. I can assure each of you that I approached Mr. Nelson and Chief McCloud with this desire."

"Mrs. Tomlin is going to assume ownership of Nelson Manufacturing," Phil announced. "For those of us who have houses, we are going to officially *sell* them to Martha as well. The paperwork is already in the works. By the end of the day today, we will display *Out of Business* signs in the windows here at the plant and lock all the doors. Oh, and we need to burn all the paper employee records."

Phil paused and looked around with satisfaction. "Nelson Manufacturing has served the purposes for which it was intended. At some time in the near future, Martha will hire a local contractor to fill the stairwell to The Basement with concrete. The original construction firm was told that they were building us a bomb shelter. She will tell them she wants the liability sealed off. The lower door will be locked, so there won't be any chance for anyone to see what we've got down there."

Denver spoke up. "But what about all of the nuclear material? Will it be safe just leaving it all underground?"

Phil gestured off to his left. "Doc?"

"A valid concern, Mr. Collins, but one which we anticipated from the very outset of this enterprise. After our final charging session, the fuel rods will be lowered into a lead-lined concrete storage vault. If the estimates that Dr. Papineau and I calculated some years back are accurate, our containment system should yield protection for many, many decades to come. Perhaps a hundred years or better."

Phil turned a page. "Thank you, Dr. Stonecroft. For those of us with cars, I would like to ask Billy to assist each of you in taking your vehicles down to Bloomington and then selling them to a car lot for a price they can't refuse. All the excess cash goes to Mrs. Tomlin. We need to liquidate as much as possible. Gather your clothing and shoes, and donate them to a shelter or a church ministry or something. If you can't, haul whatever you have left out to Mrs. Tomlin's place and store it in her basement."

He paused and looked around the room. "It is important that we do not leave anything behind. Anything from the future, take it back with you or destroy it completely. Empty your homes and apartments of any paperwork, documents, anything…*anything* that could identify you. Make sure your rents are paid up, turn in your keys to your landlords as soon as possible and clear out. Inform your neighbors that you're moving out of town. Tell them that the factory closed down. But be specifically vague about where you're moving to. Relocate to Martha's house or here at the factory as soon as you're able. We can set up cots right here."

Denver was struck with Phil's confident yet calm demeanor. *I can see why Leah respects this guy so much.*

I bet he was a great teacher back in Colorado.

Not as well-spoken as Doc, but just as friendly as the Chief.

A good mix.

"I realize that the next forty-eight hours are going to be incredibly hectic and frustrating," Phil acknowledged, "but we need to do this right. If we don't, we could jeopardize Mrs. Tomlin or even jeopardize our own futures in ways we cannot even imagine. The First Accord encourages us to

'Walk Without Footprints'. But now, maybe it's time for a Fifth Accord…as we get ready to depart we also need to *Leave Without Footprints*."

"And just when are we leaving?" Alexus implored. "I wanna get home!"

Doc rose from his seat again. "Soon, my dear Miss Daniels. Soon. In fact, you are scheduled to depart in the very first batch, so to speak."

"The first batch?" Garrett said.

Ellen jumped on the question. "Once the capacitors are fully charged, they can only hold enough juice to power four individual jumps. After that, it takes about eighteen hours to charge them back up for the next round of time travelers. It'll take a few days to get everyone home." She smiled. "And we will get everyone home."

"Who goes when?" Leah asked.

Phil glanced back down at the notepad. "Glad you asked, Mrs. Swan. Our first round of Jumpers will be…Alexus Daniels, Tori Wilkinson, Ellen Finegan…and *you*, Mrs. Swan."

"Round two?" Garrett inquired.

"Round two…let's see…Billy O'Connell, *you* Mr. Frazier, then Chief McCloud, and finally myself."

Denver shrugged. *Guess I'm on the last train out of Dodge.*

Ain't complaining.

I will see you soon, Jasmine.

"Our final batch," Phil concluded, "will be Denver Collins, then followed by Dr. Glen Stonecroft. Doc needs to hang around until the end. Just in case there are issues or problems."

"What kinds of problems?" Alexus probed. "Like the kind that killed Mr. Sheppard and Ms. Larson?!"

"Just a prudent, precautionary formality, my dear," Doc comforted. "Do not let your heart be troubled. We have performed multiple tests with one hundred percent safety and accuracy."

"I know that Doc and Ellen have already met with those of you who will be jumping here to the factory," Phil said, "but I want to reinforce the plan. If you are a non-TRS sample Jumper, you will be jumping to a safe location somewhere on these premises. Doc has assured me that they have tested your jump dates and have determined safe zones here on the property. Once you jump, you will then have to find a suitable way home, whether by bus, plane, or bicycle."

Everyone smiled.

"But seriously," he continued, "if you are jumping here to the factory, you need to take sufficient cash to aid in your return home. It will be older money, but it will still be usable money. Only take what you need. Remember the Third Accord. And if you get home a bit early, remember the *Fourth* Accord. That's a big one. What we don't want is '*honey I'm home*' to become '*honey, we're home*.' That would be...bad."

Chief McCloud fidgeted with his hat. "Hey Doc...you, uh, wanna tell everyone about the other thing? The destruct thing?"

Stonecroft's rotund face flushed in a matter of moments. "Your introduction was as delicate as a sledgehammer, Chief McCloud. But first, we prefer to label it as our Disablement Protocol."

"Sounds pretty much like the same thing. A rose by any other name would still be a bomb."

"It is not a bomb," Doc protested. "Dr. Tesla and I have constructed a series of disabling mechanisms that are connected to a basic timer. Once I initiate my own temporal rift, I will activate the timer, and approximately five minutes after my departure, the temporal apparatus will be rendered unusable for any and all future purposes."

The Chief leaned forward. "Does something blow up?"

"Well, yes…strictly speaking, Chief McCloud. A series of controlled charges are involved."

"Then…it's…a…*bomb*. B-O-M-B. Or bombs," McCloud insisted with a grin.

"An automobile engine operates according to a precisely regulated series of controlled combustions, Chief McCloud. But I daresay that I cannot recall having heard anyone in this assembly refer to a moving vehicle as a bomb."

McCloud pressed back against his seat and stretched his legs. "It's a bomb," he mumbled.

"But if you blow up or *disable* the portal," Denver began, "then what if there are other Jumpers…later? In the future after we leave. Won't that just strand them with no hope? With no way back?"

"An excellent inquiry that I will defer to Dr. Tesla," Stonecroft replied.

"To put a fine point on it, Mr. Collins…there will not and cannot be any future Jumpers. At least, not to Normal," Tesla responded.

Denver squinted. "I know you're real smart and all, but how can you be so certain?"

"If you recall, it was my experimentation in the Sandbox that drew each of you out of the temporal stream. Without my guidance, the technicians from the Pentagon do not have the background in theoretical physics worthy of activating and controlling their device." He smiled and patted his gnarled hand atop his cane. "I feared the unrestricted usage of my portal, and so I engineered certain…*safeguards*. It cannot function properly without my guidance. And you will be pleased to hear that I have no intentions of returning to the Sandbox."

"Where're you planning on goin' after we get outta town?" McCloud asked.

"I have died and disappeared once before, Chief McCloud. I am fairly confident that I can both choose and fashion my new destiny."

"Fair 'nough."

Phil Nelson closed the notebook with a curious smile and dropped it on the table. "Chief McCloud? May I indulge the group in that little convocation that we discussed earlier today?"

"Denver assures me that the danger's past," the Chief responded. "Surely one more time won't hurt. But I'm gonna have to skip out, for obvious reasons."

With a growing grin, Phil continued. "For those who can remember the good ole days, I propose a small, quiet party. A going away bash. In our usual spot. Tonight. Nine o'clock. I will have to be a bit disguised, but I would love to see you there."

Steak 'n Shake? Denver wondered.

Leah perked up. "At the corner of Main and West Virginia?"

Phil dug out his wallet and thumbed through it.

"Yes ma'am. And I'm buying."

February 8, 2006

SECURITY LEVEL: TOP SECRET

FOR: Chief Leonard Mueller, Project SATURN
FROM: Calvin Baremore, Northeast Section
SUBJECT: Identification of Spouse

Mr. Collins has had a third date with a woman identified as Jennifer Lynn Pruitt. The physical features of Jasmine Collins are consistent with those of this female candidate. Considering this fact along with the apparent necessity that the daughter will be born sometime in 2008 (with conception likely occurring in 2007) the timing and identification appears to be conclusive concerning this candidate.

With your permission, we will begin dissuading potential competition in order to protect and cultivate this relationship.

END

PS

CHAPTER 46

Sunday, December 23, 1956, 3:31 p.m.
Jump Day: One

"I'm scared," Alexus announced, trembling. "I'm really, really scared." She laid her hands on either side of her tear-stained cheeks. "I don't know if…if…I can do this. I'm gonna throw up."

"Heavens, child," Doc called out as he and Ellen worked their way to the distressed young woman through the excited crowd. "Your trepidations are perfectly natural, Miss Daniels." They embraced her from either side. "The great Roman Emperor and philosopher Marcus Aurelius wisely noted that *"if you are distressed by anything external, the pain is not due to the thing itself, but to your estimate of it; and this you have the power to revoke at any moment."*

Doc sought to gain eye-contact with her. "My child, you—*you*—have it within your power to overthrow any debilitating fear."

Terror filled her face. "I…I can't do this." She gestured beyond the door into the portal chamber. "There's no way I can…can walk through that…*thing* in there." Alexus started to collapse.

"Whoa, girl," Ellen yelled out, guiding her limp frame down into a chair. "Someone get me a cold washcloth or towel or something. Now! And something to drink!"

Leah sprang into action and returned with a rag. "Breathe," Ellen encouraged. "Big, slow, deep breaths." She dabbed Alexus' face with the cold compress. "Listen, sweetie…you are just overwhelmed, with the, the excitement of going home, and the sadness of saying goodbye to your friends." Ellen made a funny face. "And you're probably sick of all this stuffy air down here in The Basement." She winked and whispered. "Old man smells."

Martha delivered a glass of water. Leah helped her to stabilize the cup long enough for a few drinks.

"That's good, that's good," Ellen repeated with a soothing tone. "Big breaths and small sips. Feeling any better? Even a little?"

Alexus blinked hard. "Maybe. But I feel weak…and I'm still scared."

"Back up, everyone," Ellen commanded to the handful of gawkers. "This isn't a circus sideshow, give her some space."

They did and Leah knelt down, cradling one of her coworker's shaking hands. "Hey. Ever since I first met you, Lexi, I was amazed by how strong you were. Now *me*, when I first jumped here, I was a complete and total wreck."

"She was," Phil quipped from the other side of the table, which Ellen had decorated with a festive centerpiece sporting a miniature Christmas tree. "She was a wreck. I can vouch for that. Basket case actually."

"I was," Leah said. "I'm not ashamed to admit it. But you, you always talked about going home, and finishing your Journalism degree. You wanted to see the world. Write the big stories. Live the dream."

"I still do."

Leah hugged her briefly. "Of course you do. I know you do. And you will. You will. A good journalist has to follow their hunches and take risks. Sometimes to get the big story, you have to go places other people won't." Leah wagged her index finger towards the portal. "It's time to go after the biggest story ever. And it's waiting for you on the other side of that door. And when you get home, look up the archives from the *Normal Journal* and read your articles from 1956. Now *that* would be a trip!"

Alexus straightened up and ventured another sip. "Aren't you afraid, Mrs. Swan?"

"What're you talking about?" Leah blubbered, tears beginning to flow from her compassionate brown eyes. "I'm scared out of my mind. I'm shaking all over. Inside and out. But you know what? I have two precious children and a husband back home that are worth more to me than...*anything*. They're certainly worth more than putting up with a belly full of butterflies."

Alexus trembled with a nervous laugh. "My whole insides are butterflies, not just my belly."

Leah rose up without releasing Lexi's hand. "And that is okay. It's okay. You know what? In a few minutes I'm gonna walk down that little ramp and right into the arms of my family. And so are you." She squeezed the girl's hand. "We are going home. We've worked for this day. We've waited for this day. We've *prayed* for this day. Trust me, it'll hurt like crazy to say goodbye."

Leah glanced over at Tori, who was absorbed in a book, calmly unaffected by the turbulent emotion surrounding her. "We have all become close, Lexi. We're more than friends...we're family. But we need to get back to our other families. They are waiting for us. Counting on us. It's time to see them again. It's time to be with them again."

Ellen peered over at Doc and nodded with subtle discretion. He drifted back to the control panel in silence and busied himself. Tesla, aided by Denver, joined Stonecroft in his precise preparations.

After a few moments, Alexus wobbled up to her feet, steadying herself against the edge of the table.

"That's the spirit," Ellen commended. "This is gonna be the best day of your young life, girl. You just wait."

"I hope so…Miss Finegan."

Ellen clasped her and held her tight. "I know so…Miss Daniels. I promise. I'll be seeing you on the other side one day. I won't be long."

"Thank you, Miss Finegan. For everything."

Ellen inched away as the remaining Jumpers respectfully formed a makeshift line. Leah guided the frightened traveler along the heartwarming path.

"May God be with you, child," Martha offered with a tender embrace.

"Thank you, ma'am."

Billy was predictably awkward but thoughtful. "It, uh, has been a pleasure being your friend, Miss Daniels. Gonna miss ya. That's for sure."

"The same to you, Officer O'Connell. Thank you."

Alexus hunkered over and draped an arm around Tori. "You be good, Tori. Keep making those beautiful paintings. Goodbye."

The young teen spoke without rising. "Goodbye."

"It was nice working with you," Garrett said, reaching out his hand. "Take care."

She returned the gesture. "Thank you, Mr. Frazier. Sorry that I've been sick so much lately."

"Aw…gimme a big hug, gal," McCloud beckoned, arms thrown opened wide. She did and he almost swung her off her feet. "It's gonna be alright. You can bet your bottom dollar on that. A police chief wouldn't be worth his salt if he let anyone or anything hurt his people. You're gonna be fine."

"That's what they keep saying, Chief," she replied with the tiniest of grins. "Thanks for watching over us. For watching over me."

"It's what I do," he said with a wink.

She ventured a few more steps and stared up into a kind face. "Mr. Nelson. I don't even know how to thank you. I…I don't know what to say. All of us would've been lost…we would've been lost without you."

He squeezed her shoulders with a tender grip. "I told you the other night at Steak 'n Shake, and I'll tell you again, Miss Daniels…I had very little to do with it. Thank God I was surrounded by good people. Talented people. We were all in this together. I was merely the first one. That's all."

"Well, you'll always hold a special place in my heart." Alexus brought her hand to her chest. "That is, as soon as all these butterflies make some room in there."

"And that is all the thanks I could ever wish for." A wide smile broke out across his face. "Goodbye, Miss Daniels. Godspeed. Like I said the other night…I can't wait to see your name in the papers. In a good way."

"Goodbye, sir. And thanks again, for everything."

Phil motioned. "I believe the one you should be thanking is right behind you."

She swiveled about to Doc's beaming face. Alexus grabbed him and kissed his hairless scalp. "Oh Doc," she sobbed. "I will never forget your kindness, your poems…at just the right time. Thank you."

"And I shall never forget your beautiful smile and more beautiful character, Miss Daniels. May God hold you and shield you in the palm of His infinite hand."

She glanced over at the tiny Christmas tree. "You kept your promise," she said.

"Oh?"

"You said *'home by Christmas'*."

Ellen worked her way back over. "Absolutely. With even a few days to spare! An early Christmas present."

"Indeed. By the grace of God," Doc acknowledged. "In the spirit of the holiday season, salvation may be His free gift to us. But your return home is my gift to you, child. Go change the world."

"I will try, Doc."

"I have not the slightest doubt that you will," he assured.

"And Dr. Tesla," she called out. "Thank you, sir."

"May your future be bright, ma'am."

Alexus had almost reached the door when she spun about. "Will, uh, will it hurt, Doc?"

He studied her face. "Do you recall the day you jumped here to Normal, my child?"

"Yes."

"Did that life-changing temporal event cause you any pain or discomfort, beyond the immediate confusion of the moment?"

She looked down. "I, uh, I didn't feel a thing."

"Ah, yes. And such are the gentle hands of time," he replied. "They will bear you along with all the tender softness of a summer breeze."

"I hope so. You promise?"

"Ask Mr. Collins, my child. His courageous willingness has given us much more than the fleeting and fickle sensations of hope. It has provided us with confident assurance."

Denver made his way over and took hold of her shoulders. "Do me a favor. Close your eyes."

She obeyed and he lightly traced the tip of his right pinky across her cheek. "Did you feel that?" he asked.

She nodded and opened her eyes. "It kinda…*tickled.*"

"That's how it's gonna feel. A little tickle. All over." He paused. "Kind of like thousands of little bubbles all over your skin. But for just a second. And then…you're home."

She clutched his waist. "Thank you, Mr. Collins. I hope to see you when I get home."

He patted her back. "It's a date. I'll introduce you to my pride and joy. Just look us up, I'll be in New York. The Big Apple. Can't miss it, just look for the Statue of Liberty…it's the little town right next to it."

"Forget Lady Liberty," McCloud bellowed. "Just keep an eye out for the World Trade Centers. They're *way* taller."

Denver exchanged a tense glance with Doc. The aged researcher shook his head, almost imperceptibly. "Just, uh, just look me up," Denver repeated, forcing a comforting grin.

"Okay, Mr. Collins."

Phil trotted over to the control panel. "Is everything ready, Doc?"

Stonecroft adjusted his glasses and peered across the colorful array of knobs, switches, and gauges. "Miss Daniels' TRS sample has been processed. Dr. Tesla and I ran an exhaustive diagnostic series not more than two hours past. All components are operating at optimal performance and efficiencies."

"I like the sound of that," Phil said.

Doc raised and waved his hand. "Ladies and gentlemen. Please, if I may obtain your attention for just a few precious minutes. It is crucial that all present are in agreement and aware of the process that awaits us."

The group quieted down and formed a tight cluster around him. "Once we engage the capacitors and initiate the liquid nitrogen cooling system, we can sustain a stable temporal rift for not more than seven minutes. Based upon our calculations and the measurement of the mass of each traveler, we have sufficient energy stores to transport each set of Jumpers within a comfortable margin of surplus. The charging delay between sessions is substantial."

"What my over-educated colleague is saying," Ellen declared, "is that we do not have a lot of time once we open the portal. Like we said the other night, the first four of us go through, and then you will have to wait almost a whole day for the juice to charge again."

"Okay. Pretty important information. Anything else, Doc?" Phil inquired.

"Once the process has commenced, Dr. Tesla and I will be thoroughly occupied crafting the myriad of required adjustments between each traveler. We would covet your quiet consideration during this…*hectic* enterprise."

"In other words," Ellen clarified, "after the portal opens…do not bother those two men. At all."

Phil brought his hands together as if in an attitude of prayer and raised them to his lips. "I know that we are all excited…excited and saddened at one and the same time. Most of us took advantage of our gathering at the corner of Main and West Virginia the other night to express our final thoughts, well-wishes, and goodbyes. I would submit that if you have any additional farewells for Miss Daniels…Miss Tori…Miss Finegan…and Mrs. Swan, this would be the time. Their bus will be leaving soon."

Ellen wasted no time slipping alongside Denver and latching onto his arm. "The best thing that ever happened to you is about to slip right out of your life, soldier-boy. Forever."

"Is that so?"

She worked her way around front. "Yep. You see, Doc's not the only one that can do math. I've done a few little calculations myself."

He glanced down into her hazel eyes. "Calculations? So…what do the numbers say?"

"They all say that it is extremely unlikely that we will ever meet again, Mr. Collins. Think about it. I'm headed back to 1968. You…to 2014. If my mental abacus is functioning properly, that means that this gorgeous redhead would have to be over ninety-years-old when you hit New York." She traced a seductive finger along his chest and tapped on his chin. "Something tells me that, even though you are obviously drawn to older and more experienced women…wrinkles, dentures and orthopedic shoes won't be that much of a turn on."

"I could wait for you," he said, shrugging. "I mean, think about it…I still owe you for saving my life. It's the least I could do."

Her eyes widened. "Now that was fun. Playing doctor. You do have a nice chest."

Denver's eyes glistened as he kissed her forehead with a slight chuckle. "Goodbye, Ellen. Thank you. I will always remember you just like this. No dentures. No wrinkles. No old people's shoes. Just a beautiful and wonderful nurse. And a better friend."

Ellen couldn't resist reaching up and stealing a brief kiss. She peeled away from his face as if in slow motion. "And I will always remember that kiss. So long, Mr. Denver Wayne Collins."

"So long."

"I guess that's how Irish women say '*goodbye*'," Leah observed, watching Ellen shrink away. "They're very touchy-feely. Now, us Asians…we're a little more reserved. Usually."

"Well, Mrs. Swan," Denver said with a cordial hug. "Are you ready to do what must be done?"

The whites of her eyes transitioned to a crimson mess. "If you are," she whispered.

He nodded.

"Tori, dear?" she called out. To anyone listening, it was obvious that Leah was laboring to restrain an ocean of tears. "It's, uh, it's about time to go, sweetheart. Like we…talked about. Like we practiced yesterday. Remember?" Her voice cracked. "It's…time to go home."

Tori set her pencil down. "Okay."

Leah navigated towards the young girl, but then almost fell against a chair. Phil rushed to her side.

"Leah? *Leah?!*"

Wild eyes, drowning in tears, gazed up at him in panic. Her shoulders heaved while she attempted to speak, but only air escaped.

"What's the matter?" Phil implored. "Can you breathe? Are you alright? Are you choking?"

She eventually shook her head and eked out a string of breathy syllables. "I'm…I'm…okay."

"Strange way of showin' it," McCloud mumbled.

Ellen bumped the back of his shoulder before whispering, "She's worried about Tori. Be nice."

"Oh."

"I'm okay," Leah assured, wholly lacking conviction. She pivoted from the chair and plastered herself against Phil. "I can't do it. I can't let her…go, Phil. I can't. I can't."

His comforting arms folded around her. "Shhh…listen to me, Mrs. Swan. We talked about this. Tori was a gift…but a gift *on loan*. And now…now it's time to allow that gift to be returned."

"I can't."

"It's not our choice, Mrs. Swan. It's not your choice." Phil waited for a few thoughtful seconds. "That little girl over there has a family that loves her. That needs her. And she needs them. Just like she's needed you."

Leah pushed off and wiped her face with his sleeve. "It's so hard."

"Of course it is. Sure it is. But God chose you for this special mission. And He doesn't make mistakes. He gave you the strength to hold her. And now, He will give you the strength to let her go."

She hunched forward and rested her palms on her thighs. "I, uh, wish I could believe that."

"No. That's not the problem, Leah. You're afraid because you *do* believe it."

That seemed to hit her hard. Leah clamped her eyes shut and rocked back against the table. Phil's warm hand landed atop her shoulder. "Now, Mrs. Accounting Expert…it's time to balance the ledger. We have to reconcile the books of time. It's the right thing to do."

"I know," she whispered.

"Then come on. Tori's future and family are waiting. And so are yours."

Leah straightened up and bobbed her head.

"Dr. Stonecroft," Phil began, "it gives me great pleasure, after over ten years of waiting, to announce that it…is…*time*."

A reverent hush rippled out across The Basement.

"Indeed, Mr. Nelson. Indeed. First Mate Finegan? Would you do us the extreme honor of instigating the transfer of power that will inaugurate our temporal rift? And our cooling system?"

She feigned a hasty salute as a single tear careened down her fair cheek. "Aye, aye…Captain Stonecroft." Ellen's trembling hand reached forward and engaged the cold steel of the throttle. The unsettling reverberating hum, which had become so familiar of late, propagated in both volume and intensity.

All traces of levity vanished from Doc's face as he glanced at the clock. "So it begins."

The heavy door to the portal chamber yielded and swung open under the combined strength of both Denver and Garrett. Mesmerizing waves of dancing light streamed through the widening gap, bathing the crowd in shades of electric blue.

Martha pointed. "Simply beautiful."

Phil leaned into her ear. "Your favorite color."

"Alexus, dear," Ellen coaxed. "It's time. It's time to go home."

Leah circled around the table and drew alongside her terrified coworker undetected. "It's gonna be alright, Lexi. I'm right here with you." They clasped hands. "You won't walk alone. Let's go."

Alexus nodded and turned to face the portal chamber. Her entire body stiffened under the emotional stress, and Leah began to apply forward pressure. "Come on, you world-class reporter. It's time to go after the biggest scoop of your career, Lexi."

The girls' frozen feet finally broke their stalemate, sliding only inches at first. Leah capitalized on it. "That's it. It's just as simple as taking a step at a time, and…before you know it…you'll be walking home."

They passed beyond the threshold and Denver offered Leah a subtle thumbs-up. Alexus' foot hit the metal transom and she locked up for a moment.

"Hey now, that's just the walkway," Leah explained. "The walkway that will lead you home. It will lead us all home. Isn't that wonderful? I'm going home as well. I'll see my kids, my beautiful kids. And just kiss their faces all over. You'll see your family, too."

Alexus was silent, fixated on the pulsating portal.

They ventured a few more steps.

"Home by Christmas, that's what Doc promised you…didn't he, Lexi? What a wonderful present. Home by Christmas. And would you just look at that…the portal. It's even kinda shaped like a big, tall, blue Christmas tree. Not as pretty as the one Ellen decorated, but still, it's almost like a tree. Sorta."

The onlookers crowded into the wide expanse of the doorway to share in the wonder of the event unfolding before them. The two women cast deep and unearthly shadows across the curvature of the chamber behind them as they progressed.

"Almost home," Leah offered. "It's going to be just like walking through a…uh…a pretty blue waterfall. Except you won't even get wet! Or cold."

The swirling face of the portal loomed five feet away.

"Th-thank you," Alexus said.

Leah hugged her as they dared a few more cautious steps. "No, *thank you* for being so brave. And you are brave. And, my friend, you are almost home. Lookie there, you're close enough to just reach out and touch it."

Alexus froze.

"I'm scared."

"Of course you are," Leah consoled. "It's a new experience. Everyone gets cold feet about new experiences. But remember, Mr. Collins has already done it. And he came out just fine. And so will you. Actually…*better*. Because you'll be going home. Just like me."

Leah glanced back. It broke her heart to see that Tori had already been stationed in place, awaiting her turn beside Grandma Martha. Phil was rubbing the teen's hand and nodded with a calming smile.

"Are you ready, Lexi?" Leah called out.

"No," the girl replied. "But, I, uh, I'm going anyway."

Leah released her hand by degrees and began rubbing across her friend's back. "You're going to be fine. I wouldn't lie to you."

Alexus donned a resolute stare.

"Here I go."

"Yep, here you go."

After an encouraging move forward, Alexus whirled back and latched onto her. "Goodbye, Mrs. Swan." She eased her mouth right against Leah's right ear and whispered something.

Leah fought back another rising tide of tears. "I know. I know. Goodbye, Lexi."

The young woman slipped her arms off Leah's shoulders, pivoted around with purpose, and pressed ahead into the misty blue unknown. The surreal surface rippled around her gentle features and swallowed the anxious traveler in a concentrated burst of white light.

Lexi was gone.

Leah felt paralyzed.

A voice echoed out into the radiant compartment. "We only have about four and a half minutes remaining, Mrs. Swan."

She bit her bottom lip and trudged in an accelerating retreat along the suspended mesh plank. The sight of Tori, perched like a quintessential school girl awaiting the morning bus, shattered the veneer of her own resolve.

Leah searched the teen's expressionless gaze as she slowed to an abrupt stop. With trembling hands she straightened Tori's collar and patted along her arms.

Ellen glanced towards the control panel. "Are we ready, Doc?"

Five seconds passed before the reply rang out. "Affirmative."

Phil inched closer. "Do you want me to take her, Leah? I will."

A flat palm went up. "No. No. Uh, she's my…responsibility. My *gift*." Leah blinked hard. "Thanks."

He backed off. "I'm here if you need me."

"I…know." She slid her arm down and clutched the girl's hand. "Uh, alright, Tori. It's time…for you…to walk. Like we practiced. Remember?"

"Yes."

"Well, just…follow me." Leah brushed the tears out of her own eyes as she struggled to pin her wayward hair behind her ear. The pair moved forward.

"That's good, Tori. That's good. We are going to walk you…h-h-home. *Home.* Right through that pretty blue door over there."

"Okay."

"I'm gonna miss you."

More steps.

"Please….remember me," Leah pled.

They passed the midpoint.

"I'm gonna…remember you, Tori. I promise."

The mist-covered portal drew nearer.

Leah's heartrending voice cracked intermittently. "You, you will always be…in…my…heart."

More steps.

She halted and squeezed Tori's hand once more as her own hot tears shattered into dozens of glassy puddles on the textured walkway below. "You, uh, will have to…go on without…me, without me now."

"Okay."

After mouthing a silent plea heavenward, Leah released the girl's hand, one quivering finger at a time.

Tori stopped mechanically.

Leah's concern mounted. "You have to keep…going, Tori."

"I know."

"Then…you need to start walking again, sweetie."

Tori seemed fascinated by the colorful display for a moment then looked back. "Mrs. Swan. I love you."

Three seconds later the precious child vanished from both their time and their space.

CHAPTER 47

Sunday, December 23, 1956, 3:46 p.m.
Jump Day: One

Doc looked worried.

He rarely looked worried.

"Three minutes remain in our temporal window of opportunity," he called out, glancing through the throng off to his left. His unusually serious eyes flared red. "*Miss Finegan?* It would appear that…you must…depart, my dear."

The redhead released her grip on the power throttle and met the gaze of her closest friend and colleague.

"All the…*necessary* settings are accounted for," he said, wiping his face. "It is time…for you to partake…of the fruits of *our* labor." He broke down.

Ellen scrambled through the human obstacle course and seized him forcefully. Her delicate arms pinned his meatier ones to his side. "I will miss you…so, so much!"

"As will I…my dear, dear Ellen."

She swiveled back and forth, drenching his shoulder in tears. "You know…if you wait for me, I will be about the same age as you when you get back."

He pulled away and patted her heaving shoulders. "Then I will see you again…in less than forty-eight *hours,* Miss Finegan."

She backed towards the door as the people parted. "But it will be over forty *years* for me. Goodbye, you lovable little mathematics professor."

He breathed deeply. "I will see you soon, Nurse Finegan."

"I hope so. And thank you as well, Dr. Tesla."

Tesla glanced up. "It has been an enduring honor, ma'am."

Ellen observed a final survey of the sorrowful faces strewn about and nodded toward each. A few patted her on the back. Fewer could find the words to speak.

"*Two* minutes," Stonecroft proclaimed.

She faced the portal with chin held high. "Goodbye, my friends."

As brilliant bursts of flickering light flooded her beautiful face, Ellen brushed the wet hair out of her eyes and sauntered along the transom. Her confident stride and posture never wavered while the research assistant simply passed into the rift.

The portal yielded a powerful burst.

Phil hung his head down for a brief moment.

"I…can't believe she's…gone," Denver sighed.

Phil lowered his hand onto Denver's shoulder and looked over at Leah. "Now comes the hardest one, Mr. Collins. Are you ready?"

Denver squinted. "Not really…but it's time to send someone home."

"Ninety seconds!"

As if on cue, Leah rushed over and huddled together with Normal's very first and last Jumper.

"You can do this, Mrs. Swan," Phil encouraged. "Trust me."

Denver bit his lip. "Yeah…piece of cake. I hear the weather in Phoenix is beautiful this time of year. Mild temperatures, low humidity."

She punched him on the shoulder and wiped her face. "Come visit me and see…for…yourself."

"You bet," Denver whispered. "Thanks for being a patient teacher. You know, if it hadn't been for your expert training, I would never have known what a cranked paper shaker was. But now it's time for a dolly like you to lay a patch."

She grinned. "Thanks, Denver…for being a *complicated* student."

They herded her towards the portal walkway; Denver began dropping back. He caught Garrett's eye and gestured for him. "I may need you to help me," Denver admitted discreetly. "I have a feeling she's not gonna go through with it."

"Oh…you think she may need a little push?"

"A *big* push," Denver replied.

"Sixty seconds!"

Leah pivoted around and waved at the group while Phil retreated from her. "Goodbye. And…I…will miss you all!" she managed to call out.

"We love you, my dear," Martha responded as sporadic waves broke out.

Billy pushed to the front of the line. "Goodbye, Mrs. Swan."

Leah blew a kiss and rotated towards the portal, venturing a few hesitant steps. She stopped.

"Your children are waiting for you, Leah," Phil announced. "Time to go."

A few more steps.

Stop.

Doc got Phil's attention. "Time is becoming most critical, Mr. Nelson."

Phil cupped his hands around his mouth. "Almost there."

She trudged five more feet then halted.

"Keep going!"

Start.

Stop.

The intensity of Doc's unspoken plea was unmistakable. *"Mr. Nelson!"*

Denver looked around frantically. "Crap…she ain't gonna do it. She ain't gonna do it!" He snagged Garrett's shoulder and wrangled him forward. "Come on, Frazier. Gimme a hand. We need to run. *Now!*"

"Gladly."

The two men shoved through the tiny crowd and Garrett barreled towards her with Denver close on his heels. Frazier shot out his massive arms.

"Leah, now!" Denver yelled.

She collapsed down, plastering herself flat against the plank as Denver lowered his shoulder and plowed into the small of Garrett's back with punishing force.

Frazier's unprepared body lunged forward, crashing headlong through the seething surface of the portal. Leah dared to crack her eyelids open just as a blinding flash of light heralded the finale of Garrett's traumatic, yet involuntary journey.

Denver bounced then rolled up against her on the metal mesh. "You okay? I thought that lug might've stepped on you."

Leah struggled to push up to a sitting position and winced, massaging her bicep. "Oh, I'm fine. He caught the side of my arm. Nothing too bad. Not much could compete with the pain in my heart now, anyway."

He gestured. "Still, let me take a look at it."

"I said *I'm fine.*"

They both twitched when the fury of the broiling wormhole collapsed with an ear-splitting pop. She shot him a hard stare as the unnerving silence engulfed them.

"Plus, Mr. Collins…after that little stunt, you should probably be more worried about your own skin."

July 20, 2013

SECURITY LEVEL: TOP SECRET

FOR: Senior Staff, Project SATURN
FROM: Chief Leonard Mueller, Project SATURN
SUBJECT: Operation Caretaker Phase VIII Update

We are 90 days out from the motor vehicle accident that initiates Phase VIII. I am requesting an updated status from all departments regarding the following topics:

1. Preparation for operating room utilization at Montefiore Medical Center in the Bronx.

2. Itinerary and logistics for Dr. Cantore and his staff.

3. Latest field test results on all subcutaneous sensors, especially the human trials.

4. Current logistics for all monitoring technology (mobile, satellite, residential and occupational ground-based).

5. Accident event action plan with minute-by-minute itinerary of event, including First-Responder action plan.

I would like to have these on my desk within 48 hours.

END

DCI/PS

CHAPTER 48

Monday, December 24, 1956, 11:04 a.m.
Jump Day: Two

And then…there were four.

The enormity of both loss and promise weighed heavily upon Denver's overwhelmed thoughts. In less than twenty hours he had stood spectator, more or less, as seven of the most important people in his new life had gone.

I hope they found home.

If not, I hope they found…peace.

Leah's departure, not quite four minutes past, had proved a pill much more bitter than sweet. The two of them had barely slept since the culmination of the previous day's exodus from Normal. They had sat for hours in the upstairs conference room, licking each other's wounds as it were while bolstering their collective confidence.

Between Tori's uncertain fate and Garrett's certain indignation, their conversation never faltered, their emotion never waned. As she gushed about the captivating joy of seeing her children again, her hope-filled expectation found a kindred spirit within Denver. His desire to feel his daughter's embrace and to hear Jasmine's innocent laughter was almost debilitating at times. Somehow the experience of merely sharing that intense longing was therapeutic.

But now Leah was gone.

Along with Billy.

Followed by the Chief.

The roaring drone of the once-again activated portal made extended concentration challenging.

Doc's regular proclamations only added to the difficulty. *"The temporal rift has been properly calibrated for you, Mr. Nelson. Three minutes!"*

Denver glanced with fascination over at the man who had started this ball rolling over a decade before. "Your return flight to Colorado is now boarding, Mr. Nelson."

Phil released a sober chuckle. "Well, it sure seems that way. It's really hard to take in."

Martha Tomlin offered a final hug. "I shall never forget the day that you waltzed into that police station," she said. "And after a mild charade, you took me in and cared for me as your very own."

They pried apart. "It was just the two of us in those days," he reminisced out loud. "Just you and I." Phil hesitated. "So many memories."

"And I shall surely treasure each and every one of them. Go in peace, Mr. Nelson. May God bless you."

He kissed her on the cheek. "Goodbye, Mrs. Tomlin. And since I won't be here tomorrow…Merry Christmas."

She stepped back with tears flowing. "Merry Christmas."

Denver lowered a hand onto Phil's shoulder. "Well, it looks like you're all dressed up, and ready to go."

Phil looked down, admiring his own loosely fitting outfit while stroking the sleeves. "To tell you the truth, I like my suit better than the Chief's a few minutes ago."

It was Denver's turn to laugh. "I've been in the military, and I've seen more than my share of guys in their birthday suits. But his was…*disturbing*."

"I didn't look. And I pray that Martha didn't."

Denver grimaced. "I did, by accident."

Phil smiled. "As Doc said, '*naked he came, and naked he shall return.*'"

"Instead of goggles," Denver lamented, "I should've handed out blindfolds. Wow. There are just some things you can't *un*see. I won't be forgetting it anytime soon."

Phil ventured towards the portal chamber. "Well, Mr. Collins…I hope you won't forget *me* anytime soon."

"Notta chance."

They shook hands.

Phil leaned to the side and raised his voice. "I will say it one more time. Goodbye, Dr. Glen Stonecroft. And Dr. Tesla. On behalf of all of us…I thank you."

Doc peeled off his spectacles which seemed to release a river of tears. "Godspeed, Mr. Nelson. May He grant us a speedy reunion on the other side."

Tesla ambled forward, leaning on his cane. "It is fitting, I suppose, that my research brought you here. And now, our research will return you home."

Phil nodded. "We are forever in your debt. I wish I could give you more than just my thanks."

"Your gratitude is a gift…a gift of high caliber, Mr. Nelson," Dr. Tesla replied.

Something triggered inside Denver as Phil rounded the portal chamber doorway.

Gift?

Gift.

Give him his gift, Collins!

Doc slipped his glasses back on. "*Only one minute!*"

Denver sprang towards the table. "*Wait! Phil!* I almost forgot."

The dancing blue rays rimmed Phil's left side with a dazzling display as he turned back. "Wait? Why?"

Denver clutched a small satchel and rushed up to him. "It's a gift. A Christmas eve present."

Phil extended his arm and accepted the curious package with visible trepidation. "Um…thank you, Mr. Collins."

"Oh, no, no, no. Don't thank me. Actually, it's from *you*."

"Me? What?"

Denver urged him towards the walkway with increasing pressure. "Let's just say it's a nice little read for your trip home." He led him midway along the transom. "Thanks for everything. Now go."

Phil broke out in a heartwarming grin. "Goodbye, Mr. Collins."

"Until we meet again, sir."

Phil tucked the package under his right arm and strolled at a steady pace into the very heart of the turbulent temporal rift. Denver swung around after the burst of light and fought hard to suppress a sad but satisfied smile.

Enjoy the read, Phil…it was your journal, anyway.

CHAPTER 49

Monday, December 24, 1956, 2:12 p.m.
Jump Day: Two

Small fires had always captivated him.

The sensory buffet of rich colors, crackling branches, and comforting heat, all suffused with a smoky aroma that both assaulted the eyes and delighted the nose was a lifelong guilty pleasure.

Denver's father had raised him to appreciate the survival value of a campfire, but fifteen years later, Uncle Sam had sought to obliterate that unintentionally dangerous civilian mindset. Set against the velvet darkness of the Middle Eastern desert, even the harmless burn of a single smoldering cigarette could cost the lives of an entire unit of soldiers or nullify the element of surprise.

Denver tossed another shirt onto the confined blaze in the gravel lot behind Nelson Manufacturing.

But this wasn't Afghanistan.

And nightfall was at least three hours away.

And four hours until Christmas Eve dinner at Martha's.

He studied the rising flames, and stepped aside as the shifting December breeze sought to choke him with a thickening column of black smoke.

It's not a campfire, he mused.

It's more like a funeral pyre.

And it's all gotta go.

It was his last formal assignment by the remaining powers that be. Doc Stonecroft had admonished Denver to clear out and incinerate all of the leftover items from the Vault down in The Basement. Two large loads of clothing, shoes, and personal effects made the long trek from times yet unknown to a backyard burn pile on Christmas Eve of 1956.

"It is imperative, Mr. Collins, that we leave not a single trace behind. We must honor the First Accord."

Not a single trace, Denver thought. *That's impossible.*

His eyes tracked the intermittent embers and wafting ash that piggybacked upon the hot streams of smoke dissipating into the sky above him. It seemed almost poetic that charred fragments from the distant future were being intermingled with the air, water and soil of the soon-to-be distant past.

He chucked a pair of shoes into the inferno.

Big shoes.

They had belonged to Shep.

He couldn't help but picture three hastily dug graves out on the back fringes of the farm owned by Hank Bodenschatz. Denver's own hands had helped excavate two of them.

We're leaving a whole lot more than traces, Doc.

We're leaving people.

We're leaving our friends behind.

Everything about it offended his soldier's training and sensitivities.

Denver extracted a flimsy cardboard shoebox from his bag, then cast aside the tattered lid. A handful of Polaroids beside a portable tape player seemed poised as if to challenge him. He selected one with trembling fingers.

Betty.

Denver knelt, lowering the photograph down to the fire. The whole scenario seemed a sacrilege. In effect, he felt as if he was destroying the evidence of the life of a woman who had dedicated her life to discovering evidence. The tragic irony gave him pause.

Forgive me, Betty.

One by one, the white-bordered images smoked, then discolored, before blistering into brief, fiery bursts. He clamped his stinging eyes shut for a respectful moment, and then dumped the remaining articles into the heart of the blaze.

In his tortured mind's eye, he once again envisioned his lost photo of Jasmine. He couldn't begin to tolerate the thought of someone discarding that precious memento into the destructive ravages of a fire.

I love you, sweetie.

Daddy'll be home tomorrow.

On Christmas. Christmas in June.

Denver did his best to snap back to the mission at hand.

Okay, Collins…one more small bag.

He lifted the flap and peered inside.

Oh, yeah.

Wow.

The items we stole from Betty's safe.

Forgot about these little beauties.

He drew out the flip phone.

Yeah, you guys almost cost me a bit of brain damage.

Who knows…maybe you did.

I'm pretty sure I've still got a dent in my forehead, at any rate.

Denver returned the phone and retrieved a crumpled piece of paper.

Well, hello there, Mr. Five-Dollar Bill.

He pulled it closer for examination.

Yep. 2013. Torn corner.

This baby's mine.

He could still imagine the shocked face of the waitress on his eventful, first full day in town. Denver smiled wide and shoved the cash into his pocket before pitching the bag onto the fire.

Well, Waitress Katie…now that I've got my money back, maybe I'm not such a big tipper after all.

October 21, 2013

SECURITY LEVEL: TOP SECRET

FOR: Chief Leonard Mueller, Project SATURN
FROM: Wanda Trousdale, Phase VIII Coordinator
SUBJECT: Caretaker Phase VIII Update

The first 24-hours following the initiation of Phase VIII have been an unqualified success. The motor vehicle accident occurring on 20 October in New York City involving Denver Wayne Collins unfolded deliberately and precisely according to our action plan.

Dr. Cantore reports that the 12-hour procedure to implant all subcutaneous sensors "could not have gone better."

Dr. Cantore estimates that Mr. Collins will be released from Montefiore within three days.

All monitoring stations in and around Montefiore Medical Center are receiving data within acceptable tolerances. All monitoring stations within the immediate vicinity of Mr. Collins' apartment on 77th Street and place of employment are prepared to receive data.

His wallet has been confiscated and the lining will be imprinted with the necessary information by 22 October. Initial comparison of his current wallet with the wallet obtained in August 1956 reveals that they are identical with the exception of the interior items, including paper money, receipts, photos, and cards.

END

DCI/PS

CHAPTER 50

Tuesday, December 25, 1956, 8:14 a.m.
Jump Day: Three

Denver was fairly certain he wasn't anywhere near the latitude or longitude of the North Pole, but Doc Stonecroft had fashioned himself into a makeshift Santa Claus.

Of sorts.

"A very good morning to you, Mr. Collins," he offered warmly. "And can I be the first to wish you a Merry Christmas! Your first and *only* Christmas in Normal, I hope."

Denver finished bounding down the last few steps and yawned. "And Merry Christmas to you, Doc. And for the record…I like the little red hat. Will we be riding home today behind a team of eight tiny reindeer?"

Doc blushed and gestured towards his scalp. "A relic from several years of a tradition instituted by Miss Festive Finegan. She threatened to hasten from the future if I failed to don it for the last time this year."

"Where's your Chief Elf and Tinkerer?"

"Pardon?"

"Dr. Tesla," Denver explained with a smile.

"Oh, yes, yes, of course. The good doctor is performing a final inspection of the magnets and cooling system."

Denver strolled over to the table and sat down. "Is there a problem?"

"Not at all, my friend. A routine inspection."

Denver leaned his elbows onto the table and lowered his voice. "So tell me, Doc. What's he going to do? You know, once we jump ship? Is he gonna move in with Martha or what? I'm sure there's no way he can return to the Sandbox place."

Doc slid a chair closer and sank into it. "My dear Mr. Collins, you need not worry about the future of a world-renowned scientist such as Dr. Tesla."

"Well, I'm not really worried about his future. Just...*curious*, I guess." Denver paused, collecting his thoughts. "His, uh, his knowledge of us and the portal and all kind of tramples all over both the spirit and the letter of the First Accord."

Doc lifted his holiday hat and draped it against the base of the small, tabletop Christmas tree. "I can assure you that his plans and purposes are in strict alignment with both the First Accord and sound scientific principles. Trust me."

Denver toyed with a few of the ornaments on the tree. "Well, if I can't trust the word of Dr. Glen Stonecroft, then who can I trust?"

"Did you rest well?"

"Hardly a wink," Denver admitted. "Too excited, I guess. Kept thinking about seeing my daughter. You?"

"Like a baby," Doc beamed. "Of course, I am confident that the scrumptious holiday fare prepared by Mrs. Tomlin last evening contributed to my refreshing slumber."

"She really did outdo herself. Wow."

"Unfortunately in more ways than one," Doc said.

"What do you mean?"

He removed his glasses and pinched the bridge of his nose. "I have already spoken with her by phone this morning. She informed me that she felt positively dreadful. I am afraid that the emotional strain of recent events has taken a toll on her physical health."

Denver sank back against his seat. "Sorry to hear that. But I'm glad that the four of us got to have a nice Christmas Eve meal together. She seemed to really enjoy visiting with Dr. Tesla." He dropped his voice again. "So, tell me, what was the deal with those gloves last night?"

"Are you referring to Dr. Tesla's *white* gloves?"

Denver nodded.

"Well, Mr. Collins, our Serbian scientist has a number of…*eccentricities*. For reasons unknown, he always elects to wear white gloves during formal meals and engagements."

"Interesting."

Doc scanned the area behind him and then arched forward. "I had to exhort Mrs. Tomlin to conceal her jewelry, especially any and all adornments which may appear to be pearls. Even as inconsequential as decorations gilding her Christmas tree."

Denver appeared stunned. "Umm…*why?*"

Doc answered in hushed tones. "An additional eccentricity."

"Hates pearls, huh? And I noticed that he didn't eat any meat last night at Grandma Martha's. Vegetarian?"

Doc polished his spectacles on the soft fur of the Santa's cap, nodding silently.

"So, he hates meat and he hates pearls. Well, everybody hates something. For me it's spiders. To each his own. But, regardless of his *eccentricities*…it must be working for him. I mean, you guys have only been together for less than a few weeks and you've solved the mysteries of time or whatever."

"He can remain on task, Mr. Collins, for eighteen to twenty hours per day. Every day. Some days…a complete and total absence of normal rest."

"So a white-gloved vegetarian who requires little to no sleep and hates pearls. Neat mix."

Doc slid his glasses back on and then adjusted them while studying Denver's shoulder. "I say, Mr. Collins, did you encounter a nasty tumble during an athletic workout this morning?"

"Athletic tumble?"

Doc motioned. "Your attire. It appears to be stained."

Denver glanced down at his hoodie. "Oh, *that*. No, these are the clothes I was wearing when I jumped here back in August. It was only four months ago…but it seems like a lifetime away." He laughed. "Actually this hoodie is from New York in 2014. But the dirt is vintage. From the wheat fields of Normal. 1956."

Doc chuckled and slapped the table. "Ah, yes. A good year. A very good year, indeed."

"I will probably have this hoodie mounted in a glass frame or something when I get home, like a famous sports jersey," Denver commented. "Every time I look at it I will remember a musty motel in the middle of nowhere, a keystone cop, and a tranquilizer dart."

"No doubt we will all have an impressive collection of stories to recount, but alas, precious few people to share them with. If any."

Denver nodded as he slid the Santa's cap over his hair. "And if we did tell anyone our stories, they would probably lock us up in a place like they did with Phil Nelson. And then throw away the key."

"Perhaps it is far better to hold a truth contained, than to subsist as a person restrained."

Denver squinted and the cotton-ball tip of the unstable red hat fell forward, slapping his forehead. "Is that a line from a poem? Don't tell me you just made that up. Like right here. Right now. On the spot. Did you?"

"A true poet, Trailer Collins, never reveals his sources of inspiration…for they are the hidden wellsprings of his success."' Doc winked.

Denver waved his hand and flipped the hat back onto the table. "You're impossible. But I like you. I do like you."

"All jesting aside, my dear friend, I have been sifting through my collection of rhymes, seeking a most fitting verse to encapsulate our experience."

Denver stretched. "Any luck?"

Doc raised his eyebrows. "Lord Tennyson perhaps, with some modification." His round face waxed serious as he concentrated into the distance.

"'When can their glory fade?
O the wild charge they made!
Honour the charge they made!
Honour the Light Brigade.'"

Denver's head bobbed. "Not bad. I see your, uh, connection there. The Light Brigade. Kinda like us rushing into the portal of light?"

"Spot on! Precisely."

"They are spot on, and they are precise," Dr. Tesla announced while meandering back into the control area. "At least, that is the current condition of both the magnets and the liquid nitrogen cooling apparatus." He glanced up. "Oh, good morning, Mr. Collins. I thought I heard voices. At my age, you pray they are not merely in your head."

Denver rose out of his chair. "Good morning, sir. And Merry Christmas."

"Merry Christmas." Tesla ambled up to the table and rested one hand upon it. "Is the famous fugitive and criminal, Mr. Denver Wayne Collins, prepared to follow the light this morning?"

Denver sat down. "I've done it twice before. So I guess, third time's charm. And no offense, Dr. Tesla…but I hope that we *don't* have to meet again."

They both laughed.

Doc folded his hands on the table. "The parallel is striking."

Denver shot him a quick glance. "The what is what?"

"In the spirit of the holiday season, I was contemplating the similarities between our plight, and that of the first Christmas, two millennia ago."

Denver inched closer in his seat. "This I gotta hear."

"The scripture records that the Magi, the wise men if you will, were led by a brilliant source of light that transported them, after a fashion, to a particular place at a particular point in time. To find the Savior."

"I think I see where you're going," Denver replied. "And so now, on this Christmas Day, we are being transported by a portal of light to a particular place at a particular point in time."

"A most striking, if not altogether complete, parallel."

"Well, there are *three* of us," Denver noted. "But I don't think there's any chance I could be called a *wise man* by any stretch of the imagination. Plus, only two of us are gonna be traveling today, so it would be one wise man and one…*average* intelligence guy in a dirty hoodie."

Doc concentrated on Tesla for a moment and then returned his gaze back at Denver. He pushed out of his seat. "Enough talk of such things." Stonecroft strolled over and shot out his hand. "Before we part ways and times, Mr. Collins, I would like to, once again, express my warmest appreciation. I have tremendous respect for the great and perilous lengths you have been willing to be subjected to for the greater good of our little community of temporally displaced persons. We all owe you many profound debts, Trailer Collins."

Denver blushed as he rose up and returned the gesture. "I think you have it all backwards, Dr. Glen Stonecroft. This room would be filled to the brim with a bunch of hopeless, stranded people if it hadn't been for your dedication and hard work. And you, too, Dr. Tesla."

A stubby finger wagged above the table at Denver. "The inability to graciously receive an honest compliment could be considered a serious character flaw, Mr. Collins. Once returning to New York, you may want to consider seeking professional help to overcome that defect." Doc smiled broadly.

Denver shrugged. "I will if you will."

"Touché."

"Thanks again, Dr. Tesla."

"Your need has fulfilled my dream," Tesla replied. "So thank you, Mr. Collins."

Denver sauntered to the control panel. "So, is the, uh, self-destruct thing or whatever all ready to go?"

Stonecroft joined him. "Our *Disablement Protocol* has been tested and is in perfect working condition." He pointed at a small red switch recently installed near the top edge of the console. "Once this timer is activated, the portal will be rendered irrevocably damaged not less than five minutes later."

Denver nodded towards the reactor room door. "And the atomic stuff in there?"

Doc folded his arms. "The nuclear fuel rods have already been inserted into our lead-lined concrete storage system, Mr. Collins. Once we activate the temporal rift and depart, the capacitors will exhaust their entire supply of stored energy. As they say, it will be *lights out* for The Basement. Permanently."

"What was the final decision about the property? After we leave?"

Doc yanked off his glasses. "I know Mr. Nelson had a lengthy discussion with both Mrs. Tomlin and Miss Finegan regarding that very issue. I believe Martha Tomlin was going to stipulate in her last will and testament that the property will default to Ellen Finegan in 1968." He paused. "I am sorry, I was not privy to the—"

"What was that?!" Denver pushed away from the control panel. "Did you hear that?"

"Hear what, Mr. Collins?"

He raised a finger and whispered. "*Upstairs.*"

Doc and Tesla both shook their heads while maintaining silence.

"I'll be back." Denver kicked off his shoes and sprinted up the dark stairwell. His pace slowed as he reached the top and peered through both open doorways, studying what little of the factory interior he could see. With the utmost caution, he hugged the right wall and worked his way to the second doorway leading out onto the manufacturing floor. Denver paused for several seconds with his back against the wall, listening for any sound.

His head peeked around the door jamb as he performed a cursory scan of the facility. Other than the occasional rattle of a few roofing trusses, the situation appeared to be normal. Denver retreated, closing both doors with great care before descending back to The Basement.

The researchers were awaiting his return at the foot of the steps. "Was all quiet on the Western Front?" Doc inquired in his best library voice.

Denver plopped down on the last stair to slip his shoes on. "*'Not a creature was stirring, not even a mouse'*."

Stonecroft grinned and patted him on the shoulder. "A little 19th Century Christmas poetry from C. C. Moore. Well done, Mr. Collins!"

"I've learned from the best." Denver rose up and took a deep breath. "Let's do this."

"All settings arising from your TRS sample have been properly calibrated," Doc announced above the rumbling din of the activated portal. "Whenever you are ready, my friend. And my fellow New Yorker."

"Thanks again, Doc," Denver offered as he shut and locked the lower door to The Basement. He strolled into position within the threshold to the chamber. "Come see me sometime."

"If the Lord grants me another decade of physical life, I will be at the door of your apartment on 77th Street the very morning after your return."

"Now remember this date…Monday, June 16th." Denver winked. "I'll take the day off from work. Introduce you to Jasmine."

"I can feel that delightful bundle in my arms already."

Denver smiled. "Me too."

Tesla saluted. "Safe passage, Mr. Collins."

Denver returned the encouraging gesture. "Hey, Doc…do I have to walk?"

Stonecroft frowned and leaned back. "Excuse me?"

Denver's arms shot up as he shrugged. "I said, do I have to *walk*?"

"Your relative velocity, Mr. Collins, is inconsequential to the success of the temporal displacement process."

"I'll take that as a long *yes*," he replied, backing up as far as possible into the control room. Denver dropped down as if into the starting blocks on a professional track. He extended his hands out onto the smooth concrete on either side. "Goodbye, my friends!"

"Oh, my!" Doc exclaimed.

Denver rocked a few times before accelerating forward in a burst of excited energy. His sprinting feet hit the metal transom and gained speed with four more lengthening strides. He bent down for a brief instant before launching into the air, his arms stretching out ahead of his hurtling form. Denver dove into the center of the portal's swirling blue turbulence as the mist swallowed him in a terrific flash.

Doc and Tesla attempted to scramble over to the doorway.

They gawked in momentary silence.

"Well," Stonecroft said. "Denver Wayne Collins has left the building. And the century. And even the millennium."

Tesla put a hand on his shoulder. "Come. Now it is time to prepare for the final departure."

Doc removed his spectacles and brushed away a few tears collecting on the bags beneath his reddening eyes. "Yes. Yes, of course."

"Will you be at all sad to leave this subterranean laboratory, Dr. Stonecroft?"

Doc arrived at the console and busied himself. "A most curious question, Dr. Tesla. Most curious, indeed." He surveyed the room. "What began as a cement prison has transformed into our only means of actual liberation."

"Truth is often stranger than fiction," Tesla noted.

Doc grinned while adjusting several dials. "Ah…*Don Juan* by Lord Byron. More poetic references."

Tesla looked back towards the table. "Did you finish packing all the paperwork? And your research journal?"

Doc pointed. "It is all in the briefcase at the end of the cabinet here."

"Very well. I have completed my calibration."

Doc made a set of final tweaks. "As have I, my friend."

They glanced at each other before rechecking a host of settings.

"Everything appears to be in proper order, Dr. Tesla."

"I concur."

Doc shed his lab coat. "Well, my esteemed colleague…this is it."

Tesla waved his cane. "It is a shame that the annals of scientific discovery may never be privy to all that has been accomplished here."

Doc snagged the briefcase and migrated towards the portal chamber. "No. But the glory of a feat is not diminished by a lack in its recognition." He paused. "Tell me, Doctor…if the entire world knew of the splendor of our accomplishment, would it add even one further ounce of joy to your heart at this thrilling moment?"

Tesla stared up at the low ceiling for a fast second, then locked eyes with him. "Not at all, Dr. Stonecroft. Not at all."

"Indeed."

Tesla motioned at the far end of the metal ramp. "Your future awaits."

Together they began a slow plod towards the captivating fury of the flickering rift. Doc patted him on the back. "Correction, Dr. Tesla. *Our* future awaits."

"Are you certain that I will not be a burden?"

Doc laughed. "Let me repeat, once again, what I have assured you of from the very beginning. Not one soul is more deserving to reap the fruits of their temporal labors than you, my friend. I have a spare bedroom that only serves to collect dust. I would be honored."

They slowed to a full stop within arm's length of the raging blue surface of the rift.

Tesla's gaunt face wrinkled even further. "You are positive?"

Doc bowed and gestured. "After you."

A few seconds later…the portal flashed.

Twice.

Not quite twenty feet away, a silent hand slid along the complicated control console and landed upon a small red switch at the top.

She flicked it off before rubbing her ring.

It was a gift from her mother.

The End of Book Four: Crossover

EPILOG: ONE

Denver had to resist the temptation to pinch himself on no less than three occasions during the last half hour alone. The first surreal sensation overtook him when he had just lowered Jasmine down onto the shiny black rubber of the park swing. Seconds later her infectious giggling distracted the proud and thankful father and the overwhelming urge dissipated.

As he retreated to a newly painted park bench at the edge of the smooth pea gravel, a quick checkup phone call from Jennifer had aroused similar feelings. The call was tense and efficient, but cordial. An irrepressible smile broke out as he told her that he loved her.

He waited.

There was no reciprocation, at least nothing audible.

He hung up, reminding himself that he was unaffected, and stared at his ecstatic daughter. One of the two most important women in his life loved him unconditionally.

Now I've got the time to work on the other, he thought.

An unfamiliar voice interrupted his relationship musings. "A beautiful day to be at the park."

A surprised Denver shot his head to the left as an elderly gentleman sporting a charcoal gray suit complemented with a black cane hobbled up to the bench. He seemed to have materialized out of nowhere.

"Yes it is," Denver agreed. "Yes it is. And a great day to be alive."

The man gestured with his cane. "Is the remainder of this seat taken?"

Denver smiled broadly and motioned. "Be my guest."

It was a rather slow process, but the visitor finally backed up and settled onto the bench. "Looks like that precious little girl is having a wonderful time."

Denver nodded. "Oh yeah. She *loves* swings. Maybe more than she loves me."

They both chuckled.

Denver straightened up and angled towards the man. "I've been away for a while. On a…*trip*. To Illinois. Today's park adventure is just making up for lost time."

"Kids are so resilient," the man offered. "And I have a theory about why that is so. But us…we adults, we seem to be the ones who have the hardest time with separation anxiety."

Denver stared down into his lap. "Yeah. Yeah, it was tough. Very tough. Hardest thing I've ever done. Glad to be home."

The man swung his cane out towards the play area in a few wide arcs. "Jasmine certainly is a beautiful child."

It was a harmless comment, and one that Denver had heard no less than a hundred times from friends and family.

But this elderly visitor was *neither*.

"Excuse me," Denver started, "do we know each other?"

With some effort, the stranger pivoted towards him. "Well, Mr. Collins, I would say that we have had a rather one-sided relationship." They locked eyes. "I know of you, and I know your lovely wife Jennifer, and that six-year-old cutie over there."

A thousand questions and reservations crowded into Denver's mind and his blood pressure spiked. "But how can you—"

The new arrival silenced him with a sudden wave of his hand. "I'm sorry, but there isn't time to explain who I am, and why I have such an—*unusual*—level of knowledge of your life, and your family's, Mr. Collins. But, I wanted to finally meet you, and Director Mueller gave me the green light."

He stretched out his wrinkled hand and grinned. Denver returned the gesture, but his skeptical courtesy was laced with trepidation.

The man continued, "After spending years watching your life with great interest, I had to finally meet the world's most important man. And now…I have." The gentleman raised his eyebrows and leaned on his cane. "I'm not getting any younger, and at my age every moment is bonus time."

"You can't expect me to not be a little concerned here, Mr—?"

"Let's just not worry about my name or my job, Mr. Collins. I wanted to come and personally thank you for…well…giving my life *real purpose.* And that's a pretty big compliment. I used to guard the life of the President, you know." The man tried to conceal his laughter. "But you've affected not just my life, but the lives of dozens and even hundreds of people at times. Especially of late. And perhaps millions in the future. Or billions."

Denver threw his head from side to side, scanning the area for any other inexplicable, out-of-place people.

What did he say? Millions and billions of people? What?!

He glanced back at Jasmine. She appeared blissfully unaware of the unsettling conversation transpiring fifteen feet away.

"Is that all you want from me?" Denver inquired. "Just a few words and a handshake? That's it?"

The gentleman leaned forward and pushed on his cane. "It's all that I needed, Mr. Collins. Our technicians have already received what they required." The old man was on his feet after a few moments straining. "And now, I must be on my way. It has been an honor."

The roar of a starting engine echoed out from the parking lot directly behind the bench. Denver glanced over his shoulder as two men exited a black SUV and guarded an open door to an empty backseat. In silent confusion Denver studied the mysterious visitor as he ambled away across the manicured grass. He started to turn around to check on Jasmine when something small caught his eye across the bench. He grabbed the oddly familiar item and sprang up.

"Excuse me, sir!" Denver called out while navigating around the bench. "Excuse me. You dropped this, sir."

The well-dressed gentleman halted and gazed back with a contented smile.

"Keep it, Mr. Collins. It was your wallet anyway."

EPILOG: TWO

Perched beneath the expansive overhang, the pair of Marines decked out in dress blues stood in stark contrast to the building's bright façade. The sentry on the left nodded as his counterpart executed a well-rehearsed motion and opened the glass panel door for the visitors.

An elderly gentleman leaned upon his cane and surveyed the interior of the structure with nostalgic satisfaction.

Sixty-six years, he thought. *It's been a lifetime. Yet it seems like yesterday.*

"Right this way, Mr. Schaeffer," a second, much younger man offered, gesturing subtly towards the far end of the exquisite foyer. The white-gloved Marine sealed the door behind them without a sound.

"May I remind you, Director Mueller, that I have walked these hallowed halls and studied every square-inch of this vital real estate a hundred times over. And then some."

The Director smiled and continued into the next chamber. "Not since Truman, I believe."

"I know my way around the White House," Schaeffer retorted.

"I doubt it. Make a left. I think Nixon remodeled the West Wing Lobby in the early 70s."

Mueller was right.

Schaeffer hated to admit it.

"I will get there," he called out, somewhat annoyed. "Just not as fast as you."

The pair continued down a modest hall and made a hard right through the door at the next junction. Another sentry stationed beside a wide doorway halted their progress. The delay allowed Schaeffer time to saunter up to Mueller and the two colleagues exchanged silent glances. They didn't wait long.

The door swung wide as a female aide stepped out and motioned. "Good morning, gentlemen. He will see you now."

Mueller spoke for them both. "Thank you, ma'am. After you, Mr. Schaeffer."

They disappeared into the room and the guard closed the door. Neal paused and inspected the furnishings and décor of the most famous office in the world. He couldn't help but notice the alternating tan and beige stripes adorning the walls.

That's new.

He studied the enormous taupe rug, trying his best to read some of the quotations woven into the white border.

And that.

Mueller cleared his throat. "Good morning, Mr. President."

Obama rose from his desk and navigated around it. He smiled broadly. "Director Mueller." They shook hands. The President rotated to his left, reaching out. "And former Director Schaeffer."

"It's a pleasure and an honor, Mr. President."

"I've heard so much about you. Your service and career are legendary. At least, to those of us who are privy to those types of legends."

Neal smiled and nodded. "Fame is the first casualty of secrecy, Mr. President. By design. And by necessity."

Obama settled onto a couch and gestured for them to sit as well. They sank into an identical furnishing just across a dark brown coffee table.

"Thank you for making time for this briefing, Mr. President," Mueller began. "I fear no sense of exaggeration when I tell you that it will probably be the most important conversation that has ever occurred in the Oval Office."

Obama's eyebrows shot up. He hesitated before responding. "Strategies that have ended world wars were debated in this very office, Director Mueller. And Kennedy made decisions that prevented a nuclear exchange with the Soviets from just about where you are sitting." He leaned forward with a cynical glance. "Care to reassess your last statement?"

Mueller shook his head as he laid a briefcase on the coffee table. "Not in the slightest. With all due respect, sir, what we are about to reveal will seem like a fairy tale, like science fiction. I am still having trouble accepting it myself."

The President brought his hand to his chin and laid a single finger across his lips. "You have my full attention."

Schaeffer took the lead. "Fifty-eight years ago, President Eisenhower authorized the implementation of the most ambitious and far-reaching initiative in the history of American intelligence." He paused. "Operation *Caretaker*."

"I don't recall having been briefed on this particular program, gentlemen."

"Only three past Presidents have, sir," Neal clarified. "Eisenhower, Reagan, and Bush. Bush *forty-three*."

Obama crossed his legs. "And what circumstances qualify me to be the fourth?"

Mueller took over. "Because Operation Caretaker has officially concluded its six decades of research on your watch, sir."

Obama was obviously studying both of their faces. "A...*successful* conclusion, gentlemen?"

"Unimaginably so, Mr. President," Mueller replied. "The results of this initiative are what brings us together today."

"In 1956, the late Director Ross and I gained access to a wallet that had been lost by a very special individual," Neal said. "A time traveler, Mr. President."

"A *time traveler*?"

"Yes, sir. From 2014."

"A person traveled from this year—*now*—back to 1956?"

"That is correct. His name is Denver Wayne Collins."

Obama was stoic, no doubt punctuating his skepticism with a loud exhale. "Gentlemen, this is starting to sound a lot more like fiction, and a lot less like science."

Neal slid the briefcase closer to himself and popped the latches. He withdrew a large black and white photograph and dangled it from his fingertips. "This is a photograph of Denver Wayne Collins. Taken in November of 1956. In a holding cell at Area 51. Before he escaped on that very same night."

Obama hunched forward and slowly retrieved the aged picture. Neal selected another print from the briefcase. "And this," he slid it across the table. "This is *another* photo of Mr. Collins."

The President picked it up and compared them side by side.

Neal sought to suppress his grin. "The second photo...was taken just over a week ago." Obama glanced up at him. "In New York, Mr. President."

"You are saying that this—*this*—is the same man. Except that these were taken about sixty years apart?"

Neal nodded.

Obama noticed something. "What's this gash on his forehead?"

"Let's just say that it took a little bit of aggressive behavior to convince him to stay at Area 51." Neal fished out two more prints and handed them to Obama, then tapped on one of them. "This is a photograph that we found in Mr.

Collins' clothing back in 1956. The other was taken not quite seventy-two hours ago. In a park near Brooklyn. Her name is Jasmine. She is a spunky six-year-old."

"His daughter?"

"Yes, sir," Mueller answered. "An only child."

The President continued to study the evidence. "It's difficult to wrap one's mind around it all."

"I can assure you it is true, and has been verified," Mueller added. "As you know, both the CIA and the Pentagon have sought to achieve temporal displacement. Project SATURN and the Sandbox are testaments to that valuable and elusive goal."

"I believe that the Sandbox program was dismantled in the late 50s," Obama countered.

Neal interrupted. "Mr. President, Operation Caretaker took a more patient and proven path. With the certain knowledge that a jump in time was going to actually occur, most likely in 2014, and with the exact identity of the time traveler also perfectly known, Caretaker sought to exploit those facts."

The President lowered the photos to the couch before folding his arms. "You've been waiting since 1956 to see if your predictions were correct? That's a hell of a wait, boys."

Schaeffer raised his own eyebrows and tapped his hand atop his cane. "In our defense, I did mention we were patient. But we weren't just waiting. Once Denver Collins was born, we spent over thirty years guiding his life, shepherding his path and choices, until the all-important occasion of his mysterious jump back in time. And his return."

Obama seemed interested. "I imagine that this was all done without his knowledge or consent? Or did he sign up for this?"

Both visitors glanced at each other. Mueller spoke up. "He did not know, Mr. President. But it was necessary. It was justified."

The President pressed for more. "And why did we have to manipulate his choices and so forth? I assume he is an American citizen?"

Mueller nodded. "He is. This intrusive manipulation, Mr. President, was necessary due to the fact that his jump in time could or would alter the future. Just his presence in the past potentially modified the future. To guarantee the highest probability that this one man's life would be the same again, we had to control his choices and even global events. We needed to ensure that his life in the present matched the wallet we found in 1956. So that we could monitor Denver Wayne Collins…the only verifiable time traveler."

"Which global events?"

"It's all very complicated," Neal replied, avoiding the question. "But, Mr. President, the result of Operation Caretaker has been an unqualified success. Under the illusion of a car accident, our surgeons implanted dozens of sensors within Mr. Collins' body. His apartment, vehicle, and even his office at work were rigged with a staggering array of sensors and scanners. Over the last several months, his every move, his every action has been monitored, tracked…studied. We've utilized satellites, trucks, human intel, everything."

Obama rested his hands on his knee. "And what did we get in exchange for this ultimate violation of human privacy?"

Mueller's eyes brightened. "We got everything, sir."

"Define *everything*."

Neal struggled to sit up and carefully deposited his cane on the coffee table. "We captured the data from the moment of his jump. And return." Neal's eyes glistened as a subtle smile worked its way across a face wrinkled by the passage of time.

"And now, Mr. President…we can repeat it."

EPILOG: THREE

Sunday, June 29, 2014, 1:19 p.m.
Corner of Main and West Virginia
Normal, Illinois

Thirteen hours of driving west had been split unevenly across two apprehensive days. He tried to pawn off his exhaustion as road fatigue, but the shallow attempt at personal deception caved to reality.

Denver was nervous.

In his defense, the mesmerizing and (at times) blinding rain storm he had endured since Fort Wayne hadn't helped matters to any great degree. Scenarios careened through his idle driver's mind in a maddening mix of excitement and anxiety.

What was it gonna be like?

Would it be like before?

He made a right at the final light and sloshed through the curb runoff as he eased into the parking lot. It was the right address…it appeared to be the wrong building.

Monical's Pizza?

Denver grabbed his new iPhone and double-checked the location while he rolled to a stop. *1219 South Main Street.* His eyes continued to deny what GPS had just confirmed.

Steak 'n Shake is now a pizza joint?

He raised the gear shift into park and killed the motor with a reverse flick of his key. As the wipers ended their final dance across his windshield, he was engulfed in silence for the first time in several hours. Denver arched forward and rested against the steering wheel as he slid his sweaty palms across his jeans. He strained to peer past his own rain-splattered window in a bid to identify the patrons milling about inside the pizza parlor. The glare of the overcast across the expansive glass of the restaurant made it difficult to see anything, let alone anyone.

He glanced down at his phone.

1:22 p.m.

Alright. Let's do this, Collins.

He snagged his keys along with his phone and jogged across the lot through the pelting downpour. A young family pushed through the front entrance as he held it open for them and nodded while they exited. His pulse raced and he couldn't seem to catch a steady breath.

Get inside, Collins.

Only the most basic layout of the structure struck him as the least bit recognizable, the remainder was wholly unfamiliar ground. He ventured a few cautious steps inside.

This is so strange. I just ate here a few weeks ago!

But, of course, he was right and he was wrong.

It hadn't been a few weeks.

Denver Wayne Collins hadn't walked these floors in nearly sixty years. He closed his eyes for a brief moment and remembered the surviving handful of Jumpers who had assembled here for a final round of milkshakes just before their bittersweet departure.

But that was back in 1956.

A baby cried two tables to his left and it snapped Denver out of his recollection. He scanned the few dozen disinterested faces scattered about. The sudden realization that not a single soul in sight was aware of this surreal moment in history was a terrible burden. He denied himself the luxury of mulling that painful thought over too many times.

If they only knew…

He tried his best to step aside in the narrow aisle as a pitiful figure in a wheelchair attempted to roll by. The elderly man was missing all of his hair and one of his legs. Denver made reluctant eye contact and nodded politely in an awkward exchange.

The man stopped rolling abruptly. "Well, it's about time you showed up."

Denver shot him a double-take.

That voice…

"Didn't figure you'd recognize me," the man lamented. "Without my red hair and most of my freckles, can't say that I blame ya. Plus this dang chair."

Another voice from the far corner of the room caught Denver off-guard. "Aw, for Pete's sake! Leave 'em alone, Billy! I'm sure that Mr. Collins needs a few minutes to let it all sink in."

I know that I know that voice!

Denver glanced over and spotted the grinning source of the rebuke. He was probably forty pounds heavier and capped with a thick mop of white hair, but there was not a single doubt that a much older Police Chief James McCloud was seated at a table along with another elderly man.

Denver felt a warm hand grab his. "It's so good to see you, Mr. Collins," Billy called out from below. He dropped his volume down. "You haven't changed a lick in sixty years!"

The tears flowed hot and fast as Denver returned the gesture. "It…it is so good to see you too, Officer O'Connell. Really good!" He knelt beside the wheelchair and managed an awkward yet heartfelt hug.

Billy pushed back. "Well, come on, you cry baby. The gang's been waiting to see ya. For a long time." O'Connell swiveled his chair around and navigated back to the corner.

McCloud and the other gentleman rose in unison. The Chief was obviously fighting back his own flood of tears. He stepped forward.

"It, uh, it probably seems like only yesterday when I tranquilized your ass in that wheat field in the middle of a chilly August night, son."

A visibly trembling Denver discovered that a reply was virtually impossible. The elderly McCloud grabbed Denver's shoulders. "A few months ago for you, but for me, that was…oh, almost twenty years back." He leaned to his right. "That was what? Over thirty years for you?"

"About twenty-five years, James," the other man said. "Welcome home, Mr. Collins."

Denver couldn't miss the telltale birthmark on his wrinkled neck. They shook hands as Denver cleared his tight throat. "Th-thank you, Mr. Nelson. It, uh, it's good to be home. Couldn't have done it…without you, sir."

"It's a nice sentiment, but wholly unnecessary, Mr. Collins," Phil replied. "We all had a part to play, we all contributed." He motioned with his hand. "But please, let's all sit down. I'm sure you have quite a laundry list of questions. Oh, and *thank you* for my parting gift. That journal has been a constant source of joy and nostalgia for me and the others here. Especially at our reunions."

"Reunions?"

McCloud spoke up. "We try'n get together every three or four years. Mainly here in Normal."

"Oh."

"So what questions, Mr. Collins?" Phil asked.

Billy arced around to Denver's left and slid out a chair for him. "Well, let me start it," O'Connell chimed in. "It's kinda hard to hide the changes in my life, and it sure is uncomfortable to ask about it." He pointed at a leg that wasn't there. "Tony Bennett sang that he left his heart in San

Francisco. Well, William O'Connell here left his leg on the Ho Chi Minh trail. February of '71. It's been me and the rolling throne ever since."

A new voice interrupted from several feet behind Denver. An older female voice. "Are you already boring our latest arrival with your war stories, Billy?"

Denver launched out of his chair and spun about.

"Leah! Leah Swan!"

He ran up to her and they embraced for several seconds. Her big brown eyes flooded instantly as she brushed the salt and pepper hair out of her face. "I have missed you terribly! Not a day, not a single day has gone by that I haven't thought about you, Denver Wayne Collins." She pushed him back. "Now, let this old woman take a good look at you."

His mind reeled with the visual contradiction. Less than a handful of weeks before he had said goodbye to this same woman, but a woman years younger...*decades* younger. His memories flashed to her TOC training, at the factory, at the jail. He recalled their long drives out in the country, her tenderness for Tori, her broken heart at the mental hospital, her joy several weeks later.

She snatched his hand. "Oh, and it's Leah *McMullin* now. I lost my first husband about fifteen years ago. But, don't worry, I'm fine, and remarried, and now my kids have kids. Who would've thought...Leah the grandmother?!"

Denver's chuckles mingled with his tears. "Well, you look fantastic for a grandmother. Really great."

She waved her hand. "Oh, go on. And you—*you* look exactly the same as my last memory of you. Which is a pretty good memory."

He pivoted around and made room for her to pass by. "I, uh, I imagine that Doc is no longer with us? I never heard from him."

McCloud intercepted the response. "2009. He had a stroke late that summer. Sharp as a dang tack til then. Doc almost made it to Thanksgiving. Passed on his birthday, actually." The Chief fished around in a coat draped over the back of his chair. "And, speaking of Doc," he muttered just before pulling out a crumpled envelope. "Here. He wanted you to have this. I've been holdin' on to it for years now."

Denver hesitated to take it.

"It's not a bomb, Mr. Collins," McCloud laughed as he slapped it against Denver's hand.

"I'm the bomb expert," Billy quipped. "Avoid them at all costs."

"It's a letter," the Chief continued. "Remember those things? We used to actually write 'em before the days of smart phones'n all." He folded his beefy arms. "Right after the stroke, Doc figgered he wasn't gonna make it to see you again. The writing probably ain't very pretty, but I guarantee you it's from the heart."

Denver nodded, overwhelmed. "Thanks…really." He stashed the precious parcel away and glanced around. "And…Ellen? Lexi?"

"We lost Ellen to breast cancer," Leah answered with quiet discretion. "Actually two rounds of it. They thought she had it beat. But, it came back with a vengeance. She survived long enough to see Nellie here jump back."

Phil leaned onto his elbows and rubbed his chin. "Ellen always said I was like her second father." He paused. "It was a difficult reunion. When I made it back, she had become far older than me." A few somber moments later, he gazed over at Denver. "It really messes with your head, as I am sure that you are experiencing, Mr. Collins."

Denver sighed. "Uh, yeah. My eyes and my brain are having quite a disagreement right now."

"It'll pass," Phil noted. "Takes a while."

"I'll take your word for it."

"It does," Leah added. "Takes a while, that is."

"We lost Martha in 1966. I own the property now," Phil said. "It's an empty lot for the most part. We can go visit it afterwards if you like."

Denver paused. "Sounds good. Uh, what about Alexus?"

"After jumping back, she finished her degree in Journalism," Leah answered. "She worked for a few papers, then network news. Lexi ended up as a war correspondent in Afghanistan."

"Tell 'em the rest," Billy said. "About the kid."

"What kid?" Denver asked.

Leah flushed. "Uh, Alexus had a baby. About six months after she jumped back."

"That's wonderful," Denver replied. "Wait…*six* months?"

"Uh-huh," Leah mumbled. "A boy."

"But that would mean…"

"*Uh-huh.*"

Denver scanned all their faces. "But…who?"

Leah raised her graying eyebrows. "Shep."

"No."

"Yes. Trust me…I know. She told me. The day she left."

"Wow."

Billy cleared his throat. "There's more. Tell 'em."

"Well, Alexus disappeared doing what she loved," Leah explained. "She just…vanished. In Afghanistan. In 2004. Probably kidnapped. That's what the State Department thinks."

Denver bit his lip. "That's terrible. I've been there. Not a great place for a woman."

"About twenty-five years ago, Mr. Collins, you once told me that the Midwest was more dangerous than Afghanistan," Phil said.

"That was only a few weeks ago," Denver countered.

"Not to me, my friend."

"Speaking of people being held against their will…Garrett's still up the river," the Chief interjected, dropping his voice noticeably. "He was supposed to get out several years ago, but he got involved in a riot or somethin'. Imagine that. Hurt a few guards. I think one of his fellow inmates died. Anywho, they *extended* his government-paid vacation."

"So he did jump from prison, like we suspected?"

"Uh-huh," McCloud replied.

"Well, I hate to admit it," Denver said, "but I'm a bit relieved he's still there."

"You should be," the Chief exclaimed with a wink. "I bet ole Frazier's still got a bruise where ya smacked him."

Denver frowned. "Maybe I should change my name."

McCloud stretched and raised one eyebrow. "Might not be a bad idea."

"We've never been able to find Tori," Leah lamented.

"Really?"

She nodded. "Phil has a theory about that."

"More of an educated guess than a theory, Mrs. McMullin," Phil replied. "It may very well be that Tori jumped from much farther into all of our futures. She may not even be born yet. So Mr. Collins, you probably should have been calling her *Trailer* Wilkinson. Maybe we all should have."

Leah blinked several times and gazed out the windows. "I would trade just about anything for even a hint that she's okay. The unknowing haunts me sometimes. Every single time I encounter someone with autism I remember her. I usually cry."

Denver patted her hand. "Listen to an experienced war vet. You can't second-guess yourself, or worry about things that you don't have any control over. It'll eat you alive."

"He's right about that," Billy added.

The Chief raised a glass. "To the Final Five."

Everyone looked at him. "The Final Five," he reaffirmed. "Count for yourselves. It's simple. There's just five of us left."

"Maybe *six*," Leah added. "Tori's out there. Somewhere. And so's Lexi. And you shouldn't argue with a former accountant when it comes to numbers."

Billy scrunched his face and wagged a finger across the table. "And don't forget about Frazier. He may be on ice but he's still kicking."

"*Final Six or Seven* just ain't got the same ring to it, folks," the Chief announced. "And people in prison don't count, deputy."

"Tori's out there, Chief," Leah said.

"And when we find her, we'll change our group's name. Til then, we're the Final Five." He raised his glass higher. "Long live the Final Five."

Denver cried out, "Here, here." The others loosely echoed the sentiment.

"Tell us about Jasmine," Leah prodded.

"She's still a daddy's girl. I think I held her for like three days straight after I got back. We've taken several trips, spent hours on end at the park."

Leah laughed. "I did about the same!"

Denver stared into his hands. "Things aren't great with my…*wife* and all. But, you do what you can. I can't make her love me."

Leah adopted an understanding smile. "The heart takes time to change. Sometimes people are…*slow* to forgive. I have experience with such things, if you remember."

"Yep."

"Take it slow, Denver. It'll work out."

"That's what I keep telling myself."

Phil seemed to enjoy a long drink and motioned across the table. "So, now that we've covered most of the obvious questions, Mr. Collins…are there any pressing questions gnawing at you?"

"Well," Denver began, building up to a large smile. "My first question, Mr. Nelson, is if you're paying the tab today? Like you did the last time I was here."

Everyone laughed. Phil raised a hand. "My money doesn't go as far as it used to. And I've given up gambling. I don't seem to have the same luck. I can't predict horse races like I used to." He paused for the group to calm down. "Any other *legitimate* questions, Mr. Collins?"

Denver leaned forward. "It's complicated. I sure wish Doc was here. Or Tesla. I have at least a million questions about time travel and all."

"A *million*?" Phil repeated with a stunned look. "I may be a retired school teacher from Colorado, but I don't know enough about time travel to answer that many questions. I might be able to tell you a couple of things."

"A couple? No offense, Mr. Nelson, but *two* isn't quite a million," Denver remarked. "But it is a start."

Phil locked eyes with him. "Well, there are two things you should know about time travel. First, it's impossible. And second…it's terrifying."

The End of Back to Normal: Series One

For more information, visit:
www.MovingImagesPublications.com

ABOUT THE AUTHOR

As a science fiction movie fan and insatiable reader from his earliest memories in his birth state of California, Randy McWilson draws inspiration from a wide spectrum of interests and influences.

The reverberating echoes of Cold War espionage, explosions in scientific advancement, and strong, complex themes permeate his literary offerings. The historically-inclined reader finds a thrilling tale founded upon the rich fabric of both actual and alleged events.

He occupies his non-writing hours with a diverse range of hobbies: geology, theology, philosophy, history, and art.

McWilson currently lives in Jackson, Missouri, with his wife, Amanda, three children, and several pets.

BACK TO NORMAL: SERIES ONE

Book One: Paradigm Rift

Book Two: Tradecraft

Book Three: Proximity

Book Four: Crossover

www.ingramcontent.com/pod-product-compliance
Lightning Source LLC
Chambersburg PA
CBHW030421310726
48979CB00009B/1554/J

9780997791716